THE CAVE

A BERRY SPRINGS NOVEL

AMANDA MCKINNEY

HH TISEVICH

Paperback ISBN 978-1-7324635-8-5
eBook ISBN 978-1-7324635-7-8

Editor(s): Nancy Brown

https://www.amandamckinneyauthor.com

DEDICATION

For Mama

ALSO BY AMANDA

THRILLER NOVELS:

The Stone Secret - A Thriller Novel

A Marriage of Lies - A Thriller Novel

The Widow of Weeping Pines

The Raven's Wife

The Lie Between Us

The Keeper's Closet

The Mad Women - A Box Set

ROMANCE SUSPENSE/THRILLER NOVELS:

THE ANTI-HERO COLLECTION:

Mine

His

ON THE EDGE SERIES:

Buried Deception

Trail of Deception

And many more to come...

LET'S CONNECT!

Text AMANDABOOKS to 66866 to sign up
for Amanda's Newsletter and get the latest
on new releases, promos, and freebies! Or, sign up below.

https://www.amandamckinneyauthor.com

THE CAVE

After getting trapped in a remote cave, two strangers must work together to survive while being hunted by a ruthless killer...

Life is full of surprises, rescue swimmer Owen Grayson knows that better than anyone, especially when he's forced to take an indefinite military leave and return home to pick up the pieces of his dad's latest mistake. As Owen struggles to settle back into his roots, he is called to a remote cave where he's pulled into a mystery that hits a little too close to home. As the clues begin to unravel, it becomes apparent that the cave is hiding secrets worth killing for... and everyone on site has a target on their back.

Coming off a bad break up and an even worse few days, Forensic Anthropologist Dr. Sadie Hart is brought in to excavate human remains found deep in the treacherous mountains of Berry Springs, in a cave rumored to be haunted, nonetheless. When her team stumbles upon a dead body before they even reach the cave, Sadie quickly realizes this is going to be no ordinary job—especially when she meets a particularly charming Adonis who's hellbent on becoming her next mistake.

A storm hits, trapping Sadie and Owen inside the cave with nothing but a flashlight and a small backpack with provisions... and someone who wants them dead. As the odds stack up against them, Sadie begins to fear she and Owen will become the next pile of bones found deep in the catacombs of Crypts Cavern...

1

SHE WAS BEAUTIFUL. Alluring, magical. A commanding force who had a way of reminding you how little and vulnerable human life was. How she could chew you up and spit you out without so much as a happy ending. She was powerful, relentless, unforgiving, and tonight, she was in one hell of a mood.

Owen knew her well. He loved her, respected her, and had found a home with her even though she'd take everything from him in a moment's notice, then build him back up, only to destroy him again. She was addictive, an adrenaline rush second only to jumping out of a MH-60 Jayhawk at a hundred feet, then getting pelted with a 120-knot rotor blast. He'd seen the bodies she'd devoured in her wake, watched the friends and families cry. But the truth was, he'd be nothing without her. She'd made him into the man he was today. For better or worse.

She was a bitch of a mistress, and Owen's gut told him they were in for a helluva fight tonight.

Owen buckled the waist belt, giving it a quick tug before moving onto the chest straps. The helicopter dipped, dropped, then lifted again causing him to glance up at the pilot, Lieutenant Potts, who was laser focused on the controls glowing through the dark night. A flash of lightning streaked the sky in the distance, sparkling off the rain-streaked windshield. Up ahead, the lights of a capsized sailboat—the only light in the black, swirling water—swaying back and forth on its side, at the mercy of her angry waves.

Yeah, she was in one hell of a mood tonight.

Petty Officer Williams handed him a dive mask, and Owen pretended not to notice the tremble in the rookie's hand.

From the flight deck, Potts's voice crackled through the radio. "We've got a second round of storms coming in at one-hundred twenty kilos. Need to get a move on this, boss."

"Almost ready. What've we got?" Owen strapped on his gloves.

"Surface winds of fifty-two, nine foot swells. I'm as low as I can go in this wind."

Owen cast a side-long glance at the rookie's rounded eyes. "Another walk in the park, kid." He winked as the prominent Adam's apple in the rook's throat bobbed.

Lieutenant Foster, a two-thirty tank of muscle with an attitude to match, pushed past the rook, shoving him to the side. His steely eyes met Owen's, and after a quick shake of his head, he checked Owen's gear one last time. The helo dipped again, sending the rookie stumbling. Owen caught him by the arm and yanked the kid to him.

"I need you to pull it together, Williams. You've trained for this, kid. We're search and rescue swimmers. This is it, *this* is what we do. Grab your fucking balls. You've got this."

Williams blinked, then steeled himself and nodded. "Sorry, boss."

Owen turned toward Foster, who was in charge of operating the hoist. "I'll bring the kid up first, then the mom, then the dad."

Foster nodded—*I'm ready.*

"When you are, Potts."

"10-4. Target is directly below us. Remember, names, Gary, Beverly, Timmy McCarver. One yellow lifejacket in the water, next to the boat."

"One?"

"One."

One lifejacket for a family of three didn't bode well.

Owen removed his radio, pulled the wet suit over his head, and secured his mask. The door opened, sending a freight train of whirling wind and rain inside.

It was go time.

Owen looked down at the black water swirling twenty-five feet below, only visible by the white caps of the crashing waves. He scanned the water, looking for the family who'd been tossed overboard. The spotlight from the helicopter illuminated a wide circle over the water but through the slanted rain, visibility was shit. He'd just have to trust his team.

Just another walk in the park, his own words echoed in his head as Foster counted off on his fingers—*one, two, three.*

Owen shimmied to the edge, and after a quick inhale, dropped off the platform, plunging into the water below. The wind was strong, relentless, the bitch of all bitches. After a thumbs-up to the crew, the helo rose, taking most of the rotor spray with it.

Owen zeroed in on the capsized sailboat circled with a yellow spotlight. A four-year-old boy, his mother, and father had made the poor decision to ignore weather warnings and take the boat out for the evening. They'd drifted further than expected, and, to no one's surprise, got caught in the storm. The Coast Guard received a mayday twenty minutes earlier, before the boat had capsized. Owen wondered if this would still be a rescue mission, or body retrieval at this point... assuming the other bodies were even found.

A massive wave roared toward him, and he dove under, waiting for it to pass as it crashed down on him, tossing him like he was nothing—a small speck in the middle of an endless black sea. After years of training, years of leading rescue missions, the force of the ocean never ceased to amaze Owen. And for a man who liked control, the irony wasn't lost on him. He'd fallen in love with a force stronger than him, bigger than him. The only thing he could count on was that she was unpredictable. Like most women in his life.

Like this mission.

Owen came up for air, fighting the churning water around him, then dove again pushing through water that felt like thick molasses, twisting and turning him with each stroke. Finally, he reached the boat.

"Help!" The shrill scream carried though the howling wind like a beacon.

Through the sheets of rain, a man waved wildly from his death-grip on the mast, his bright yellow life jacket reflecting in the spotlight. Owen dipped under again, careful to stay away from floating debris.

"Mr. McCarver, I'm US Coast Guard Search and Rescue," Owen shouted over the crashing waves once he reached the mast. "Where is your wife and son?"

Eye's wide with shock, McCarver's face was pale, panicked, wild. The man opened his mouth, but shut it when they rose with a wave and were splashed by buckets of water. But, by the look on the man's face, Owen knew what was coming before he even said it.

"She's…" he spat out ocean water. "He… Timmy, my boy, he slipped off, into the water… she dove in after him. I tried to stop her! I *tried*—"

Shit.

Owen turned and scanned the dark water, catching a glint of reflective material a few yards out.

Child first.

"I'm going to get your wife and boy, first. I'll be back for you. Keep the life jacket on, stay on the mast. I'll be back."

As he turned to go under, a wave crashed over them, a Mack truck barreling across the sea. Owen breached— McCarver was gone.

Shit, shit, shit.

He dove under, gripped the man under the shoulders and pulled him up. Coughing, spitting, gasping for air, McCarver swatted, grabbed and pulled at Owen. "I'm drowning," he gasped. "I'm drowning."

McCarver had at least thirty pounds on Owen but when survival instinct mixed with adrenaline, it felt more like an eight-hundred pound grizzly bear wrapping around him.

"You're not drowning. *Gary,* I've got you."

With every second that ticked by with Gary McCarver trying to crawl onto him like a damn life boat, the storm was getting worse and Owen was losing time searching for the rest of the family. So, he made the snap decision to save the father first, then go after the family.

"*Sir,*" he slipped behind and wrapped his arm around the writhing panic attack, "I've *got* you."

He looked up at another wave about to barrel onto them. Owen clenched his jaw as he gripped the yellow life jacket a split-second before the wave hit. They both went under, then bobbed back up.

"I'm going to take you to the basket and pull you up." He

yelled as he turned, kicking his fins wildly against the whipping current. The rain had picked up, reminding him of Potts's warning about the lightning. The helo hovered above, swaying in the storm as the ocean swayed in the opposite direction. McCarver continued to pull him under despite Owen's repeated warnings not to. It took three tries to get ahold of the rescue basket, before Owen could even secure the man into it. Water pelted them like shards of glass hurling through the darkness. Owen gave the signal moments before the basket began to rise.

One down, two to go.

As he started to turn away, a light from the helicopter cabin caught his attention—a bright red light waving back and forth.

Kill the mission.

His gaze shifted to a flash of lightning piercing the sky, closer now.

Kill the mission.

Just then—a distant scream.

All or none, he thought as he turned and dove back under allowing his instinct, his sixth sense, to guide him knowing that every second longer he spent in the water put his crew's life on the line.

A mother and child.

Adrenaline flooded his veins as he fought through the storm, the waves, and the fatigue numbing his legs.

"US Coast Guard. Where are you?" He yelled over the wind, the helo spotlight scanning the water, nowhere close to his location. The lights from the sailboat barely illuminated the radius of the boat itself.

A second passed...

"Over here!"

Owen would never forget the sound of the woman's

scream for the rest of his life. It wasn't only panic... it was a wild, primal tone, a terror he'd never heard before...

And then he found out why.

With one arm wrapped around a life preserver, a mother gripped her four-year-old boy, dangling lifelessly over her other arm.

"He's *dead!*" Her eyes met his across the black churning water. *"He's dead!"*

The boy's skin was pale, lips blue, eyes closed as his head bobbed against the water.

And then... the world went black. A pitch-black inky dark. A darkness only being out in the middle of the ocean could provide. The capsized boat had finally lost electricity, and with no light to guide him, he had a nice little problem on his hands. One shift of location, one big wave, and that boat could crash down on top of them, killing them in seconds flat. He looked up at the spotlight shooting out of the helo, scanning the ocean for him.

They were a good twenty yards off.

Fuck.

Owen swam toward the hysterical screams.

"Ma'am! I'm here, I'm going to get you out of here." Kicking, he reached forward until—*finally*—he made contact.

Frantic arms swatted at him. "He's dead! *He's dead! My boy is dead."*

Eclipsing the father's panic, this woman was hysterical, which was obstacle number one. The second obstacle was that if the child was dead, there was no way in hell she was leaving the boy's body. Obstacle three—about ten more minutes and they'd all be at the bottom of the Atlantic Ocean.

"Keep hold onto the life preserver, and onto me, Mrs. McCarver," he said as he felt the thin arm of the limp body next to him. "I need you to let go of your son. I've got him."

"He's dead!" She continued to scream, but a well-timed wave knocked her grip just enough for Owen to pull the boy to him. Owen wrapped his arms around the little, cold body, fisted his hands and shoved them into the child's sternum. Again, again, using each kick under the water as leverage with each thrust of his fist.

Another wave, another force under the water.

He shifted the boy and blew five rescue breaths into his mouth, then turned him again.

His brain was screaming at him to get back to the helo *and* out of the path of the sailboat.

One more, Owen. One more fucking try.

As his fist bored into the tiny chest, the spotlight found them just as water spewed from the child's lips.

"My *baby!*" She screamed as the child wailed like an infant.

For a split-second the world froze around him as he looked into the boy's eyes, now full of life. A wave pulled him back to the moment and his determination switched to tactical—he had to get the fuck out of there.

"I've got your son—"

"Is he alive?" She squeaked.

"Yes, ma'am," he yelled over the rain and screaming child. "I've got him. You have to trust me."

"I have to—"

He locked eyes on her. "You have to trust me. Do you trust me?"

She stared at him with round eyes, helpless, exhausted, fatigued... but *hopeful*—another moment he would never forget.

"Yes." She nodded. "Yes."

"Good. Let's go."

Owen looked in the direction of the sailboat—total blackness—called a Hail Mary and with one arm hooked around the child and gripping the life preserver with the mother, they swam to the rescue basket dangling a few yards away.

Two more waves crashed over them until he finally gripped the basket. Thankfully, the mom was a tiny thing and Owen was able to allow her and her son to ride up together. He watched from the churning water as the mother gripped onto her baby boy, swaying in the wind.

Alive.

Once they were safely inside the helo, Owen was hoisted inside. It took both Williams and Foster to get him into the cabin.

Owen ripped off his mask, his gaze darting around the cabin until he spotted the boy—he was okay.

He looked around at his team, tending to the family—they were okay.

Okay, Owen, okay.

Extreme exhaustion waved over him like an unstoppable force. He fell to the cabin floor, chest heaving.

Williams kneeled down beside him with a grin the size of Texas. "Holy shit, man," he yelled as the door closed and the helicopter lifted.

Holy shit was right.

"Hell of a way to go out, man. A fucking legendary last mission." He patted Owen's forehead before taking his seat in the front.

Legendary last mission.

His *last* mission.

Owen's gut clenched—not because of the near-death experience he'd just had, or because of the adrenaline crash, but because he was about to walk away from the only thing he'd ever loved.

Owen rolled down the windows as he bumped along the pitted dirt road. The mild, autumn breeze whipped around the cab of the truck, the spicy scent of fall triggering memories—some good, some bad. He mindlessly swerved around a pothole—the same one that had given him multiple flat tires growing up. He looked around the dense woods that surrounded him, the last of the day's sun spearing through the thick canopy of trees. The Ozark Mountains were a canvas of yellow, orange, and red leaves, each desperately hanging on to the past, before their time was up.

Like his was.

He turned up the radio in an attempt to distract the nerves threatening to grab ahold of him. Nerves make you messy, and if there was anything Owen wasn't, it was messy.

He inhaled deeply—what a cluster fuck.

It had been two weeks since he'd saved the McCarver family from the Louisiana coast. Two weeks since he'd signed the papers that released him on indefinite military leave. Two weeks since he'd received a call that his dad had been arrested for his third fucking DWI, and after a short stint in jail, was being forced by the judge—his father's old high school buddy—to enter a sixty-day rehab program.

His *dad*... in *rehab*. His mess of a father who after his mom walked out on him, went into a deep liquor-induced depression throwing away everything and anything positive in his life. The man had given up on everything except booze.

Lester Grayson had spent his life serving his country in the Navy, just like his father—Owen's grandfather—did. Owen was born between his father's deployments, to a nineteen-year-old girl who'd decided it would be fun to go home with a sailor after a few too many whiskey shots at the local bar. That single decision turned into a baby boy they'd named Owen. Despite the birth of his first and only son, Les continued his career in the military, but only after deciding it was probably best to marry Sheila—he had knocked her up, anyway—in jeans and T-shirts at the county courthouse. And so began a tumultuous relationship of a man who put his country above all else and a woman who never wanted his baby in the first place.

Owen spent his childhood roaming the mountains of Berry Springs, doing everything he could to avoid being home where arguing was as common as empty whiskey bottles. The woods, the mountains, were his home... until his uncle, Ray Grayson, taught him to swim in the lake just below their small cabin.

At seventy miles long and including over five-hundred miles of shoreline, Otter Lake was one of the main tourist attractions in the small, southern town. Splitting off into dozens of rivers and creeks that wound through the treacherous mountains, the lake was speckled with soaring bluffs, deep valleys and miles of caves.

Before school, Owen would swim four miles every morning, despite the temperature. He taught himself how to fish and eventually bought a small fishing boat, where he spent most of his evenings. The water was his peace, his solitude, his escape from the chaos of his house.

Owen found his new home in the water, so it was no surprise that the day after graduating high school, he enlisted in the Coast Guard, spending the next fifteen years of his life as a rescue swimmer on an elite Search and Rescue team stationed in Louisiana.

He'd found his one true love in the ocean, and he'd

found his family in his teammates, and despite several trips home to bail his father out of jail or to attend funerals, Owen had vowed never to return to the Ozark Mountains. For good, anyway.

That was until he'd received the call about his dad's latest fuck up, and was informed that his father had not only spent the last year of his life drinking himself to death, but also barely paying his debt to the bank, stopping payments altogether over the last few months. Owen was at risk of losing his family home and the family business while his dad went away.

"Let him lose everything, Grayson. It's his fuck up, not yours," his Coast Guard buddies had told him. *"Maybe this is what he needs to finally wake up,"* they'd said.

But just like the times he'd made the ten hour drive from his base in New Orleans to bail his dad out, or just like the times he'd wired money when the man couldn't make ends meet, Owen couldn't turn a shoulder to his dad. Never had been able to. Because the truth was, Owen knew what serving decades in the military did to a man. Owen knew the sacrifice and respected it. Owen knew the weight of seeing dead bodies, watching men die in your arms, and making life or death decisions in the blink of an eye. It fucked with a man's psyche. Some men were stronger than others, but they were all bonded by a common thread— serving their country.

Commitment.

Honor.

Respect.

That's why he'd come back.

Owen shook the thoughts away as he braked next to a rusted mailbox with more dents in it than his Chevy.

L. Grayson

The damn lid didn't even close. He pulled out the stacks of mail, noting more than one red envelope.

Nothing good ever came from a red envelope.

After taking a second to jimmy the lid closed, then adding a new mailbox to the running shopping list in his head, he stared at the narrow dirt driveway that led to his family home.

Tall oak trees grew like a tunnel over the drive, swaying in the autumn breeze. Dead leaves covered the ground. The underbrush was thick, with snarled bushes, rotting logs and tree limbs. A massive tree had fallen inches from the ditch, probably during the last ice storm, he guessed.

Owen tossed the mail on the passenger seat and turned into the driveway. It had been five months since he'd been home last, and based on the mailbox and landscaping, he couldn't wait to see what condition the house was in.

He descended the long driveway with one elbow hanging out the window, and memories of his childhood racing through his head. He passed the pine tree where he'd carved his initials, a mound of moss-covered boulders where he used to play cops and robbers—with himself, of course. A hundred-year-old oak tree that he used to climb and nestle himself in-between the branches with a Coca-Cola and a Hardy Boys book that he'd read a thousand times. So many memories, yet, as he drove down the dirt road, he realized they were all lonely memories. No family trips, no brothers, or sisters. Not many friends' parents were willing to drive that far into the woods just for a playdate. Hell, Owen had felt alone his whole life.

Just like he did now.

As he descended deeper into the valley, he eyed the old barbed wire fence that ran along the sides of the road, and hit the brakes.

I'll be a son of a bitch, he thought as he peered out the window at the long, black hair caught in the wire, and just beyond that, two massive bite marks on the tree. The black bears had moved in... which meant two things—his dad apparently didn't make it past the liquor cabinet when he was home, and two, the Ozark Mountain ecosystem was thriving.

Of all the times Owen had played in the woods as a child, he'd only seen a bear one time... and that was nothing compared to the mountain lion he'd come across one morning while hiking. It was all part of what made the woods magical to him—you never knew what you'd find.

Bears, elk, white-tailed deer, coyotes, were just a handful of the creatures that roamed the mountains. And although his home turf was the opposite of his address on the ocean, the woods were just as beautiful. Well... they *would be* after he spent weeks of back-breaking work getting the land up and running again.

He pressed on, driving deeper into the woods, when finally, the musty scent of lakeshore filled his nose.

Home.

A steep dip in the terrain, then a sharp corner, and the woods opened up to a small clearing speckled with maple and pine trees. Old, wooden fencing ran along the yard of his childhood home—the small cabin he stood to inherit one day.

Shaded by tree cover, the two bedroom, two bathroom log cabin was nestled in a small cove just above the lake. A pebbled walkway in the back led down to a dock, complete with a humble fishing boat.

Home.

Owen parked next to the single-car standalone garage,

which was packed with boxes, old furniture, and whatever else his dad didn't have room for, and got out of the truck.

The woods were still, quiet.

The sound of the water lapping against the dock in the distance pulled him back in time—a familiar song of his past. A breeze swept past his skin, rustling the trees above as he fisted his hands on his hips and gazed at the decrepit house.

Rotted planks ran throughout the wraparound porch, the front window was cracked from God knows what, and there were dozens of shingles missing around a rock chimney. Leaves scattered the front porch, piling on the crooked porch swing that, apparently, his dad never used.

Owen grabbed his camo backpack from the bed of the truck, slung it over his shoulder, and walked up the aged wooden steps that led to the front porch. He kicked the pine needles and cigarette butts away from the front door as he slid the key inside.

With a deep breath he pushed through the heavy wooden door.

Stale, humid air hit him like a brick wall. Musty, dirty, was his first thought—his second was *holy shit.* The house he'd grown up in was an absolute wreck. Newspapers, beer cans, and magazines covered the leather couches that sat in front of floor-to-ceiling windows that looked out to the lake. Dust particles danced in the dimming sunlight spilling in through the smudged, dirty glass. The back deck was in the same shape as the front. A kitchen that hadn't seen a sponge or a can of Comet in months sat to the right, and beyond the massive rock fireplace to the left were two bedrooms—and based on the clutter he could see on the floor, also hadn't been cleaned in months.

He dropped his bag onto the dusty floor and blew out a

breath. His father had given up. What man just gives up on life? Hell, his father had raised him to get up after every fall. No kissing or coddling, just wipe yourself off, and get back up.

What the hell happened to his dad?

Owen looked around the house, recalling their last conversation at the funeral, months earlier.

He knew. Owen knew exactly what had happened to his dad... and that thought brought a surprising pang of guilt. Maybe if he had stayed around after everything had happened. Maybe if he had never left in the first place...

Owen pushed the thought aside. *One thing at a time... one thing at a time.*

He made his way to the kitchen, set the stack of mail on the counter, killed a line of ants, then yanked open the fridge. Beer, more beer, boxed wine, wine coolers, and hot dogs. Owen grabbed a Shiner, popped the top and stepped outside onto the back deck.

A camping chair lay on its side next to an empty beer bottle filled with cigarette butts.

He walked to the middle of the deck, to a spot where he could see the lake through a break in the trees. After taking a sip, he leaned his forearms on the railing and gazed out to the water, sparkling under the setting sun.

He could not believe he was back here.

He could not believe the twist his life had taken.

He could not believe the knots in his stomach.

One thing at a time, Owen...

And with that thought, he ignored the unease coursing through his body and began making the long list of things he needed to get done.

2

wo months later...

THE EARLY MORNING light cut through the trees, illuminating the bodies on the ground like a horror show in its final act. Vultures swooped overhead, circling, circling, circling, waiting for their chance.

Sadie looked up at the two massive black and brown buzzards, with their muted red faces and dirty beaks. "Morning, Bert, Ernie. You're up early today." She popped the rubber band from her wrist and haphazardly tied back her long, brown hair before pulling a face mask over her nose and mouth.

No matter how many times Sadie visited the body farm, she never got used to the scent. Gut gobbling birds she could handle, but the rancid smell of human decay made her stomach flop like a fish out of water... and after the morning she'd already had, her stomach was already in knots.

Make that gut clenching twists, following by weepy panic.

After entering her eight-digit code, Sadie stepped

through the ten-foot security gate. Dead leaves crunched under her feet as she made her way across the dying grass—a fitting environment for the farm's residents.

Sadie walked up to her newest resident—7395—and tilted her head to the side, looking the body over.

Maggots slithered in and out of the eye sockets, gathering on the teeth of a crooked opened jaw, as if the corpse was in mid-scream. The puffy Y-incision from the autopsy marked the torso, the grey flesh moving with maggots.

She pulled out her pocket weather meter and recorded the current weather conditions.

Temperature: 68F

Humidity: 47%

Wind Speed: SW 6mph

Dew Point: 45%

She had just begun taking soil samples when she heard footsteps behind her.

"Holy *shit.*"

Sadie stiffened, steeling herself for the onslaught of jokes to come. When there were none, she glanced over her shoulder at Griffin Olsen, a twenty-something wide-eyed, eager resident student that had been assigned to her team as an intern for the fall. With shaggy brown hair, a six-foot, lean body sculpted from years of marathon training, and wide-rimmed glasses over bright green eyes, Griffin had the nerdy-hot-guy thing going for him, and the women of the lab took notice. Griffin was outspoken, cocky, and sure as hell wasn't one to miss a joke.

Had he seen the morning paper? Read the gossip columns that wrote about her life as if they knew her? As if they'd known what had *really* happened? As if they had any *right* to display her personal life for the world to see?

"Morning," she said with a touch of skepticism. And

after waiting a moment, she stood and continued, assuming he wasn't up on the latest gossip, "You're here early."

"Have to keep up with you, boss," he said, staring down at 7395.

Her gaze shifted to his hands. "One of those for me?"

Griffin tore his eyes away from the decaying body and handed her a travel cup of coffee, keeping the larger one for himself. "Sorry." He stepped next to her, his eyes boring into the corpse at her feet, like a car crash. He couldn't look away. "That dude has *doubled* in size since yesterday."

"Is it a triple?" Her sole focus now being on the much-needed caffeine kick she was about to get.

"Triple chocolate mocha, extra drizzle, made especially for one of the *top forensic anthropologists* in the country."

She frowned, cocked her head.

Griffin winked. "According to Ben the barista, of course. You should have seen his face drop when I walked in without you." He strapped on a face mask. "Dude's obsessed."

"He's obsessed with the tip we leave him every day." She lifted her mask and sipped, savoring the warm tingle of chocolate and cream on her tongue, then replaced the mask and squatted down next to 7395.

"He's obsessed with what he can't have. The guy knows who you're dating... I mean, come on."

The muscles in Sadie's shoulders tightened, like intertwined ropes being twisted tighter, tighter, tighter. She took a quick breath, looked down, then changed the subject.

"So, anyway, yes, *dude* has doubled in size since yesterday. He's in the bloat phase, which usually occurs within the first few days of death. We were lucky to get this one so soon."

"And it's the bacteria from the cells that makes him swell, right?" Griffin kneeled next to her.

She took another sip. "Sort of. Right after death, the fluid in the cells leak out, feeding the bacteria. Then, the bacteria converts the insides of the body to gas basically, which causes the body to bloat." She pulled the pen from behind her ear and pointed to the "dude's" coppery-colored limbs. "See here? This is marbling, from the sulfur in the body, created from the bacteria, too."

"And I'm assuming that's the smell, too."

Sadie grinned under her mask. "Yep." She stood. "I just recorded the weather stats and took a soil sample. We'll need to do this every morning. Be sure to log it in his file before the end of the day."

Griffin nodded. "You got it, boss."

Sadie stood and looked at the dozens of bodies, each in different stages of decomposition, lying under metal cages so that scavengers couldn't partake. A few bodies lay in the shade, a few in the sun, a few on a man-made creek, and a few in tubs of water at the bottom of the hill. Each body strategically placed to analyze and record each stage of decomposition.

A body farm was everything worst nightmares were made of, except this was very real.

And very important.

A gust of wind followed by a grinding *creak,* pulled their attention to a nearby tree.

"God, that's creepy," Griffin muttered as they stared at the decomposing body hanging by its neck from a tree branch. With every gust of wind, the dead body swayed back and forth, scraggy scraps of hair attached to a decaying face blowing in the wind while the rope groaned at its weight.

Sadie walked to the tree with Griffin on her heels. "It's important to recreate different homicide—or suicide—scenarios so we provide the best analysis we can to law enforcement. Bodies that decompose in the air are a lot different than ones on the ground. Even after the bones begin to drop from the body, or perhaps after all of them drop, we can still tell that the majority of decomposition happened in the air—which would imply a hanging, which would be huge in an investigation." The body caught in the wind again, turning in circles now. "But yeah, I'll give you that. It's pretty damn creepy."

Griffin turned away from the grotesque image floating in front of them. "Anyway, I came down here to make sure you had everything you needed for your presentation that starts in thirty."

"Thirty minutes?" She glanced at her watch. "Damn, okay, I need to print a few things out..." She slid her notebook into her pocket and began making her way through the bodies, "... and look at something else beforehand."

"Anything I can help with?" Griffin fell into step next to her.

"No thanks." Her mind started racing with everything she needed to get done. The job never slept, and neither did she.

After getting her doctorate in forensic anthropology years earlier, Sadie had jumped at the opportunity to intern with KT Crime Labs—a privately funded forensics laboratory with one of the largest body farms in the country. That internship had turned into a job offer, which she'd accepted on the spot. She was living her dream, committing herself to every case she worked. As the years ticked by, Sadie had begun to make a name for herself, and was given more and more responsibility, earning the label of a workaholic. And when the only other forensic anthropologist in the area left his job at the state crime lab, local law enforcement agencies were calling on her to do work that typically went to the state. Before she knew it, Sadie was working fifteen-hour days just to keep her head above water. But that was okay, she was doing something that she truly loved—helping solve homicides.

And it wasn't like she had a family waiting for her at home, anyway.

Or hell, even a dog.

They pushed out of the gate and began walking up the hill. "Did you get the campers reserved for the excavation this afternoon?"

"Yep. Well, only one. The other's already been reserved. I'm packing my tent. Supposed to be seventy-five in Berry Springs over the next two days, nights in the mid-sixties. Perfect camping weather. Nothing like fall in the mountains."

"Okay, mountain man, I'll sleep in Chitty Chitty Bone Bone, and you get the rocks. Fine by me. Although, you might feel differently when you wake up next to a hungry black bear."

"Bear?"

She grinned. "Yep... snakes, coyotes, mountain lions..."

"Oh, my."

Sadie laughed.

"Like you wanted to share anyway," grinning, he slid her the side-eye.

"Hey, I don't mind one bit."

"Yeah, right, little Miss *anti-social.*"

"Some of us have work to do in the evenings."

"Well, some of us need to be social with everyone else."

"And watch the bottom of the whiskey bottle disappear?"

"Exactly... Hey, so that reminds me. Are you going to ask Kimi to join us?"

"Kimi, as in, that new forensic pathologist, Kimi?"

"Do we have anyone else at the lab named Kimi?"

Sadie rolled her eyes. Griffin's smartassery was already legendary at KT Crime Labs. "Hadn't really thought about it."

"I think she's from the area. Or lived there awhile, at least."

"How do you know that?" Smirking, she looked at Griffin.

"Unlike you, I care to get to know my fellow KT co-workers."

"Yeah right." She laughed. Kimi Haas was close to a decade younger than Sadie and had recently accepted a position with KT Labs where she was still in the training period, and was expected to assist with as many cases as possible to learn the ropes. Sadie wasn't a fan of anyone on her team dating—or dating in the workplace in general—but from the moment Griffin had laid eyes on the black-haired, dark-eyed, legs-for-days newbie, Sadie knew he was a goner.

"Anyway, considering she knows the area, I thought it would be good to have her."

"Okay, fine, I'll invite her along. But no funny business, Mr. Charming."

"You can't just turn this off, Miss Hart." He winked and flexed a bicep.

"What a gentleman."

"Hey, what can I say? Mama raised me right."

"Then *mama* also raised you to keep your eye on the

ball, and off young, impressionable women's asses, so you can keep a paying job."

"Message received, boss."

They walked up the front steps that led up to the sprawling, three story mirrored building that was home to KT Crime Labs.

"Alright," Sadie said as they pushed through the glass door and stepped into the marble lobby. "I'll be in my office after my meeting, then we'll hit the road around noon to head to little ole' Berry Springs..." She emphasized her southern accent and tipped an invisible cowboy hat. "Maybe get some cheese grits while we're at it."

Griffin laughed.

"I'm hoping it's just a one-nighter."

"Me, too. One night in a tent's enough for me. Good luck at your meeting. Kick ass."

Sadie stepped into the elevator as Griffin disappeared down the hall.

A one-nighter. Just one night digging up bones in remote mountains that were rumored to be haunted.

As the shiny elevator doors closed, she looked at herself in the reflection.

Just one night to leave this place behind and pretend the last twenty-four hours never happened.

3

*A*FTER KEYING IN her security code, Sadie stepped into the lab and clicked on the lights. The *click, click, click,* of the wall clock echoed off the blinding white walls as she grabbed a lab coat. Not a soul around, which wasn't surprising considering it was only seven in the morning. And this morning, of all mornings, Sadie needed silence. Solitude. Hell, she needed a bottle of wine and a ten foot rope.

Her computer came to life with a buzz and she inwardly groaned as she watched the emails populate one by one, several marked "important."

Shocker.

Careful to avoid the internet, Sadie glanced at her to-do list—almost as long as her unanswered email list—and decided to take five minutes to cross a few things off before her meeting.

Sadie grabbed her laptop, an evidence box from the cabinet, then made her way to the microscopes. After removing the manubrium bone from the box and placing it onto the slide, she shifted back to her computer and pulled up the related case. She settled into a chair and clicked through the file, reading each document for the umpteenth time.

Something wasn't adding up.

In deep thought, Sadie blew the top of her eight-dollar triple shot mocha cappuccino, then took a sip.

She set down the coffee and shook her head. No, something definitely wasn't adding up.

With determination giving her a jolt of energy, she peered into the microscope, then back at the pictures. Then repeated, again and again.

Click, click, click... Seconds turned into minutes as she studied and analyzed, as she was trained to do.

Case number 7890 was of a human skeleton found in an abandoned barn in a remote area twenty minutes out of town. The woman, Jennifer Miller, was identified by her high school class ring that was dangling on her middle metacarpal. According to the case file, Jennifer's boyfriend, who lived just seven miles from the barn, was issued a restraining order before she went missing the next day, never to be seen again. When the body was excavated, the medical examiner suggested Jennifer had possibly been stabbed in the chest. According to the interview transcript, the boyfriend admitted to owning multiple hunting knives, and to *not* having an alibi the night Jennifer went missing, but he did not admit to murdering his girlfriend. They needed more to prove that Jennifer's boyfriend stabbed her to death. That's when the bones were sent to her.

After ten minutes, Sadie blinked, pulled back from the scope and rolled her neck from side to the side. The shades and lines of the bone were beginning to blur together.

"Hey, Sadie?"

Sadie squeaked like a mouse, her arm jerking, spilling her coffee onto the table.

"*Shit!*" She jumped up—her seat flying backward—as Sam, the front desk receptionist, darted over.

"Grab the scope!" Sadie threw her body over the table, using her lab coat to soak up coffee threatening to destroy thousands of dollars of equipment. The liquid scorched her stomach as a handful of napkins rained down on her.

"Here, girl, here!" Sam tossed the napkins like dollar bills at a strip club, then grabbed the microscope.

"Shit, shit, *shit,*" Sadie whined as she wiped up the mess —well, most of it. She straightened and looked at Sam, holding the microscope above her golf-ball sized eyes.

"I am *so sorry,* Sadie."

"You saved the bone, that's all that matters." Sadie took the scope, the smell of chocolate coffee permeating the air.

"But not your clothes."

No, not her clothes. Sadie grimaced as she looked down at her white lab coat now covered in coffee and chocolate swirls. As she opened the coat to assess the damage to her brand-new, white silk blouse, she heard—

"Dr. Hart..."

Sadie glanced up just as a large silhouette stepped into the lab.

Sam flashed Sadie an *I'm-sorry* look, before clearing her throat and saying, "Sadie, this is Detective Dave Arbuckle with Clement PD."

Her jaw clenched as the silhouette came into view. "Yes, we've spoken several times but haven't officially met."

Chest puffed out like a man with something to prove, the two-hundred and fifty pound detective strode across the lab—as if he owned the place—the dim lab lights reflecting off his freshly shaved head and the gold tips on his alligator-skin cowboy boots.

"Detective Arbuckle came by to see if you had any updates for him on case 7890."

At seven o'clock in the damn morning.

Arbuckle's mustache twitched as his gaze lowered to Sadie's coffee-covered lab coat.

Dammit. Fantastic first impression. And Sadie had learned quickly that her first impressions were very important, considering everyone that met her was expecting a fifty-something year-old male. Not a thirty-one-year-old brunette with a smattering of freckles that no lightening cream could make go away.

She squared her shoulders and thrust out a hand. "Nice to officially meet you—"

"Do you have an update for me?"

Her brow cocked as she pulled her hand away from the bear-trap grip.

"Well, Detective," meeting his brisk tone with an attitude of her own, "In the voicemail I left for you—at four-thirty yesterday afternoon—I told you that I would have something for you by the end of today." She glanced at the clock to make her point, then back at him.

"Okey-doke, then," Sam sucked in a breath. "Uh, Sadie, I'll leave you two alone. Sorry about..." she pointed her finger along the chocolate streaks on Sadie's lab coat. "... all that. And Detective, I'll show you out when you're ready."

A grunt in response.

As Sam scurried out, Arbuckle crossed his arms over his meaty chest and settled back onto his heels making sure there was no mistake that he came here to get answers.

Just like all the others, Sadie thought. Each case was more important than the next, each bone needing her undivided attention at that exact moment. It was as if they thought all she had to do was glance at the remains and, with a twinkle of her nose and a handful of fairy dust, she was able to instantly tell the person's entire life story. Well, forensic anthropology didn't work like that, and apparently Detective Arbuckle didn't get that.

Yes, he was just like all the others, but there was something more to this one... an undercurrent of sexism, mixed with ageism, in his voice every time they'd spoken over the phone.

And sexism and ageism were two things Sadie didn't tolerate.

She continued, "I'm not finished examining the bone, as I said on the voicemail. I'll have the report to you this afternoon..."

Her attention was pulled to a steady *drip, drip, drip,* breaking the silence. She frowned and glanced over her shoulder.

Sadie gasped as she turned to the equipment where a steady stream of coffee ran off the side of the counter onto the electrical outlet on the wall.

Dammit!

In one swift move, she grabbed the used napkins from the trash can, squatted down and mopped up the remaining mess, feeling the man's disapproval boring into her backside. Her sneakers squeaked on the slick floor as she stood.

Dammit, dammit, dammit.

Resigning to the disaster of her morning, Sadie blew out a breath just as the detective stepped past her.

"That's the bone, isn't it?"

"Yes, it is. I was just looking at it before you walked in." She forced the fluster aside—she was damn good at what she did and she wasn't going to let this guy, or her shit-morning, knock her off her game.

He looked at her, some of the air deflating from his chest. "I'd really appreciate some sort of update, Dr. Hart. There have been significant advancements in the case, and this is the missing piece of the puzzle."

"Well, you might not like this piece, Detective." She pushed past him and sat in front of the scope. "It's my understanding you believe the victim was murdered, correct?"

"That's correct, based on, among other things, the restraining order issued to her boyfriend the day before she went missing."

"And you determined her identity by the jewelry found in the grave, correct?"

"Right."

"Miss Miller was eighteen years old, correct?"

"Correct."

"And your assumption is that she was stabbed to death, correct?"

"That's your job to determine that."

She leaned into the scope. "Well, based on your notes in the file, the initial assessment was that she was stabbed. Your words, exactly."

"Fine. That's right."

Sadie leaned back and swiveled her chair to face him. "The markings you noted on the sternum that led you to believe the victim had been stabbed are not kerf marks."

"Kerf marks?"

"Right. The markings are not from a tool, detective, they are from scavengers."

Arbuckle's bloodshot eyes widened. "Are you sure?"

"I'm one hundred percent sure." She slid back and stood. "Have a look."

As the detective stepped forward, she continued, "There

are two types of scavengers, carnivores and rodents. The scores on the bone that you noticed are from rodents."

He peered into the scope.

"You can see multiple small striations—not just one, as assumed by the naked eye—and they are all perfectly parallel. Made from teeth, not a knife." She waited a moment to let the news sink in.

"And you've checked the rest of the skeleton for marks?"

"Yes."

"No marks?"

"No tool marks. That's correct."

He looked at her. "You're sure?"

She nodded to the scope. "Take another look. The bone is fractured just below the clavicle notch. Can you see the small dot at the tip of the fracture?"

A second passed and she glanced impatiently at the clock.

"Oh. Yeah, I see it. Kind of."

"I believe that's a puncture mark from a carnivore, based on the size, my guess is a feral cat."

"So you're saying multiple animals gnawed on this bone."

"That's right. It's understandable that someone untrained jumped to a stabbing scenario, but that isn't the case with Jessica Miller."

The detective pulled away, frowning. "The DA's got a full case built against the boyfriend. A restraining order issued the day before she went missing, a barn seven miles from where he lives—a barn that he admitted to hanging out in with her. Damn kid even collects knives for Christ's sake."

Sadie didn't say anything. It wasn't the first time her analysis had changed the course of an investigation—whether law enforcement liked it or not.

Arbuckle ran his fingers over the top of his bald head. "If she wasn't murdered, what the hell happened?"

"Well..." Her voice trailed off as she weighed how much to tell the detective at this point.

"Well, what?"

"There was something that stood out to me with this case."

"What?"

"You are one hundred percent sure on her age and identity, correct?"

"Yes."

"Okay, then... so, her bones show a significant amount of deterioration. If it weren't for the confirmation of her identity through the dental records, I would have pegged this skeleton to be in her thirties, maybe even older."

"So... okay... what does this tell you?"

"Well, I found that interesting, right? So I sent one of her teeth off to the toxicologist for analysis."

"Toxicologist?"

"That's right. You see, with that much bone deterioration at such a young age, there's a few things I look at—disease for one. But also—and my gut was tugging me in this direction—I consider drug use. Specifically, opioid use."

"You are shitting me."

"Nope. There are multiple studies indicating the adverse effects of opioid addiction on the body's process of formation and destruction of bone tissue. A severe opioid addiction destroys bone tissue."

"And your toxicologist can confirm that by examining her teeth?"

"Possibly, yes."

The detective's gaze darted to her computer. "Well? What did he say?"

"I haven't heard back yet, which is why I was waiting to call you back." She picked up the phone. "If you can give me a minute..."

The detective cocked a brow and moved to the doorway, just out of earshot as she made the call.

"Adam here."

"Hey, it's Sadie." She turned her back and lowered her voice.

"Well, good morning, sugar."

Sadie rolled her eyes. A die-hard shameless flirt, Adam was on his fifth year at KT as a crime lab technician, specializing in courting every single woman that crossed the front doors.

"I need a favor."

A chuckle on the other end of the phone. "Meet me for coffee in the cafe and we'll talk about it."

Sadie grinned at his perseverance. She'd lost count how many times the guy had asked her out, or tried to con her into a "meeting date" in the office cafe.

"I can't. Got a meeting in—*crap*—seven minutes. Hey, I sent a tooth over yesterday for a toxicology scan. Any way you can push that to the top of your list? Case number 7890, submitted by a Detective Arbuckle."

"Case number 7890..." his voice trailed off as Sadie heard the *click, click, click* of his keyboard.

"Well, you're in luck, sweetheart. It's done, but I can't release the results yet until Fischer has a look at them. You know how he is..."

"Come on, just tell me..."

"*Hmm*... how much is it worth to you?"

She groaned. "*Fine*... I'll bring you coffee every morning... for a week."

"This sounds interesting. What kind?"

She clenched her jaw. "Whatever kind you would like, *dear.*"

"The high dollar stuff. Not that syrup from the cafeteria."

"High dollar. Deal."

"And a blueberry muffin."

"Done."

"Annnd... a chocolate scone."

"Done. High dollar coffee, blueberry muffin, chocolate scone and a gallon of insulin to pull you out of your diabetic coma."

He laughed. "I don't have diabetes."

"You will if you keep eating like that, Chubs. Now, what did the report say?"

"That your girl liked to party—heroin and fentanyl in her system."

"Wow, seriously?"

"Yep. You know it takes, like, one grain of fentanyl to kill you."

She nodded, and glanced at the detective, who was glancing at his watch.

"Thanks, Adam."

"Adam, I think I'm going to make you call me Mr—"
Click.

Arbuckle crossed the room. "Well?"

"Jennifer had heroin and fentanyl in her system." She watched the detective's eyes widen, before shaking his head and laughing a humorless laugh.

"Died of a drug overdose. Oh my *God,* the DA's going to love this."

A part of her wanted to say she was sorry, wanted to say she understood how many man hours had gone into the investigation already, to only get thrown on its head.

He stared at her for a moment. "I've never been in their shoes, but I'm thinking an overdose would be a hell of a lot easier to stomach than someone murdering their daughter." He stuck out his hand. "One step closer to closure for Jennifer's family. Thank you, Dr. Hart."

She smiled just as the lab door opened and Sam slinked inside as if she was entering a snake pit. "Dr. Hart, your seven-thirty..."

The detective pulled his hand away, nodded, then strode out of the lab, and Sadie mentally crossed one thing off her to-do list.

"I'm *soooo* sorry. He just barged in." Sam hurriedly crossed the room.

"It's okay. All part of it." She began gathering her things.

"As if you needed that this morning."

Sadie froze, turned like a ballerina on a music box, and zeroed in on the magazine rolled in Sam's hand.

Shit.

Sam's face pulled into a tight frown as she lifted the magazine.

"Is that Ozark Digest?"

"Yeah..." she nodded.

"*Unbelievable.* I don't know how they included it in this print. It just happened."

"It's on a few of the blogs too."

"I know." She closed her eyes and shook her head, her stomach churning. The headline *KT Crime Labs heir splits with "neurotic" anthropologist girlfriend after unwilling to commit* would forever be burned into her brain—and the punching bag in her gym, for that matter.

"Surprised there hasn't been a company-wide email out yet." Sadie glanced at her inbox.

"No, not *yet.*"

"I was joking."

"Oh. Sorry." Sam closed the inches between them and lowered her voice. "I mean, do you think they'll *fire* you, Sadie? Will Evan have you fired? Because if so, I know a good lawyer..."

It was the same thought that had been running through her mind since she'd read the first headline as she'd settled in for her morning coffee. She'd almost thrown up all over her duvet. She knew, in her heart, there was a definite possibility they'd find a reason to let her go. She was a fool to think that kind of thing didn't happen in the corporate world.

She was a fool for sleeping with the billionaire owner's son.

Idiot, idiot, idiot.

It was a serious lack of judgment. A serious slip up, that *seriously* made her question her sanity. What had she been thinking?

She was better than that.

She was better than *this*.

Screw the blogs, screw the headlines.

And screw this conversation.

"Well, life goes on either way, I guess. I've gotta get to my meeting, Sam..."

"Okay, well, listen, I won't let the gossip run rampant, okay?"

Yeah, right.

"I'll stick up for you, and I'll let you know what everyone's saying."

"Don't worry about it." Sadie grabbed a stack of folders from the counter.

"Uh, do you... uh... need a new lab coat? You smell like Dunkin' Donuts."

At least she didn't smell the way she felt—like shit.

"No, I think there's spare ones in the bathroom. Thanks, Sam."

"Okay, well, let me know if you need anything."

With that, Sam left Sadie standing in a puddle of coffee and misery—and almost late for her meeting.

After pressing print on a few documents, Sadie ran to the bathroom and slipped out of her coffee-covered lab coat, frowned at her stained—destroyed—silk blouse, then pulled open the cabinet only to discover there were no extra lab coats in the bathroom.

You have got to be kidding me. She slammed the cabinet closed and released a hysterical cackle, because at that point there was nothing else to do. She put her hands on her hips and stared in the mirror...

Her gym bag!

Sadie turned on her heel, ran out of the bathroom, grabbed her gym bag and frantically sifted through the contents. Black leggings, an inappropriately low-cut tank top, and—*yes!*—a T-shirt!

She yanked it out while running back into the bathroom, ripped off her blouse, then slid on the T-shirt, and looked in the mirror.

I like big bones and I cannot lie.

The back read:

KT Crime Labs

Body Farm

"Oh... My... *God.*"

The world was officially against her.

After wiping down her arms with paper towels, she gave herself another look, cocked her head, then knotted the bottom of the shirt at the hip. Cute? Hip? Horrific? She stepped back—well, it was going to have to do. She yanked her shoulders back, then gave herself a manly thump on the chest before darting out the bathroom.

You got this, Sadie.

By the time she gathered her printouts and sprinted down the hall, she was exactly two minutes late to her meeting.

With a quick inhale, she pushed through the conference room doors.

The chatter stopped as all eyes dropped to the kitschy T-shirt.

Sadie bit the inside of her cheek and walked to the head of the table, and she wondered if they were staring at her because of her wildly inappropriate meeting attire, or because they'd never seen a female scientist before.

The thought gave her the kick in the ass she needed.

She was always game for a challenge.

"Morning, gentlemen," she said, tipping up her chin.

Her boss, Ronnie Sharp, director over the Bones Unit, stood, and after giving her a cocked expression that she wasn't sure was about her late arrival or her T-shirt, or perhaps both, he made the introductions.

"Gentlemen this is Dr. Sadie Hart, our forensic anthropologist. Sadie has recently accepted an offer to lead a new project we've started that re-opens notable cold cases. We're hoping a fresh set of eyes along with continual advancements in technology will help solve these cases that have gone unlooked at, for decades in some cases. Sadie graduated top of her class at the University of Tennessee, is a member of the American Board of Forensic Anthropology, has headed up dozens of excavations, and travels the country giving lectures on forensic anthropology." Then, with a sarcastic tone, he said, "Sadie also enjoys mochas, long walks on the beach, and Sir Mix A-Lot, apparently."

A few snickers around the room as she cut a side-long glance at her boss.

He continued, "Sadie, this is Special Agent Miller and Special Agent Brown with the FBI, and Sheriff Andrew Dunn, with Carroll County."

"Pleasure to meet you all," she said, looking around the room as Ronnie took his seat next to Special Agent Miller who hadn't looked up from his cell phone since she'd taken her place at the head of the table. His demeanor was as stiff as his navy button-up with iron lines down the sleeves and the razor-perfect edges of his freshly trimmed salt-and-pepper hair. Miller was a stark contrast to his counterpart whose faded, wrinkled pinstripe was rolled up at the elbows, suggesting he'd already had a hell of a day, and didn't give a shit about appearances. Brown was younger than Miller, with fine lines beginning to form along a tanned face and eyes with a hint of steel from spending too many hours a day hunting evil. A former military man, she guessed, and kind of cute if she was being honest. Across from the agents sat Sheriff Dunn, a walking stereotype with a handle-bar mustache perfumed with the mint-flavored snuff that sat snuggly in his front pocket.

Hell of an audience.

"As Dr. Sharp just mentioned, I've been working extensively on re-opening cold cases and using new technology to bring those cases back to life, and hopefully close them, and provide closure to the victims' loved ones. This includes cold case 7327, which is why we're here today." She slid a thumb drive into the computer and clicked on the projector.

"As you all know, I've determined the bones you submitted are from a young, Caucasian boy, age range ten to twelve years old, with a height of fifty-four inches. Estimated TOD is between thirty and thirty-five years ago." She walked across the room and flipped off the lights as all eyes followed her every move. Then, she clicked on the projector and opened the crime scene photos where the bones had been found a week earlier. "Per the case file I reviewed, this was the location of the grave, correct?"

"That's right. In a field, in the lower delta of the state. Very remote area."

"And there are no missing boys in the area that match this profile at, or around, the TOD?"

"That's correct."

She nodded. "So based on that information, or lack thereof I should say, I ran a stable isotope analysis on the bones."

"Stable... what?"

"Stable isotope analysis. This type of test is a relatively new development in forensic science. There are two types of isotopes, radioactive and stable. Radioactive isotopes decay over time and become untraceable, whereas, stable isotopes do not decay and remain at the level they were when the victim died."

"And how does this help us?" Agent Miller asked.

Sadie clicked a few keys on the computer and brought up an image of stable isotope ratios. "Isotopes are every-where, in everything—soil, water, air, *everything*. As we age, the tissues in our body constantly replace and renew, and the isotopes that are in the food we eat, water we drink, and air we breathe become a part of our tissues, including our bones. When the body dies, radioactive isotopes decay, while stable isotopes stay at the exact level as when the person took their last breath. This is where I come in."

She clicked another slide. "You can see here, there are many different kinds of isotopes, but for bone analysis, we typically look at carbon, nitrogen, hydrogen, and oxygen isotopes. Carbon and nitrogen help us understand the dietary signature of a victim—what he or she ate, drank. For case 7327, his carbon levels were notably elevated, with the nitrogen levels being abnormally low. This tells me that the boy was most likely a vegetarian, with possibly a significant amount of fish in his diet."

Eyebrows raised around the room.

She continued, "Now, this is where things get fun. Or, interesting I should say. With hydrogen and oxygen levels, we can determine where the victim lived in the last years of his life by analyzing the isotopes in the water he drank, then, comparing that to the precipitation of various geographic locations." She clicked to a picture of a map. "Based on the amount of oxygen isotopes in the boy's bones, I can determine that 7327 grew up on, or near, the ocean, or lived there recently."

"*What?*" The sheriff leaned forward.

She nodded. "I thought this was interesting, too, considering the bones were found hundreds of miles from the ocean."

"So, our boy is a vegetarian pre-teen who possibly grew up on the ocean." Agent Miller scribbled on his notepad.

"I'm not finished." Sadie held up a finger, then clicked to a map of the US, a red circle around the Gulf of Mexico. "So, with the information I had—Caucasian male, between the ages of ten to twelve, around fifty-four inches in height, residing near the ocean—I did a search in NamUs, the database for missing and unidentified persons, pulled a list of names, and then I narrowed *that* list down by the estimated time of death, which cut the list in half. Then, I looked at which of those missing boys lived near the ocean and zeroed in on the areas closest to the Arkansas Delta. I came up with forty-seven names."

"Holy shit..." Agent Brown's eyebrow arched.

"Not done," she said, feeling a rush of renewed energy. "During my search, I came across the name Josiah Macon. Does this name sound familiar?"

Head shakes around the room.

She clicked on a black and white mug shot. "That's Josiah Macon, otherwise known as the Bike Killer, who's serving three life sentences in Texas for the raping and murdering of three young boys, ages ten, ten, and twelve." The room was dead silent. "So, I did a search of missing boys in the locations where Macon is said to have stalked his victims and found the name of a Blake Paulson." She clicked to a photo of the poster that had been plastered around the boy's hometown thirty years earlier. "From there, I asked one of our guys to create a facial reconstruction based on the skull." She clicked to the picture.

Her boss grinned with pride, as Agent Miller's, Brown's, and Sheriff Dunn's mouths dropped.

The facial reconstruction photo and the actual photo of Blake Paulson were a mirror image.

"Then, I checked out the family of the missing boy, and bingo, they're vegetarian."

A solid five seconds of dead air ticked by until—

"Holy. *Fucking.* Shit." This from Agent Brown.

Her boss turned to her, "Unbelievable work, Dr. Hart."

"Dr. Hart," Agent Miller stood and extended his baseball-glove sized hand. "I'll remember the name."

After Sadie handed out her official report, Agent Miller and Agent Brown left the room to take calls, with Sheriff Dunn following while pulling the snuff from his pocket.

"Nice job," Ronnie said, as he picked up his coffee from

the table. "And, hey..." he leaned in. "Try not to worry about it."

Her stomach hit the floor. "Try not to worry about what, exactly?"

"You know... the Evan deal."

The Evan deal. Fumbling for words, she felt the heat rise to her cheeks, which her boss apparently noticed because he changed the subject.

"Ah, one more thing before we head out. Any update on case 7370?"

"Uhhh..." her brain scrambled to recall whatever case he was talking about as she tried to ease her racing pulse. Her freaking boss had read the blogs about her failed relationship with the owner's son.

Geez.

She was *humiliated.*

"You know, the woman that was recovered by Otter Lake around Berry Springs?"

She blinked. "Oh, yeah, sorry." The images of a woman's skeleton found in an exposed shallow grave flashed through her head. A father and son had discovered the bones at twilight while fishing five months earlier. Like nothing short of a scene in a horror movie, they'd edged their boat through the weeds along the shoreline, only to discover the arm and half a human skull breaching the mud as if trying to dig out of its grave. Rumor had it the boy didn't speak for two days, and if Sadie had to guess, didn't sleep for much longer than that.

"No, nothing more than was in my final report. All bones accounted for except for one molar. Two fractures just above that, on the maxilla, suggest blunt force trauma."

"Indicating a homicide."

"Right, that, and the fact the woman was buried in an

unmarked grave." Sadie remembered the details, perhaps because the woman was estimated to be around the same age as herself, or maybe it was because not a single person had come forward with any information, and not a single family had claimed the bones. The case went cold and was added to Sadie's long list of cold cases. Five months later, the woman still had no ID. And that didn't sit well with Sadie. A life cut short, wasted, forgotten and honored by no one. No vigilance, no funeral, no respect.

It was as if she were a ghost.

Local and state law enforcement had done everything they could to put a name to the bones, causing the local gossip to run rampant. Some said she was part of a coven of witches rumored to live in the mountains, some said she was an escapee of a local mental health facility—who confirmed no missing residents—and some even suggested the bones belonged to a discarded science experiment cour-tesy of aliens. It had been five months and people still talked about the bones found at Otter Lake.

One thing was for sure, someone knew something. Someone buried her body.

Someone was hiding something, and as long as the gossips deemed the young woman worthy of conversation, she still had a chance for justice.

"What makes you ask about it again?"

"Had a voicemail from Sheriff Crawly about it."

"Does he have an idea who she was?"

"Not sure. You can ask him about it when you see him later today."

"Later today where?"

"At the excavation in Berry Springs. He's the one working the case of the bones found in Crypts Cavern. Lots of skeletons in Berry Springs, apparently." He scratched the top of his head. "Crotchety fella..."

"Crotchety?"

Ronnie's phone rang. "Gotta get this. Good luck today. Be careful driving in the mountains." He put his hand on her shoulder in a way that made her cringe. "Might be good to get out of here for a couple days. Let everything die down."

Die down.

As Ronnie left the room, Sadie was left thinking about the young woman whose identity consisted of the numbers 7370, and she made a mental note to ask the "crotchety" sheriff if he'd made any advancements in the case.

Because if there was anything being a forensic anthropologist had taught Sadie, it was that all secrets come to light sooner or later.

4

GRIFFIN GLANCED OVER his shoulder as he reached for the door marked 'Janitor.'

"Morning, Griff."

He quickly pulled his hand off the knob. "Morning, Sam.

"Good luck on your dig later today."

"Thanks." He lifted his cell phone, pretending to be checking his texts as the front desk receptionist sauntered down the hallway.

Phew. That was close.

One last look behind him and he slid past the door and closed—and locked—it behind him.

"Geez, where the hell were—"

"Shhh..." Griffin felt his pulse kick as he crossed the five-by-five room, sidestepping a mop bucket, and red biohazard bag, and silenced his latest obsession with a long, slow kiss.

She tasted like vanilla and mint, the combination reminding him of Christmas morning. The blood funneled between his legs as he gripped the back of Kimi's head, fisting her hair in his hand.

"Did you..." she whispered between kisses.

"Yes," he whispered back, fumbling with her black, leather belt.

Kimi pulled away, her eyes sparkling, "So, I'm going? Sadie said I could come to Crypts Cavern with you guys?"

"Yep." He made his way down to her neck, smelling the sweet floral scent that had kept him up at night since Kimi Haas joined the team at KT Crime Labs. He'd never forget seeing her for the first time, crossing the white marble lobby, the morning sun streaking through her black hair, long, and as soft as silk. She wore a white blouse, with the sleeves rolled up just enough to get a peek at a small flower tattoo on her forearm, and a black pencil skirt showcasing tanned legs and curves that were something straight out of a music video—back when hot chicks were still the main feature.

Kimi Haas was young, smart, sizzling-hot, with just enough attitude to add fuzzy cuffs and a leather whip to his insta-fantasy as they'd met eyes for the first time.

A fantasy he'd made happen not forty-eight hours later after inviting her to happy hour—he'd always thought KT should have a welcoming committee, after all. Since that bed-breaking evening, Griffin and Kimi had taken their sexcapades beyond the bedroom, into the office, her car, his car, and most recently the janitor's closet. Being with—make that inside—Kimi Haas had become his reason for living, breathing, and shaving parts of him he'd previously never thought a razor should be within three feet of.

Kimi was exciting, uninhibited, and one-hundred percent non-committal.

His perfect woman.

She kicked off her black six-inch heels as her pants fell down to her ankles.

Griffin groaned as his hand trailed her hot-pink panties. "You know I love pink."

After sliding off his shirt, she grinned, "You know I like a man in a wrinkled, button-down short-sleeve shirt with a stained breast pocket."

"It's in the trash. You'll never see it again," he muttered as he cupped her over her panties, his thumb running along her inner lips, his fingertips pressing into the bottom of her candy apple ass. "Better yet, let's take it outside and run it over with my truck."

"I'd rather take a ride on this first," she said with a smirk as she grabbed his balls so hard one flew up and caught in his throat.

He smirked. *Damn* he loved this woman.

"Get this fucking thing off." He fumbled with one of the million teeny-tiny silver buttons that ran down her blouse.

"Just pull it over my fucking head... but watch my makeup."

"I'll watch your makeup slide all over my dick."

She tipped her head back and laughed. "God, we're corny. Get your pants off."

With him wearing only a pair of black socks pulled up to his shins, and her, only two toe rings on her feet, Griffin pressed his lips to her plump, red mouth, as she wrapped a hand around his erection, and began sliding back and forth.

"I have a meeting in five minutes." She muttered.

"I only need two."

Kimi grinned through his kisses. "Oh, be still my heart..."

He cocked a brow, "Not for me... for you."

Eyes locked on hers, he got down on his knees, propped one of her legs up on a metal rack, then slipped underneath her. He looked up at her eyes, flaring with heat.

"One minute, you can time me."

She glanced at the clock ticking on the wall. "Go."

With his pride on the line, Griffin slid his hands up her leg, then cupped her ass as he kissed her inner thigh.

"Forty-eight seconds..."

His tongue slid to her inner lips, barely tracing the sensitive skin with the tip of his tongue, before pressing into her.

"Oh, Griff..." Her breath had picked up, the heat radiating from her tanned skin.

Slowly circling her clit—his favorite spot—he inserted a finger... then two.

A soft groan escaped her mouth, hardening him like a steel rod.

She was hot, tight, her wetness sliding around his fingers as he pressed harder, licking over her, faster and faster.

"Shit... *baby....*"

Baby. It had become his favorite word in the English dictionary because it meant she was close.

He slid in another finger, sending her squirming and gripping the walls. A can marked with a skull and crossbones began tipping back and forth, but he didn't give a shit. He'd take a shower of acid just to watch this woman come.

Five, four, three, two...

"I'm going to—"

Her whisper trailed off as her warm release rushed over his fingertips.

He savored the moment, the taste, then pulled away.

Her sleepy eyes twinkled. "Cutting it pretty close."

He stood, trailing his wet fingers over her stomach. "You complaining? Because we've got another four minutes—"

She flung her arms around his neck. "Fuck me. Shut up, and fuck me."

The words were like a shot of speed to his system. He

gripped her waist and slammed her back against the wall as she wrapped her legs around him.

He crushed his lips onto hers and speared into her. Her fingernails digging into his back as he pulled out and pushed back in. No preamble, no patience, no mercy.

Back and forth, her warm wetness tightening with each thrust, sending tingles flying over the sheen of sweat coating his skin. Her hands trailed down to his ass, grabbed, and pushed him in deeper. He grit his teeth, pounding her so hard her head banged against the concrete wall.

His head began to spin, something clattered to the ground—hopefully not the skull and crossbones spray—and before he could release the breath he didn't realize he'd been holding, he exploded himself inside her, another small piece of his heart stolen.

*S*ADIE GLANCED NERVOUSLY at the camper in the rearview mirror as she passed the *Welcome to Berry Springs* sign.

Almost there.

She'd towed campers many times before, but as they'd neared the Ozark Mountains, the roads became curvy and the shoulders had shrunk by a good six inches—which was ironic.

Somewhere over the course of the ninety-minute drive, small-talk had dwindled and Kimi had become emerged in whatever game was the latest craze on her cell phone in the back seat. The incessant *ding, ding, ding* making Sadie want to *drive, drive, drive* into oncoming traffic. The background noise had a different effect on Griffin, luring him into a hypnotic sleep in the passenger seat. Guy sure seemed abnormally tired the last few months.

And that was just fine with her. Sadie had rolled her window down, allowing the crisp, autumn air to sweep through her hair, little by little releasing some of the stress of her epically shitty morning. She'd spent most of the morning hiding in her office. The few people that she did come into contact with stared like she'd sprouted snakes from her head. Although, Medusa probably got more sympathy. What Sadie got was a bunch of gossiping women chomping at the bit to giggle, speculate about her firing, and add to the humiliating experience of a break-up gone public. And some, she had no doubt, were plotting how to woo the newly single trust fund baby. Good luck with that hot mess.

Then, after a mind-numbingly boring lunch seminar, Sadie ran to her house, took a quick shower to wash all traces of triple-chocolate mocha from her skin, then changed into clean pants, hiking boots, and a KT Crime Labs T-shirt. After grabbing her overnight bag, she locked up her apartment, more than ready to get out of town.

Maybe her boss was right—a little time out of the office was exactly what she needed.

Maybe her day would turn around.

Sadie checked the GPS as they rolled into town, then turned onto Main Street—the main drag that split the center of the small, country town.

Small, and country it was.

Sadie had heard about Berry Springs—a nature-lover's tourist destination, known for its hiking, camping, fishing and just about anything else one could do outdoors—but had never been. She rolled to a stop at the town's only stop-light and looked around.

Jacked-up pickups, a handful of Suburus, and even a few ATVs speckled the parking spots along the town's square, which appeared to be the hub of Berry Springs. Colorful mums, pumpkins, and hay bales decorated the store fronts, and Sadie noticed a few ghosts swaying above a jack-o'-lantern in the window of a jewelry store. A family on horseback made their way across the sidewalk as if it were a normal form of transportation. Four elderly men in flannel shirts and cowboy hats sat in rocking chairs outside of Tad's Tool Shop, no doubt waiting for their wives to leave Bonnie's Bouffant, a hair salon across the street. A *Happy Fall Y'all* sign decorated the front of Fanny's Farm and Feed, which was next door to a charming restaurant named Donny's Diner, where blue-checkered curtains hung from windows that spelled out the daily specials. Today, get your homemade pumpkin pie and bottomless coffee for only $1.99. A heck of a deal in any Southerner's book. Red booths peeked from the window where a gray-haired woman in a white apron and a bun on top of her head laughed hysterically, before leaning in for a whisper.

Sadie watched a man open a door for a group of women, tipping his cowboy hat in greeting.

It was as if she'd stepped back in time, to the small, black-and-white town of Mayberry.

The light turned green, and after taking notice of the county coroner's office, she followed the narrow two-lane road out of town, and into miles and miles of dense forests and soaring mountains bright with autumn's colors. It was beautiful scenery, and she might have enjoyed the drive if it weren't for the camper attached to the back of her SUV. Every sharp turn, every steep descent made the knots in her shoulders squeeze like a pretzel. Rocky cliffs hugged one side of the road, the other, steep drop-offs that made her stomach dip.

She looked in the rearview mirror at the camper for the hundredth time, its tires hugging the center line.

God help anyone coming from the opposite direction.

After white-knuckling a few more hairpin corners, she

followed the directions onto a narrow dirt road at the base of a mountain.

"Where the *hell* are we?" Griffin sat up, rubbing his eyes.

"Morning." Sadie glanced at the GPS as her SUV bottomed out—for the *third* time—on the pitted road. After making sure the camper was still attached, she replied, "The Ozark Mountains."

Griffin gripped the *oh-shit* handle above his window as they hit another bump. "Yeah, but *where?*"

"I think we've officially crossed into no-man's land, or mountains, I should say." She was pretty sure Griffin was going to have to physically remove her hands from the steering wheel once they reached their destination.

"What time are we supposed to meet the sheriff?"

"Three. According to the GPS, we've got a few more miles on this road, but I think we'll make it on time."

Griffin looked in the backseat. *"Whoa..."*

Sadie glanced at Kimi in the rearview mirror, her head resting against the headrest, a green ring circling her mouth.

She braked as Griffin undid his seatbelt and turned around. "You okay?" He asked Kimi.

"I feel like I've been on the Gravitron."

"If you were on the Gravitron, you'd be vomiting cotton candy, funnel cakes, and cherry Slurpees all over your Keds."

"Oh *God,* don't talk about funnel cakes," she groaned, gripping her stomach.

"Speaking from experience?" Sadie grinned.

"Maybe... maybe two experiences."

Sadie rolled down all the windows and made a mental note that their new-hire got motion sickness. "You need to puke?" She asked.

"No, just get us there."

"Okay, but if you do need to, I can pull over, or, better yet, puke in Griffin's bag."

"*Nice,* boss," he muttered.

Sadie slowed at a fork in the road. "Which way?"

After tossing Kimi a bottle of water, Griffin sat back in his seat and looked at the GPS. "Left." He glanced at his phone. "*Dammit.*"

"What?"

"No freakin' reception."

She sighed and shook her head. Of course there were no luxuries like cell phone reception in these mountains.

"We'll have the wifi hot spot in the camper, and the SAT cell."

"Thank God for modern technology."

Sadie thought of the gossip columns and how someone's personal life could be splashed online for the entire world to read in under one minute. At that moment, she didn't know how grateful she was.

"Thank God for Dramamine," Kimi muttered from the backseat.

"You recognize the area, Kimi?" Sadie asked, trying to guide Kimi's mind away from regurgitation.

"I've never been this far into the mountains."

"You lived in Berry Springs for a bit, though, right?"

Griffin shot her a look. She narrowed her eyes and shot back. The kid was defensive and protective over Kimi. Perhaps his mama *hadn't* taught him about sticking his pen in the company ink.

"Just about a year in high school. It's a typical southern town with your cowboys and cowgirls. Small... a bit suffocating, to be honest."

"Well, hopefully we won't need to go into town for anything."

"I kinda wanted to go to Donny's Diner while I was here," Griffin said. "Great food... and I always prefer to eat with the living."

"What's that supposed to mean?" Kimi leaned forward, her black hair whipping around her face, a little color back in her cheeks now.

Griffin glanced in the backseat. "You haven't heard the legends about Crypts Cavern?"

"Indulge us," Sadie said with a grin.

"Okay, well, let's just say it didn't get its name for no reason." As if on cue, a dark cloud slid over the late afternoon sun, casting shadows across the dirt road. "So, the legend goes, sometime in the mid-to-late 1700's, during the French and Indian War, a tribe of Indians led by a warrior named Atohi, took refuge in the cave, hiding in its tunnels and rooms. The cave is huge, but super treacherous. I don't even think they let people in it now. Anyway, the legend is that while in hiding, Atohi trained his tribe to fight, using sticks and rocks he'd collect in the woods while he'd sneak out in the middle of the night. Day and night they trained, with little food, only eating the fish they'd catch inside the cave's lake. No light, except to build a fire to cook food at night. They trained in pitch-blackness, starving, scared. They started arguing, going nuts, and a few snapped, killing each other, tossing the bodies into the lake for the blind fish the size of pigs to eat. The story goes that the isolation and darkness took over Atohi, and he began killing anyone who challenged him. With nothing but a hatchet, he'd hack them to pieces in front of everyone else."

"Did you say a lake?" Kimi asked, as if that were the most disturbing part of the story.

"Oh, yeah. An underground water system runs through the cave."

"And blind fish the size of pigs?" Sadie didn't bother hiding the skepticism in her voice.

"That's right. There's a lot of fish in the water, and they're blind—never seen natural light, so their eyes never developed. And some fish will grow as big as their environment allows, especially if there's enough food and they never leave."

"How do you know all this?"

"I like my ghost stories... and haven't you seen my aquarium at home?"

"You're such a dork," Kimi muttered.

Griffin turned and winked at Kimi, then continued, "Anyway, as the British soldiers made their way into the mountains, they found the cave and not knowing that Atohi and his tribe were hiding inside, they made their way in. Atohi funneled the soldiers into a narrow corridor, and using the darkness to their advantage, the tribe killed them off one by one. You've heard of the Battle of Thermopylae? Greek mythology? You know, the movie 300, where Leonidas and his men held off an army of thousands of Persians? It was kind of like that. The English had them outnumbered and outmatched with their guns, but because of the narrow passageway, numbers meant nothing. Atohi and his tribe were rumored to have killed hundreds of soldiers."

"And by hundreds, you probably mean five."

"Or none at all," Kimi said, rolling her eyes.

Sadie laughed.

"And by the way, Leonidas died in the end of that movie."

"Well you two naysayers haven't let me finish. *So,* after killing these *hundreds* of men, the tribe threw their bodies in the lake in the cave, but kept their guns, food, clothes and provisions. This went on for days as more soldiers came to look for the ones that never returned. Atohi would hide in the shadows and pick them off one by one. The British eventually thought the cave was haunted and assembled a small army to take it by storm. Well... it was a dark, *stoooormy* night..." Griffin lowered his voice and wiggled his fingers in the air, "...and the rains came, storm after storm, inches of rain pounding the mountains. As Atohi and his tribe waited for their final battle, the waters in the cave rose, trapping them inside. The tribe traveled as far back into the cave as they could, seeking higher ground, only to perish in the black waters of the cave's bottomless lake, where their souls are said to remain locked in the cave forever."

"Oh my *God.*" Kimi slapped a hand over her eyes and shook her head.

"Let me guess... that's how the name Crypt Cavern came about." Sadie edged the SUV around a log in the middle of the road.

"Exactly. But I'm not done..."

"*No more...*" Kimi muttered.

Sadie chuckled as Griffin continued, "Okay, so sometime in the early 1900's, it's rumored that a descendant of Atohi, took his family to the same cave to tell them the story of their heritage. Well, the story goes that once inside the cave, the father started hearing voices and seeing the souls of his forefathers, haunting and taunting him in the darkness. It's said that the father claimed the spirits told him to kill his family, and with a *hatchet* and the help of Atohi, the father hacked his wife, two daughters and three young boys to death, limb by limb, then threw their bodies into the lake, before sending the hatchet through his own forehead and disappearing into the lake."

Sadie wrinkled her nose. "That's a disgusting story, Griff."

"I know, and the rumor is the family, and Atohi and his tribe haunt Crypts Cavern to this day. Everyone who goes inside risks never coming out. You know, the same cave *we're* going to."

Kimi laughed. "So *ridiculous*. Give me a *break*."

Griffin turned around in his seat. "So you're saying that you want to camp out with me beside the cave tonight, then, Kimi?"

"I'll camp out in the exact spot that the ruthless killer *Atohi* took his last damn breath."

Griffin's eyebrows popped up. "Really? Care to make this interesting?"

"Come on guys," Sadie cringed as a branch swiped the side of her SUV. "No one's sleeping in, or around, that cave tonight. Not because I care about your limbs, but I'll be damned if I towed this Godforsaken camper on these trails they call roads, for nothing. Do you know how many years this little trip has shaved off my life?"

"Eh, it's good for you. Women drivers need all the practice they can get."

"Hey!" This in perfect unison, from the front and back seat.

"Just joking," Griffin looked back at Kimi. "Seriously, I could use a new pair of hiking boots. Let's make it a hundred bucks. A hundred smackers say you can't make it a full night camping outside the cave, alone. There's an extra tent in the camper you can use."

"Make it five hundred."

Sadie cocked a brow and looked in the rearview mirror at the twinkle in Kimi's dark eyes. She was alert, and bowed up with determination. *Sadie decided that minute that she liked the girl.*

"Deal." Griffin's ear-to-ear grin resembled a Cheshire cat.

"Alright guys... that's enough gambling for the moment." Sadie tapped the brakes. "Griffin check the GPS."

They paused at another fork in the road—good versus evil. To the right, a straight road cut through mountains where a few beams of sunlight escaped the cloud cover, looking magical against the fall colors. To the left, rocks, boulders, a bleak gray, with steep cliffs and darkness in the distance.

"According to the directions, take a left here." Griffin frowned at the road that seemed to disappear into rocks. "Although between you and me, let's hang a right and say we got lost. Maybe have a little camping party before we get to work."

"As much fun as a *camping party*—whatever the heck that is—sounds, we've got work to do." She hung a left, descending into the grayness.

"Fine."

"I think we're almost there, anyway. Let's go over the notes before we meet the sheriff."

"Sheriff Crawly."

"What an unfortunate last name."

"Agreed." Griffin yanked out a folder from Sadie's purse on the floorboard. "Okay, so two teenagers found a handful of bones in Crypts Cavern, freaked, called the cops, and they called us to excavate."

"Exactly, although more than a few bones. A full skeleton as I understand it."

"A *full* skeleton? *Inside* the cave?" Kimi slid to the middle of the backseat and leaned forward, between Sadie and Griffin.

"Right. Full skeleton."

"Are they sure it's human? Heck of a drive for us to tell them it's animal bones."

"The local medical examiner—Jessica Heathrow I believe—confirmed the bones are human."

"A corpse found deep in Crypts Cavern, in the middle of remote mountains, with no cell phone service." Griffin shrugged, "Well, I've never been spelunking before. Should be interesting."

"You've never explored a cave?" Sadie asked.

"Been on a few guided tours."

"Well, that's something I guess."

"You been?" Griffin asked Kimi in the rearview mirror.

"A few times when I was younger."

Sadie hit a pothole, bottoming out again before bouncing her out of her seat and sending Kimi's water bottle tumbling to the floor.

"Geez!"

Dollar signs ran through Sadie's head. "I don't know how much further my car can take us."

Griffin looked at the GPS. "According to this, we're here. The meeting place is right here."

Sadie hit the brakes and looked around at the dense woods encircling them. According to the email, she would "see their cars" at the meet point.

She squinted, peering ahead. "I think the road curves up there." Barely accelerating, Sadie inched around the corner which opened up to a small clearing with three jacked-up pickups.

Four men hovered over a hood of one of the trucks. Heads turned as she parked underneath a pine tree.

"Finally," Kimi flung open her door.

"Grab her another bottle of water, Griff. There's no coming back from a vomiting first impression."

Kimi poured herself out of the SUV and sat on the grass, putting her head between her knees.

Sadie laughed. "Go hold her hair if she hurls. I'll go talk to the group."

"Thanks, boss."

Griffin pushed out the passenger side and kneeled next to Kimi as Sadie scanned the group of men. Tall, burly, southern—two in cowboy hats. A sheriff, two cops—she pegged instantly—and a particularly large guy hidden behind sunglasses with his attention focused on papers scattered across the hood.

According to the email, Sheriff Crawly had implied that her team would be meeting only him. What had changed in the last twenty-four hours?

She pushed out of the SUV, the knots in her back unfolding one by one as she straightened. She glanced up at the graying sky as a cool breeze rustled the trees above. Dead leaves tumbled to the ground. The winds were picking up.

"Dr. Hart, I'm Sheriff Crawly." The sheriff met her in the middle of the clearing.

In full uniform, Sheriff Crawly looked to be closing in on fifty, and based on the settling wrinkles, tanned skin, meticulously buzzed haircut, and the kind of belly that only came from six-packs found in the refrigerator, he'd spent most of those years in law enforcement. And based on the way he was scanning her from head-to-toe, subtlety was not one of his strong suits. He extended his hand, a gleam in his eye that made her want to vomit like Kimi was probably doing at that moment. "Thanks for coming out," his gaze never leaving her chest.

Geez.

She gripped his hand, then yanked it away. She'd intended to ask him about case 7370 before they went into the cave, but decided to wait until his hormones cooled a bit. Her gaze was pulled over the sheriff's shoulder like a magnet, meeting a pair of dark sunglasses that pinned her where she stood.

Her stomach flip-flopped, catching her off guard.

"Sunglass Guy" was tall, she guessed north of six-two, with dark hair, a chiseled face with a hint of a five-o'clock shadow, boulders for shoulders, and pecs that were something out of a superhero movie. He wore a gray T-shirt, khaki tactical pants, and worn ATAC boots that capped off the all-male alpha vibe emanating from him. Intimidating —no question. Completely mesmerizing, why?

"Find the place okay?"

She tore her eyes away and shifted back to the sheriff who'd spotted Kimi with her head between her legs.

At least she wasn't puking.

"Just followed your directions."

"Hell of a drive with a camper," an officer wearing a BSPD T-shirt walked up and extended his hand. A tall, thick man with looks that would send most women drooling. Hell, she probably would have if it weren't for the mystery sunglass guy that suddenly had her full attention.

"Lieutenant Quinn Colson, BSPD."

"Nice to meet you. And unfortunately, not my first time towing a camper through mountains." She glanced back at Griffin and Kimi still on the grass. "They need a second."

The lieutenant laughed, "Took me awhile to get used to the roads, too. They need anything?"

"No, just fresh air and solid ground."

"Plenty of that 'round here."

"Is this as far as we can go in?"

"Afraid so." He led her to the trucks, with Sheriff Crawly walking close behind her. A little too closely as she could practically feel him staring at her ass. The guy gave her the creeps. Crotchety? Not so much. Perverted old-man? Yep.

Lieutenant Colson continued, "The cave's about a ten minute hike in. You'll have to camp here and trek back and forth as needed."

Her gaze flittered to sunglass guy again, who's attention had shifted to the sheriff behind her.

"This is officer Owen Grayson." Lieutenant Colson motioned across the hood. "Search and rescue with the coast guard, working for us part-time until he goes back to full-time duty."

Military. Suddenly the superhero body and rigid demeanor made sense.

The officer dipped his chin, lingering on her for a minute before looking back at the sheriff who said—

"And this is Deputy Tucker, with the Carroll County patrol. Former National Guard, been with me 'bout two years now."

Wearing a T-shirt, jeans and hiking boots, the Deputy tipped his cowboy hat. He was a bit younger than the sheriff, with a long, lean, lanky build that reminded her of Gumby. The sheriff continued, "Technically Crypts is under my jurisdiction, but considering the proximity to Berry Springs, we're working with BSPD on this."

"Nice to meet you all."

She met Officer Grayson's gaze again, wanting more than anything to see the eyes behind the mask. Goosebumps spread over her skin. She turned away, feeling a flush heating her cheeks.

Holy *smokes,* who the *hell* was this guy?

She turned to footsteps coming up behind them. "And this is Griffin Olsen, an intern with KT Crime Labs, studying forensic anthropology, and this is Kimi Haas, a forensic pathologist with the lab."

"Sorry about that." Kimi innocently shrugged. "Mountain roads."

"I've got some mints in the truck if you need it," Sheriff Crawly nodded toward his truck, and Sadie noticed that he didn't linger on Kimi like he did with her. Maybe she didn't get all the chocolate coffee smell off her skin.

"I already got her a few, and some water," Griffin said sharply, with a hint of possessiveness.

Sadie narrowed her eyes, leveling Griffin with a single look, then turned back to the team. "Well, now that everyone's met, let's get to work. Do you have the cave survey?"

Crawly nodded toward the dented hood covered in papers and coffee mugs.

She stepped next to Officer Grayson, who stood as still as a rock for a moment before shifting away. It was as if she could feel the energy shooting between them. She fought the urge to slide another glance at him as the team gathered around the hood.

"So, as I said, the cave is about a ten minute hike in. And I do mean *hike.* Rough terrain out here. I hope you all brought appropriate attire, bug spray—"

"This isn't our first excavation in the woods, Sheriff."

Crawly cocked a brow, glanced at her chest again—to remind her that he could—then continued, "As discussed, the plan for today is to excavate the bones from the cave. Day two, search for any other bones, bodies, or missing bones from the skeleton recovered." He looked up at the late afternoon sun. "We need to get a move on. Don't want to lose our light. You ain't seen pitch-black until you've been out here after dark" He redirected his attention to the map. "The cave covers 5.3 miles, as far as we know, with the deepest point being 230 feet underground." He positioned a detailed map in front of her, and pointed. "As you can see the cave is home to an extensive underground water system, with the biggest part of the lake in what we call the Grand Room, which is eight stories high. The lake in this room stretches about seventy-five feet through rooms, tunnels and narrow pathways, and is bottomless."

"You don't actually mean bottomless?" Kimi cocked her head.

"Over the years, we've had several divers who have been unable to reach the bottom of the lake. One diver reached almost a hundred feet before giving up. It was too dangerous. Came across some freaky-ass creatures, though, he says."

"Sounds ominous."

"There's living marine life in the cave's waters, translucent fish, blind, and probably more species that we haven't seen. Oh, and it's also home to one of the largest bat colonies in the state."

Griffin shot Sadie a *you've-got-to-be-kidding-me* look. She winked.

Officer Grayson pulled a few bags from the bed of the truck and tossed them on the ground.

"Ah, yes," Crawly nodded to the bags. "We've got extra headlamps, harnesses, and a few other things we might need. Take one of each and put them in your packs."

Sadie kneeled at the bags, as Griffin and Kimi hovered over her. "Is the cave open to the public?" She asked Crawly.

"Meaning, do they give tours?"

"Right." She swatted a gnat zipping around her face.

"No, too treacherous. We've posted plenty of enter-at-your-own-risk signs, but people ignore them. If anything, those damn things are like flashing signs that say, 'I dare you to come inside.'"

The lieutenant laughed at this, the sheriff and the deputy didn't, the man of steel shifted his weight.

Crawly continued, "Crypts is a popular spot with the locals, to go spelunking or whatever. Can't count how many calls we've responded to out here."

"And bodies." Deputy Tucker shoved a water bottle into his pack.

"How many bodies?" Sadie noticed Lieutenant Colson and Crawly both glanced at Officer Grayson, before Crawly said, "I've been doing this thirty years, and have been called out to this cave more times than I care to remember, and pulled five bodies."

"Five?"

"Most tourists. Idiots."

Officer Grayson grabbed his pack on the ground, the metal water bottle that dangled from the side slamming into the sheriff's truck. The group went silent for a moment as all eyes shifted to Grayson.

Sadie zipped up her pack as she stood, looking at each of the men. She was missing something. They weren't telling her something, and that didn't sit well with her.

Crawly shot a warning look at Grayson, which went unnoticed. "As I was saying, there's a lot of legends surrounding the cave, as well as rumors that it's haunted. All the souls who lost their lives inside haunt those who attempt to explore it. And I can't say I don't believe it."

"Ghosts, bats, and blind fish. What could go wrong?"

Griffin muttered as a cluster of dead leaves fell onto the hood.

"Where was the body found?" Sadie asked, returning to the subject.

The sheriff pulled a pen from his pocket and pointed to the map. "Here."

Her brows tipped up. "The middle of the cave?"

"Exactly. A pair of fearless teenagers found the bones. It's nothing less than shocking they made it that far inside... which is why we're assuming the bones have never been found. No one's been that far in. You have to drop down, 'bout ten feet, into a narrow hole to find the room where the bones were found."

"Sooooo," Kimi glanced around the group. "Where are the bones now?"

"Still there."

"Still in the '*it's nothing less than shocking they made it that far*' room of the cave?" Griffin asked.

"Yes. We wanted to leave the bones undisturbed. No telling what a find it could be. Early settlers—"

"Aliens," Kimi quipped.

"But you called in a *forensic* anthropologist," Sadie eyed the Sheriff suspiciously. "So you must think there was some sort of foul play here."

"That's right." He narrowed his eyes. "The bones were arranged."

"Arranged?"

"Yes. In a circle with the letter *A* in the middle."

Sadie frowned.

"Anarchy." Griffin's eyebrows raised.

"Exactly."

A gust of wind skirted up Sadie's back, followed by a shiver. "Maybe someone found the bones after the fact and decided to have a little fun. Maybe they didn't call it in because they didn't want to be associated with it. Definitely not hard to imagine. It could have been the kids who called it in, wanting to make things a little more interesting—"

"Or maybe it was the ghosts."

Sadie grinned at Griffin, then continued, "The bones being arranged in a specific way doesn't necessarily mean a crime was committed."

"This does." Officer Grayson tossed a picture across the hood.

Sadie picked up the black-and-white photo as Kimi and Griffin peered over her shoulder. The image, taken in the cave, showed a human skull with a fracture running two inches above the left eye socket.

6

OWEN WATCHED DR. Sadie Hart pop open the trunk of her SUV and give orders to her team as they pulled packs and bags from the back.

He wasn't sure what he expected when Colson had told him they'd called in a doctor to excavate the bones, but it definitely wasn't the steely-eyed, brick-balled, smoking-hot stunner standing before him now.

He guessed she was somewhere in her early thirties—which was his first shocker—with dark, hooded, almond-shaped eyes that were as skeptical as they were beautiful. Chestnut hair against smooth, pale skin and a face with defined, strong lines that seemed to fit her personality. And the sexiest pair of pouty, come-fuck-me lips he'd ever seen in his life. Based on the worn khaki tactical pants and scuffed leather hiking boots, Sadie was no stranger to the woods. And, based on the curves in the back of her pants and the T-shirt that stretched against generous breasts, she wasn't unaccustomed to getting looks from men. But the way she carried herself, the squared shoulders, no-nonsense braid of brown hair that ran down her back—occasionally falling over her shoulder, remedied by an annoyed flick of her hand—and look of determination in her eyes told him that she'd fought for her title as doctor, almost as much as she'd fought for the respect that came along with that title. A bit prickly on the initial impression, and perhaps one of those women who'd cut you at the balls just to prove she could? No doubt about it.

He watched her shrug on a blue backpack that was half her weight, and sweep her braid to the side.

No-nonsense.

Her gaze flickered to him again, as it had done a dozen times since she'd stepped out of her SUV. Subtle, stolen glances laced with questions—or interest, perhaps. He wasn't sure.

But something inside him wanted to find out.

"What do you think?" Eyeing the excavation team, Quinn Colson slid into his backpack and stepped beside Owen.

"She's still got her spots."

"Agreed. Supposed to be one of the best around though."

Let's hope so.

Quinn leaned in. "Five bucks she's the only one who makes it to the bones."

Owen narrowed his eyes. "Nope, the intern has something to prove. Five bucks he makes it, too."

"You're on. The pathologist will be crying for her mommy midway through. Wait and see."

Owen watched Sadie stride across the clearing. Griffin wasn't the only one with something to prove.

"Ready?" Crawly hollered from the trailhead.

"Not bad to look at though, I'll say that," Quinn slapped him on the back with a chuckle, then walked away.

No, not bad to look at, at all.

Owen held back as the team passed, and after pulling on his own pack and checking his Glock, he brought up the rear.

Dead leaves and pine needles crunched underneath their feet as they fell into a single file line with Crawly, Tucker, and Colson up front, and Sadie leading Griffin and Kimi. A worn path—mostly from Owen—led the way through the dense woods, with underbrush almost as thick as the canopy of trees above, acting as a blanket, blocking the sun and dimming the waning light of day. He and Quinn had cleared the path of big rocks and branches, but it was still rocky terrain—ideal for twisting an ankle.

He glanced at Kimi's hiking boots—straight out of the box. She was the one he needed to watch out for.

Sadie spoke up, addressing Crawly, "It's my understanding the medical examiner estimated the bones to be less than a year old, correct?"

"'Round there. Even less than that, she implied, anyway."

"Anyone reported missing in the cave during that time?"

Owen's gaze darted to the sheriff, who hesitated.

"Not in Crypts Cavern," Crawly said with a tone that did more than suggest that there was more to that story. Owen bit the inside of his cheek as they walked in silence a moment. Sadie didn't know the half of it, and he intended to keep it that way. For now, at least.

Sadie glanced back at Griffin with an expression that told him she'd picked up on the immediate tension. Her gaze slid to him, before turning back around.

Dr. Hart didn't miss much.

"So, what about the anarchy angle?" Griffin readjusted his pack as they climbed over a fallen tree.

"No anarchist reported missing in the cave," the sarcasm thick in Crawly's voice.

Griffin looked at Kimi and rolled his eyes, not bothering to hide his distaste for Carroll County's finest—which knocked the kid up a few notches in Owen's opinion.

"I *meant,* are there any notable groups around here?"

"Not that they'd advertise. This is the Bible Belt, after all. We've got a few groups we're looking at, but step one is your analysis of the bones."

"Anarchists typically wouldn't hide in the shadows," Kimi said. "In fact, I'd think it'd be the exact opposite. It's a movement to a lot of people—not something they do behind closed doors."

Griffin looked over his shoulder and winked. "And here I thought you were Baptist."

"No, she's right." Deputy Tucker chimed in. "Anarchists are typically vocal about their disdain for hierarchy, God, law enforcement, whatever. They rebel against authority and more often than not believe violence is justified to those who believe in law and order."

Quinn glanced back, met Owen's gaze, then turned back.

"It's typically someone who hates control and fights for freedom, as they see it. It's a common grassroots belief in many anti-government groups, militia groups, terrorist cells."

"They thrive on chaos." Quinn nodded. "Chaos, to them, is freedom. Do what you want, kind of deal."

"Punk-ass misguided kids looking to make a reason for their selfish ways." Crawly grumbled.

"Misguided youth is the foundation of terrorist groups," Sadie said.

Owen watched her scan the woods around her, her brow

knit in deep thought, her full, pink lips pinched. She moved through the woods easily, eyes up, confident, with an awareness about her usually reserved for his buddies in the military.

"Any Native American anarchist groups in the area?" Griffin asked.

"Ah, you've heard the legends." The sheriff glanced back with a smirk. "Not that we know of."

"You said there's been divers in the lake, right? Did they find anything? Bones?" Kimi stumbled on a rock and caught herself on a tree.

Owen watched Griffin shoot a grin back at Sadie as she shook her head. They were a close team, but it was no doubt Sadie was the leader. No pissing matches there.

"No bones, but don't think for two seconds that the town isn't already dying to know if the bones are Native American or not."

"Gossips have already said it's Atohi's tribe, or his ancestors," Quinn looked back grinning. "Limbs and all."

"Okay guys, the terrain gets rough up here."

Sadie, Griffin, and Kimi both craned to see the front of the line. Up ahead, a drop-off that marked a steep ravine with jagged rocks, fallen limbs and slick moss. Owen had climbed down it more times than he could count as a kid and could do it with his eyes closed now, but the thirty foot almost vertical drop would no doubt pose a challenge to hikers who spent most of their time in labs.

Crawly shouted over his shoulder, "We'll have to hike down this afternoon, but I'm getting a rope bridge secured by tonight for your guys." He stopped at the edge of the ravine. "Colson and I will go down first and help y'all down. It's not too bad, plenty of tree roots and crevices to grip onto. Just go slow. Grayson, you got the rear?"

Yeah—his gaze slid down Sadie's back—*I've got the rear.*

They gathered at the edge of the ravine while Colson, Crawly, and Tucker descended down, using the branches and roots for balance.

"So, you were with the Coast Guard?" Kimi stepped next to him as they watched the men carefully maneuver the rocks.

"Yes, ma'am."

Griffin shot him a look, followed by a glance from Sadie.

"A rescue swimmer?"

He nodded.

"You've got the shoulders."

Another glance from Sadie, but this time, a tug at the corner of her lips. *Those lips.* A breeze blew a rogue strand of hair across her face. She swept it back, her bright blue eyes twinkling in the sunlight.

Kimi continued, "My dad was a swimmer. Same build."

"Why'd you get out?" Griffin asked, inching closer to Kimi.

Owen glanced down the ravine. He never was a fan of small-talk, especially when it involved his father. "Timing."

"Timing?"

"Alright," he said as Quinn and Tucker reached the bottom, thankful to be returning to the subject at hand. "Who's first?"

"I'll go." The kid with something to prove stepped up to the edge, his manliness priority one.

Crawly had positioned himself on a large bolder in the middle of the ravine, ready to help if needed... or watch Sadie's ass the entire way down. Fucker.

"There's foot holds all the way down. Hold onto the branches and roots for stability."

"Got it," Griffin grunted as he turned and began climbing down.

Kimi stepped up next.

"As soon as he reaches Crawly, you'll head down."

She nodded, focusing on the trees past the ravine, instead of him. He followed her gaze for a moment, into the miles and miles of dense forest that surrounded them, wondering what had pulled her attention.

"Alright, next!" Crawly called up as Griffin passed his location.

"Kimi, you're up."

Kimi blinked, the distance behind those brown eyes refocusing to the present. "Sorry, okay, yeah." She gripped his hand, and he guided her down past the steepest dip.

"Grab here, then here. Good job."

When he was sure Kimi had found her bearings, he climbed back up. Sadie gripped the straps of her backpack as she watched her team zigzag down the ravine. She avoided his eye contact. Confident to steal glances in a group, but locks up one-on-one? Challenge accepted.

"You ready?" He asked, excited to get his hands on her.

Her focus remained on her team, unaware he'd just spoken to her. The woman had been staring heat waves of interest into him minutes earlier, but now, total ice queen.

What the hell?

He frowned, noticing her rigid stance, her quickened breaths, her right foot hooked under a rock.

And then it hit him.

Sadie was scared of heights.

He fought the chuckle threatening to bubble up. He couldn't help it. It surprised him.

He cleared his throat. "Dr. Hart—"

"Sadie." She snapped.

Jesus.

"Uh, Sadie, okay. You ready to head down?"

Her tongue rolled along the side of her cheek as she stared at the valley, still as a statue, except for the rapid rise and fall of her chest.

Scared was an understatement. This chick was terrified.

Dammit.

His training kicked in as the playful glances they'd exchanged earlier faded to the background. He stepped closer.

"Sadie," he lowered his voice and spoke slowly as he would to a preschooler. "We have a heights issue here, don't we?"

Her neck snapped to him like a Cobra striking, her eyes narrowed, ready to fight. "Heights issue?" Her tone was high, her words quick, and he knew her adrenaline was pumping a mile a minute. She looked back down at the rocks.

"It's okay. I'm going to be with you the entire time, okay?"

"No, no, it's okay. I can do it." Her voice shook.

"Well," he casually shrugged, "I've got to get down myself, anyway, so..."

Her hand darted out and gripped his arm. She looked at him, a desperate plea in her eye. "Look. No one knows, okay?"

"No one knows what?"

"You know..." she nodded to the ravine.

"That you have a fear of heights."

"*Shhh.*" She hissed. As if everyone could hear them down below.

"Your team doesn't know?"

"Right. I... don't want them to know. *God.*" She closed her eyes. "It's so *stupid.* I can't believe..."

"It's not stupid. Fear of heights is one of the most common phobias, followed by public speaking."

"Oh. Well, that I can do in spades."

Yeah, he had no doubt this woman could mesmerize a crowd for hours.

"*This* you can do, too."

She inhaled, held, then blew it out and looked below, still gripping his arm. "I think they know something's up."

He glanced down at Colson, Tucker, Griffin, and Kimi who were at the bottom, and then at Crawly in the middle, staring up with a *what-the-fuck* look on his face.

"No they don't, but hey, if you need some time, I can tell them to go on and we'll catch up. Hell, I can go back to my truck and get ropes and you can just ride the breeze down if you want. No big deal. This isn't a big deal."

The words seem to hit her. "You're right. This isn't a big deal." She squared her shoulders and narrowed her eyes, her chin jetting out like a little girl forcing herself up after a fall from her bicycle. "Let's do this."

He couldn't fight the grin this time. Cute was quickly mixing with her sex factor.

"Good girl. Alright, give me your pack."

"What? No."

"It'll be easier to climb down without it." He reached forward—

"You remove this pack, I'll remove that hand."

Cute like a rattlesnake. His grin widened. "Alrighty, then. Okay, I'm going to go down a few feet first, like I did with Kimi, and I'll inch you down little by little. The key here is to take it slow. There's no rush. Screw them. Alright, here I go, okay?"

She nodded, her nostrils flaring as she inhaled.

He kept his eyes on her as he lowered himself past the

first tree, its roots snarling along the jagged edges, then past the steepest dip. Then, he locked his foot in a crevice.

"Okay, Sadie, it's go time."

"Go time," she repeated in a whisper, her skin pale as a ghost now.

"You got this. Hey. *Hey.*" He waited until she looked at him. "You've got this."

She continued incessantly nodding—like a neurotic tick —as she turned and squatted, and it took every bit of his restraint not to reach up and pinch the thing.

"Grab the rock in front of you there, yes... good job, now, step down..."

No step down.

"Step down onto the ledge."

No step. Sadie was frozen like a toy fireman locked in a ladder-climbing position.

"Sadie. Step down."

Nada.

Fuck.

He took a second to assess the footholds, then shifted his weight and shimmied onto a ledge that was barely wide enough to hold his big toe. After confirming it was free of moss—*thank God*—he released his weight, grabbed onto a tree root and placed his hand on the small of her back.

"I've got you now." He edged closer and wrapped his arm around her waist—a *tiny, deliciously curvy* waist—and gripped. "I've got you. Step down."

Her body trembled, every vibration pulsing against his skin like some erotic aftershock of an earth-shattering orgasm. He wished.

"I've got you," he whispered in her ear. "You're safe." He lingered a moment, fighting the urge to trace his tongue down the porcelain lobe. The trembling eased, then, in slow motion, she lowered down onto the first ledge.

A couple of cheers sounded from below but she didn't flinch. Hell, he doubted if she even heard it. Sadie was in the zone—exactly where he wanted her to be. Well, besides in his bed.

"Good job, Sadie." He caught a scent of her perfume. Light, understated, fresh. *Sexy.*

"Oh my God. This is *crazy*..." she whispered, as if to no one in particular.

"Hey..." he whispered back.

Sadie turned her head, her face an inch from his. Her big, blue eyes locked on his, panic melting into a touch of surprise as she stared back. It was as if time stood still for a moment. A lump caught in his throat as he opened his mouth, and instead of saying whatever the hell he had planned to, he searched her face as she did the same.

Holy hell.

She ran her tongue across her lips and his zipper almost popped open.

Pink flushed her pale cheeks, then, as if pulling an ice-cold beer away from him in the middle of the Super Bowl, she looked away, leaving him... surprised, confused... and wanting more of whatever the fuck just happened between them.

"What?" Sadie asked quietly, staring at the rocks two inches from her nose.

"What?"

"You said hey."

"Oh." What the fuck was he going to say? "Uhh, just... good first step, let's keep going."

She nodded, that tongue of hers darting around her

cheek again. A nervous tick apparently, and also, an uncontrollable force that wiped every bit of his good sense away.

"Alright, right foot, next step. I've got you."

She nodded, and this time, moved a nanosecond faster than before. Progress.

Baby steps.

Keep up the rhythm.

"Okay, now left." He kept his arm around her to prevent another wax figure freeze scenario. And also, because he liked the feel of her body pressed against his.

She descended with him, each movement smoother than the last.

Keep the movement fluid, the mind busy.

"So, you do a lot of public speaking?"

A handful of seconds of dead air ticked by.

"Usually, yes. Conferences, colleges. *God*, Owen—Owen, right?"

Ouch. "Right."

"I am so freaking *embarrassed.*" She shook her head. "This is... I'm usually not this bad. I mean, if I'm not in the lab, I'm working outside, on cases just like this. I've hiked my whole damn life."

Her tone was changing from terrified schoolgirl to utterly pissed off.

"Don't worry about it. Sometimes phobias creep up on you. Trust me, I've seen it."

"You have?"

"Absolutely. We do a lot of jumping out of helos..."

She cut him a glance laced with annoyance.

"Okay, bad visual. Anyway, it's part of our job. We train hundreds of hours for missions like that. I've seen grown men, who have jumped dozens of times, completely freeze up for no reason. Begin questioning everything they'd learned, every mission they'd run. Everything."

She nodded, the white of her knuckles starting to resemble flesh again.

Good.

He continued, "It happens. Even in front of your *team.*"

She rolled her eyes at herself. "Yeah, but I'm betting you didn't have to cradle your team members like babies like you are with me. I'll *never* live this down."

"Well, it'd be hard to cradle when jumping out of... you know." Pause. "But can I tell you a secret?"

Another glance, this time with perfectly sculpted eyebrows popped.

"If I were standing behind a podium with a microphone in my mouth, I'd need to be more than cradled, Dr. Hart."

She smiled now. "You're afraid of public speaking?"

"Terrified. Don't like the attention. Rather be tossed in the middle of the ocean during a great white feeding frenzy than give a formal presentation. So, yeah, our roles would be reversed, trust me." He cocked his head and grinned. "Actually let's expound on this, shall we? You cradling me behind the podium... but you'd have to be on your knees—"

She rolled her eyes, again, and slapped him, momentarily forgetting she was deathly afraid of heights. Talking was loosening her up. Mind over matter.

He laughed and loosened his grip around her waist. She could do this.

"Alright, alright." He moved down, guiding her with him. "Anyway, I'm just saying, it happens to the *manliest* of men. In life or death situations sometimes."

"But we're not saving anyone's life here, and this is no *helo.*"

"Doesn't matter. Same thing. Fear is a bitch. And that's

all she is, a bitch that creeps up on you at the worst time and turns your head to mush, taking away every ounce of self-control you've spent years fine tuning."

She stopped, turned with a grin, a mischievous spark in her eye. "Sounds like you're very familiar with this kind of bitch."

"We all have our weaknesses. But it appears that this little bitch is no match for you anymore, Sadie. I'm barely holding onto you anymore."

As if on cue, she slid on a loose rock, clawing at him like a cat on its ninth life. He looped his arm around a branch and hooked her with the other.

"Geez, Owen. Don't tell me that," she seethed.

He laughed, affording him another *fuck-you* glance.

He was beginning to like this little attitude on her.

"Okay, sorry. You're doing great, though—"

"Don't let go."

"I won't. You have my word. We're almost halfway down."

She ground her teeth and nodded. "Let's get it done."

"Okay, right foot... left... right..."

He watched the steely determination in her eyes, the *lets-get-it-the-fuck-done* attitude written all over her flushed face. No more fear. No, this woman was pissed off and irritated now. She'd overcome her weakness and was now very aware of the fact that not only could she not have made that first step without him—although she could have, she just didn't know it—but that now everyone was aware she needed help.

Her pride was hurt, and he realized in that moment that this was a woman that took pride and self-respect very seriously.

"Not a fan of heights, huh?" Crawly chuckled out as they passed him at mid-point.

Owen shot him a look that had his eyes popping. "What?" The sheriff mouthed.

Owen shook his head and glanced at Sadie, who was fuming. Yeah, she'd heard it.

Her pace quickened, her moves suddenly hasty and careless.

"Hey, slow down a bit."

She ignored him, so he quickly climbed lower and angled himself under her, so he could catch her if she fell, or, fall directly onto him. If it had to be one or the other, he hoped for the latter.

"You got it, boss!" Griffin hollered out.

"Almost there, girl!" Kimi yelled from the bottom.

He willed her team to shut the hell up, knowing that acknowledgement of her fear was the exact opposite of what she needed at that moment.

"A few more steps. Almost done." He said calmly before jumping off, onto the ground.

He stepped in front of her team, arms out, ready to catch her, but the moment her foot hit the ground, he backed off, knowing that's what she'd want.

He recognized the split second she took to acclimate herself with the steady, solid ground—it was the same moment he took every time he'd jumped out of a plane—before squaring her shoulders and turning.

Her face was beet-red, her jaw clenched with fury. At herself, he knew.

"You alright?" Griffin was first to address her.

"Yeah. Sorry." Short and curt, as she moved away from the team.

Kimi reached out her hand, a smile plastered to her face. "Didn't realize you were—"

Owen quickly stepped forward and cut her off. "Back up guys, Crawly's coming down."

He casually tossed Sadie a bottle of water.

"Thanks," she said quietly, eyes on the ground, as she twisted the cap—as if she were forcing herself to say it.

He gave her a quick nod and stepped away, knowing it would be awhile before he received any more of her cute, stolen glances.

If it ever even happened again.

7

SADIE FELT OWEN'S eyes boring into her backside as she stomped through the woods trying to erase the last ten minutes of her life.

Hell, the last twenty-four hours of her life.

What the *heck* was her problem? It felt like the entire world, including mother nature was out to get her today.

Sadie had been terrified of heights since she was a little girl, but was usually able to conceal the crippling fear behind her charming wit, and an additional swipe of extra-strength deodorant.

Not today. Today she had the strength of an osteoporosis-riddled nasal bone. Today she'd been mule-kicked by her weaknesses—bad decisions consisting of smart, good-looking men who happen to be the heir to the company where she works...and heights.

She was off.

Not herself.

Sure it had been a rough day, *and* she was in jeopardy of losing her job, but since when did she turn into a puny, dainty excuse for a woman who couldn't control her own fears? Or, her decisions for that matter?

She was embarrassed.

No, *humiliated.*

And not just because her team and a bunch of burly rednecks saw her shaking like a damn chihuahua, but because of the chiseled-jaw stranger who'd helped her down. Helped? Who was she kidding? The guy pretty much carried her down.

How completely, utterly humiliating.

Her stomach rolled and she looked down. *Fantastic first impression, Sade. Fan-freaking-tastic.*

After Sadie had regained her composure once she'd hit the ground, the vibe of the group had shifted as they'd started back through the woods. Perhaps seeing her acting like a flailing idiot had sucked out the playful energy, or maybe they were feeling the same prickle on the back of their necks as she'd been feeling the further into the woods they journeyed. Maybe it was the ghost stories, the skeleton in the cave, or the thick trees that shaded the slanting after-noon sun, making it seem later than it was. Either way, there was something about this area that had silenced everyone. Something in the air.

Well, that was just fine with her. No more small-talk, and soon enough this horrible day would be in the past and she could start over, fresh and renewed tomorrow morning. A new day. A new day to regain the last shred of authority, pride, and self-respect she was so desperately clinging onto.

Because she couldn't take any more emotional pain today.

Or, in her foot for that matter. Sometime during the hike, a pebble had worked its way into her boot. With every step, the tiny devil-rock pushed itself deeper and deeper into her arch, until finally, she felt the sting of flesh splitting.

Sadie shifted her weight, trying to hide her limp until she couldn't stand it anymore. Up ahead, the terrain was becoming less dense and rockier, with large boulders spearing out of the hills and cliffs.

Great, more climbing, and she'd be damned if she was going to do it with this shard of glass in her foot.

She veered off the path, eyeing a large rock a few yards into the woods.

Owen stopped. "You alright?"

"Yeah. Just..." She wasn't sure why, but admitting that she had a rock in her shoe seemed like the cherry on top of her mortification. "...need to check something."

Check something? Out in the middle of the damn woods? *What the heck, Sadie?*

He frowned, turned toward her.

"Go on ahead," she said over her shoulder, the knight in shining armor thing starting to wear on her. "I'll catch up in a sec."

"You sure?"

YES. "Yeah, I'll be right there." She wanted to take off in a damn sprint through the woods and not stop until she hit a sandy beach somewhere with endless Mojitos.

She walked a few steps, then glanced over her shoulder. When she was sure no one was watching, she gave in, limping her way across the dead leaves, beelining it to a boulder with a flat top.

Voices faded, the breeze halted, an eerie stillness gripping her.

She slowed, almost instinctively, her senses piqued.

The hair on her arms prickled, along with the ones on the back of her neck.

Her instincts were screaming at her.

She stopped and looked around, before climbing onto the rock.

Her breath caught in a garbled gasp.

Sadie froze, staring down at the half-eaten man staring up at her with one eye, the other had been pecked out by God knows what.

With dark brown hair and lifeless gray skin, the young man—teenager, Sadie guessed—wore a blue flannel button up, shredded to pieces around a fleshless arm and midsection, revealing bone and rotting chunks of internal organs. His neck and cheek had been chewed through, maggots slithering through the missing eye socket. The boulder had preserved the kid's left side of his body from whatever scavengers had dined on him, revealing dirty jeans and a bandana stuffed in the pocket.

Her eyes widened as she noticed the two dark red dots staining his flannel—one at the heart, the other in the stomach.

"*Oh, my God,*" she breathed out.

A hand touched her arm. She screamed and spun around, her heart jumping out of her chest.

"Step back, Sadie."

"*Owen.* Oh my *God,* he's... *he's...*"

Strong hands gripped her shoulders, lightly pulling her back. "Climb down. I need you to move back."

She stumbled backward on her butt, her eyes locked on the body sprawled out on the ground ahead of her.

A loud whistle shook her from her daze, followed by Owen's deep voice booming through the air.

"*Colson! Over here!*"

Owen's hand slipped from her shoulder and interlaced her fingers. After a little tug, he led her a few feet away.

"You okay?"

She blinked, turned toward the sound of footsteps coming toward them.

"*Hey,* Sadie, you okay?" Owen lightly grabbed her chin.

She looked back at the man who was laser focused on *her.* "Yeah. Yeah, I'm okay." She inhaled deeply, hoping the fresh oxygen would push the fog from her brain. "Yes, I'm fine."

Quinn jogged through the brush with Crawly on his heels. Griffin, Kimi, and Tucker were a few feet behind.

Shit. She did not want her team to see this, especially Kimi. Snapping to action, she pushed past Owen, Quinn, Deputy Tucker, and Sheriff Crawly as they stepped up to the scene.

"What's going on?" Griffin peered over her shoulder as chatter ensued around them.

"I..." She shook her head in disbelief of what she was about to say. "Found a dead body."

"*What?!*" Kimi's mouth gaped.

"A dead *body?* What the..." Griffin strode past her, but his attempt to look over the boulder was blocked by the sheriff.

Crawly guided them back several steps as Lieutenant Colson stepped away, pulling his cell phone, and Owen and Tucker kneeled down next to the boulder.

"I'm gonna need you guys to stay back here, alright? This is officially a crime scene."

Sadie nodded, her stomach twisting in knots. She lifted her gaze, meeting Owen's as he walked over to her.

"Can you walk me through what just happened?"

She swallowed and nodded as Griffin consoled Kimi next to them.

"I had a rock in my shoe, so I was just going to sit down,

take my shoe off and shake it out. When I stepped onto the rock... that's when I saw him. And then, there you were.... the blood on his shirt, did you see that? Looked like bullet holes."

Kimi gasped.

"Someone was *shot* out here? *When?*" Griffin's patience was waning.

"Looks recent," Sadie said, then looked at Owen. "Right?"

He gave a quick nod, keeping his gaze on Griffin, then shifted back to her. "There's about to be a lot of people out here—"

"Dammit, no reception." Quinn held up his phone.

"We've got a SAT phone." Sadie slid out of her pack and pulled it out. The fact that she was able to help eased some of the anxiety vibrating through her.

Quinn jogged over and took the phone. After sliding Owen a quick glance he looked back at Sadie. "It's hunting season here. Looks like the kid caught a few stray bullets. Should have been wearing a hunting cap or jacket." He shook his head. "Nothing for you folks to worry about." He turned to Owen, "A quick second?"

After a few quiet words, Owen returned.

"Crawly and I are going to take you guys to the cave entrance, where we've got our local SAR guys there waiting to take us into the cave. Tucker and Colson will wait here for everyone else. You'll hang out there until we get the go from Colson, then we'll head in."

Griffin glanced up at the sky. "Gonna be dark in a couple hours."

"Sure is. Doesn't make much difference in a cave."

"It's not an issue," Sadie said. "We'll get to work whenever you're ready."

Just then Crawly stepped up, his face pulled with intensity. "You ready?" He asked Owen.

"Yep. You guys ready?"

Sadie nodded, then gave Griffin's shirt a tug when he wouldn't budge. Sadie followed Owen and Crawly back through the woods, with Griffin and Kimi in a deep discussion behind her.

Voices hushed, Crawly said something to Owen.

Sadie strained to listen.

"You recognize him?" Crawly asked.

"You mean the half of the kid's face that wasn't eaten off? No, you?"

A moment passed.

"Yeah, I recognize him."

Owen looked at the sheriff, watching him for a moment as they stepped onto the trail. "Who is it?"

"Brian Russell. Seventeen years old. A senior at Berry Springs High."

"And what it is about Brian Russell that's got you all bowed up, Crawly?"

The sheriff looked at Owen and narrowed his eyes. "Brian Russell is one of the two kids who found the bones in Crypts Cavern."

8

"CRYPTS IS JUST ahead."

Sadie peered ahead at the jagged rocks against the wooded landscape. A mountain of boulders pushing their way up from the ground, seemingly out of nowhere. Moss and vines snaked their way up the sides, a trickle of water running down the highest point. Normally, she would think it was beautiful, magical even, but not today. Today, the air was thick with unease from finding a teenager shot to death only yards away. Today, the air was thick with what felt like impending doom.

Griffin and Kimi hadn't uttered a single word since leaving the body. They hadn't heard Crawly tell Owen that the body belonged to one of the boys who discovered the bones in the cave, and Sadie wanted to keep it that way. She wanted their eyes on the ball, mainly so that they wouldn't be distracted and they could get the hell out of the woods faster. She'd decided she was going to have Griffin take the excavated bones back to the lab this evening for two reasons: One, help speed things along, and two, if there was a connection between the bones and the poor murdered high school student, they needed to know the ID of the bones ASAP, to help find the boy's killer.

Murdered or not, Brian Russell was found within walking distance from a human skeleton that had been discovered in a cave...rumored to be haunted. Innocent hunting accident? No way.

The curse of Atohi? She had no doubt the entire team was thinking it. Sadie never put much stock in supernatural powers but she couldn't help but replay the story Griffin had told on the way down.

Regardless of what was going on, Sadie had a job to do. And in all honesty, it might be her last case at KT Crime Labs.

Owen helped them over a large rock where the ground dipped, leading to a jagged black *V* that marked the cave entrance—posted on each side, *Enter at Your Own Risk* signs. It was the opposite of what she expected. Based on the description of the cave by the sheriff, she expected a large opening leading to an even larger tunnel. Wrong. The entrance to Crypts Cavern wasn't wide enough for two people to walk through. It was narrow, jagged, and dark. Her stomach tickled with nerves.

As they gathered on the rocks, a man, covered head-to-toe in dirt, emerged from the cave entrance. He wore a beanie with a headlamp strapped around it, and a long braid of dark hair down his back. The bright red spelunking jumpsuit he wore was complete with various straps and harnesses, barely visible through the grime. The small pack strapped to his back was dripping.

"Ah, you're here."

"Thanks for dressing up," Owen grinned and shook his hand, the two obviously friendly.

"Knapp." Crawly dipped his chin in greeting as the cave dweller zeroed in on her.

She shifted her weight.

"This the excavators?"

Crawly nodded. "This is Dr. Sadie Hart, a forensic anthropologist, Kimi Haas, forensic pathologist, and Griffin Olsen, an intern with KT Crime Labs. Guys, this is Aaron Knapp. He heads up the local SAR Team—Search and Rescue—here in Berry Springs."

Aaron shook each of their hands, Kimi wiping hers on her pants after.

Crawly continued, "Aaron's here to help guide us through the cave. As I said, the bones are in no-man's land, so to speak."

"Pleasure to meet y'all," his eyes lingered on Sadie's for a moment too long. She glanced at Owen, who—based on his clenched jaw—had taken notice.

"You, too," she said, seconds later feeling Owen's presence close behind her.

Aaron shot Owen a wink, before his face dropped to a frown as he looked back and forth between Crawly and Owen.

Noticing the look, Sadie inquired, "What's going on? You guys look like you just came from a funeral."

"Let's talk for a minute." Owen guided Aaron away from the group.

"Man, can you freaking believe this?" Griffin shook his head. "I'm telling you guys. That cave. It's cursed."

"Look, you guys can head back to the camper if you want. I can excavate the bones alone."

"No way," Kimi shook her head. "We're not *leaving* you here."

"That's right. Besides, who's going to help you over the

ravine later?" Griffin grinned, and although Sadie wanted to slap him, she appreciated his attempt to lighten the mood.

Their attention was pulled to another man emerging from the cave. Wearing the same amount of dirt and grime as Aaron, this one wore a blue suit that fit snuggly around his wide shoulders and thick chest. Wisps of sandy-blonde hair spun out under a beanie that read *I be cavin'*. Sunlight cut through the trees, illuminating bright blue eyes against tanned skin, a sharp nose and jawline that screamed all-male. If it weren't for the mud splattered all over his face, she'd peg him as "sexy beach bum." He looked around until he spotted Aaron and Owen making their way across the rocks.

"Guys, this is Kyle Paschal, a fellow SAR team member who will be helping us out today," Aaron introduced.

Sadie looked back and forth between Aaron and Kyle. Both carried an authority and confidence of men who were in their element, which she assumed was a necessity for any search and rescue guy. But that was perhaps the only similarity. Aaron was tall and lanky, with leathery skin that contrasted his sparkling personality. She guessed he was mid-forties, and although she'd usually peg a man with a pony-tail as having a mid-life crisis, she didn't see that with Aaron. Instead, she saw a rugged, woodsy type of man who considered a haircut not only an annoying task, but an assault to who he truly was.

Kyle, on the other hand, was built like an ox with an obvious aloofness—or shyness, she wasn't sure—that was apparent the moment he stepped out of the cave. Aaron ran the show. Maybe because of the age difference, she decided, guessing Kyle was in his mid-twenties.

A little less sparkle and enthusiasm in Aaron's face

confirmed what Sadie had expected—Owen had pulled Aaron aside to tell him about the body they'd just found.

Kyle nodded, swiping his face with the back of his hand, only transferring more black and grey speckled goo.

Bat shit.

Great.

Lieutenant Colson jogged out of the tree line and onto the rocks. "Go ahead guys. Team's almost here." He sent Owen a nod before disappearing back into the woods. If she had to guess, the reason the lieutenant had ordered them to wait was so he could take a look around the nearby woods, and ensure no one was lurking in the shadows. Which confirmed what Sadie had suspected—Quinn didn't really think an innocent hunter was responsible for Brian Russell's death.

"Okay." Aaron clapped his hands together. "Let's get this show on the road. Have any of you guys been spelunking before?"

"Only guided tours for me." Griffin shifted his weight.

"What about you two?"

"We've both been in caves a few times, but nothing harness worthy."

Aaron smiled. "Got a bunch of newbies. Alright, Owen told me you all have been briefed about the cave, so you understand that it has a vast underground water system, and is pretty damn treacherous in some places. Definitely no walk in the park, so I'll need your full focus at all times. You'll have a whole team around you, so feel free to ask us for help anytime. We'll get you guys to the bones, then give you space until you're ready to come out. The cave is a cool sixty-two degrees so I hope you all brought light jackets. First off, is anyone claustrophobic?"

All eyes shot to Sadie.

"Sorry to disappoint but the entertainment ends at heights."

Griffin chuckled.

"Okay good," Aaron continued, "There's a few tight spaces we'll be squeezing through. And," his gaze cut to her. "There are a few drop-offs and a few places we'll need to climb, so..."

"I'll be fine."

"Alrighty then." Aaron's brow cocked before continuing, "Here's the lay of the land—past the entry there's a short tunnel that leads us to our first bridge, after crossing that, we turn down another tunnel to a narrow pathway that we'll have to squeeze through. Next, it's the lake, otherwise known as the Grand Room, then a bit of a climb and dip to the Anarchy room."

"Anarchy room?"

"Sorry." He flickered a glance to Owen. "That's what we've dubbed it. The room with the bones." He turned back. "Any questions?" When that was met with silence, he continued. "Okay, so do you all have your harnesses and head lamps?"

Nods around the group.

"Are we going to be rappelling?" Kimi asked.

"No, but like I said, there's some significant drops, and we'll be crossing a few bridges and climbing over a few spots. It's good to be prepared. But it'll be a slow hike to the bones. A slow, tight hike, that is," he said with a grin. "So, I'll head up the group, and Kyle will bring up the rear. We've already strung a rope through."

"For what?"

"You'll attach your harness to it—safety reasons. One, so you won't get lost. There are dozens of tunnels and turns throughout the cave, that take you in a dozen different directions. This will mark the path. Second, like I said—drop-offs."

Sadie's stomach clenched. This trip was turning out to be almost worse than her morning.

Almost.

"How long is the hike to get to the bones?"

"Around fifteen minutes."

"There and back?"

"Nope. There." Aaron tightened his pack. "Try not to touch anything, stay close and connected to the rope, and we should be good." He turned, then turned back, "Oh, one more thing. Anyone scared of bats?"

Kimi froze, Griffin laughed, and Sadie grinned. Motion sickness and fear of bats—check.

"Don't mess with them, they won't mess with you. Goes for all wildlife for that matter."

Kimi whispered something to Griffin as Sadie glanced at Crawly and Owen huddled in the short distance. Owen's tight expression and arms over his chest marked the obvious tension between the two. With a subtle shake of his head, it was as if something had been decided and they split off.

Watching them closely as well, Aaron said, "Everything alright, boys?"

"Yep." Crawly spat on the rocks. "Grayson will join you all in the cave. I'll regroup with Colson, and we'll get the rope bridge secured before you guys come back out."

"Sounds good. Like I said I'll head up the line, Kyle will be in the back," he looked at Owen. "Hell, Grayson, you go at your own pace. You don't need us."

Owen nodded and tightened his pack.

"Okay, let's help the newbies get into their harnesses and we'll get going."

After Aaron and Kyle checked everyone's harnesses, lamps and packs, they stepped into the cave, the cool, moist air sending a chill up Sadie's spine. They were secured to the ropes, then fell into line, with Owen sliding in behind her.

She expected him to make a smartass comment about the drop-offs, but instead, he checked her straps. No eye contact, no discussion—just a few butterflies as his hand swept over her skin.

"Alright guys, click on your head lamps and... bottoms up."

Six yellow beams of light illuminated the cave, darting around the shiny, dark walls. They descended down the tunnel with Aaron leading, Kimi then Griffin, then Sadie and Owen, with Kyle at the end.

The light from the entryway faded behind them and what closed in around her was a pitch-blackness, thick enough that it seemed like she could reach out and grab it. No light this deep underground, and the thought made her wonder if it was like being in a casket.

The gray cave walls were slick, shimmering in the headlamp beams. Thousands of stalactites, some as thin as icicles, some as thick as tree limbs, hung down from the ceiling. The same amount of stalagmites speared up from the floor, threatening to trip them with each step. Along the walls, a *drip, drip, drip,* echoing in the silence.

The cave entrance was narrow, with a low ceiling that made her wonder how many inches long bats were.

"Stalactites come down from the ceiling, right?" Griffin's light shone above.

"Yep." Aaron hollered back. "And stalagmites come up from the floor. Watch out for those. Easy way to remember it is—stalactites cling *tightly* to the ceiling, stalagmites *might* someday reach the top."

"Clever."

"I'd like to think so. Alright guys, we've got our first bridge coming up."

The sound of rushing water mixed with the drips. Sadie's eyes rounded as all headlamps illuminated a thick log over a six-foot wide river of flowing water.

A bridge?

Kimi shot Sadie a look that said *Holy. Hell*—her thoughts exactly.

"She's sturdy. Trust me. Kyle and I have been over her a hundred times. Just two steps and you're across. If you fall," he grabbed the rope, "you're all harnessed in. No need to worry. Let's go."

She felt Owen step closer behind her as the front of the line crossed. Again, not a word as he helped her onto the log, his strong hand gripping her pack as she stepped across, with long, confident strides.

A small victory.

They continued down another tunnel.

"Okay, first tight squeeze coming up."

Sadie craned her neck to see ahead, but only the bobbing lights from the headlamps cut through the darkness. Her foot slid on a slick spot, the cave floor becoming more wet and uneven the further in they went.

"Hold onto the rope for stability," Owen said quietly in her ear.

Goosebumps flew over her skin like a wave of fairy dust.

Just the man's voice sent every sexual sensor in her body to blast.

She walked a few more steps just to prove that she could, then wrapped a hand around the thick rope, feeling it slide through her palm with each step. He was right, it made her feel more secure.

And so did *he,* she realized.

Griffin stopped ahead of her. With a thud, she slammed into him not realizing she'd been gazing at the walls instead of keeping her eyes up.

"*Oomph.* Easy girl."

"Sorry. What's going on?"

"Why are you whispering?"

"Oh." She cleared her throat. "I don't know. Why'd you stop?"

"We all did. I think he's helping us through this spot up here."

She looked over Griffin's shoulder as Owen and Kyle struck up a conversation about hiking gear behind her. As far as she knew, they hadn't told Kyle about the teenager found in the woods. Why, she wondered?

"Hey," Griffin turned to her, inching closer.

"Why are *you* whispering now?"

"Because I have a confession."

"You're Atohi reincarnated, aren't you?"

"Yes, and instead of hacking off your limbs one by one, I'm going to force you to stand on the edge of the Grand Canyon for twenty-four hours."

"Jerk."

He laughed. "So..." then his face sobered up. "So, remember when they asked if anyone was claustrophobic?"

"Yeah..."

"I kind of am."

"What does *kind of* am mean?"

"Like, I probably should have brought an extra pair of shorts."

"That's disgusting. Why didn't you say something?"

"Same damn reason you closed up like a pissed off clam after you finally made it down that ravine. It's embarrassing."

"Touché." It felt good to joke about it, she realized. "Well, crap... want me to make up some excuse where you have to go back to the camper and wait for us there, or something? I can handle the excavation."

"No..."

The line moved forward, and even in the dim reflection of the light against the walls, she could tell Griffin's skin had paled.

"No, I can do it... just..." he looked nervously ahead, then back at her.

"Look," she said firmly, grabbing his arm. "Mind over matter. That ravine almost made me vomit my lunch up, but I did it. You can do it, too. Mind over matter. And listen, if it gets too bad, just go back." She chewed her lower lip in deep thought. "Ah, okay... if you feel like you're starting to have a panic attack or something, um, use the code, um... I like big bones and I cannot lie, and I'll—"

"What?"

"No good?"

"No good, Sadie."

"Fine. Oh, I got it. These flashlights have a strobe light option. Click it on for a minute—just pretend it's an accident—and then I'll start your exit strategy. We'll get you out of here in no time."

"Okay. That's better than I like big bones. Some of these rednecks might throw me into the lake if I said that—"

"Griffin, you're up."

"Mind over matter," she whispered as Griffin stepped up to the narrow pathway that cut through two jagged rocks.

She cast a glance over her shoulder, where Owen was staring at her with a small smile over his sexy, kissable lips.

She smiled back, knowing he'd heard every word.

After Griffin successfully passed his first big hurdle of the day, and the rest of the team squeezed through the pathway, they made their way deeper into the cave, where a distant roar began to drown out the silence.

"What the heck is that? Water or—"

Before the words left her mouth, Sadie rounded a corner and the cave opened up to a massive dome stretching at least a hundred feet above a body of water as black as ink. A waterfall cascaded down the side, slithering and splashing along the jagged rocks. Aaron shined his light as the rest of the team entered the room, standing on a small platform just above the underground lake.

She was awestruck.

Millions of stalactites looked like dripping wax from the walls, which appeared to have levels, like floors, that led to more tunnels. It was like an underground atrium. Except with bats and blind fish... and ghosts.

"This is beautiful," Kimi said almost breathless.

"The Grand Room." Aaron continued to shine the light as he spoke, yelling so that they could hear him over the water. "So this is where most spelunkers turn around." He turned and shone his light over a rickety wooden bridge a few feet above the water that hugged the far wall and lead across the water to the other side. Sadie counted at least ten planks missing. "As you can see, the lake extends past this bridge and through that tunnel, and goes on throughout the rest of the cave. There's a lot more rooms like this, but definitely not for the inexperienced explorer."

Owen nodded. "I'd say eighty percent of calls BSPD has

received are from people slipping and falling in this room alone."

"So where are the bones?" Kimi asked.

Aaron shone his light on a wall. "About ten yards back there."

"Back behind that rock wall?"

He tilted the light to reveal a small, thin opening about eight feet up. "Back there."

Griffin cut her a look.

"This is going to be the trickiest part, but Kyle and I already tested it out. You'll use a ladder to get to the opening, then slide through on your stomach, and I'll be on the other side to help you down to the room. But, first, we cross the bridge."

The line crossed the bridge, the rotting, aged wood slick on the palm of Sadie's hand. The darkness of the water below helped ease her anxiety—*only two feet deep,* she lied to herself. *Only two feet deep.*

They huddled onto a small platform next to the wall, and watched as Aaron tossed a rope ladder over the slick rocks and secured it on a thick stalagmite. Then, with Kyle's help, skillfully climbed over.

Kyle checked with Aaron, then turned to Kimi. "Alright, you ready?"

Kimi nodded, and the last big hurdle began.

It was more than ten minutes before Sadie made her way to the front of the line. It wasn't so much of the height of the climb—she could handle ten feet—it was that if she fell, she'd likely slip off the drop off that led to the black water that was only inches from where they were climbing. And that fall was how many feet? She didn't want to know.

"Make sure to test your footing before you release your weight," Owen said softly in her ear.

"Ready?" Kyle stretched out his hand and as she stepped to the ladder, she felt Owen's body close behind her.

Her hand trembled as she gripped the rope, the unsteadiness of it adding to anxiety pumping through her veins.

Kyle gripped the ladder steady and before she could protest, Owen's hands slid around her waist.

"Step. Let's go," he said, climbing beside her, without a rope.

She nodded, inhaled.

First step... second... third. Her muscles tightened with each step and by the time she hit the fourth rung, her entire body was vibrating from the inside out. Her legs were like lead weight.

"Do not look down." Her neck snapped back to position, but not without noticing exactly how close they were to a drop off into the lake.

"Step. *Go.*"

His strong, commanding voice was like a slap in the face.

Fifth step... sixth... seventh.

"Good job. Now pull yourself onto the opening and Aaron will help you down on the other side."

His voice was a buzz in her ears as she gripped the rocks and slid herself over, her stomach twisting... but that was nothing compared to what waited for her on the other side.

9

OWEN HUNG BACK, watching her work, the laser focus broken only by the occasional question by her teammates. A neurotic mess on the ravine, nerves of spaghetti in the cave, but when it came to analyzing bones? Sadie was an absolute pro. And that was good because Owen hadn't slept a wink since the bones were discovered the day before.

They'd placed their flashlights strategically throughout the Anarchy room—or, tomb perhaps was more fitting—to illuminate the bones. Griffin had used the word creepy, Kimi, chilling. In his opinion, creepy and chilling were an understatement.

The skeleton had been desecrated, disjointed—as if tortured and ripped apart—with each bone placed like pieces of a puzzle. The leg, arm and rib bones—although he assumed Sadie had much more fancy names for them—had been used to make a large circle in the center of the room. Inside the circle, the bones had been placed to depict the letter *A*, the middle horizontal line made with hands flanking either side of the skull, its black, eyeless sockets staring up at them.

The only thing missing were the candles and voodoo doll.

Creepy. Chilling. Damn straight.

Haunting.

Aaron and Kyle had left them alone and ventured further into the cave, while Owen stayed in the room. Why? Because he couldn't wait to hear Sadie's assessment of the bones. But more than that, there was no way in hell he was leaving her alone after a young man had been gunned down outside. The young man who reported finding the very bones she was excavating. It didn't sit well with him, or Lieutenant Colson.

At least forty-five minutes had passed, when finally—

"The fracture above the orbital bone happened post mortem and is not the cause of death."

"What?" He stepped closer to her as Griffin and Kimi looked up from the bones they were analyzing. "So you're saying this guy wasn't murdered?"

"I'm not saying that. I'm simply saying that this bone fracture did not cause the death, or contribute to it as the sheriff had suggested earlier."

"How can you tell?" Owen asked.

She sat back on her heels and wiped her forehead with the back of her gloved hand. "There are three categories of trauma in skeletal remains. Anti, peri, and post-mortem. Anti—before death, peri—close to, and post—after." She hesitated, as if trying to figure out how to dumb down the definition for him. "One of the main ways to determine which is which is to look at the amount of healing around the bone. If there are signs of healing in the bone, the trauma happened before death. I'll have to confirm this with my microscope of course, but," she pointed with a thin, silver tool. "Can you see here how this fracture looks jagged, or crumbly-like?" She looked over her shoulder, as he squatted down and leaned closer. "That indicates that this particular injury was done post-mortem because bones tends to be more dry and brittle after death, especially as time goes on."

"So maybe the skull was hit with something after death?"

She shrugged. "Lots of possibilities when a skeleton is months old and has been exposed to the elements."

"Could the head have been hit just after the time of death? Possibly already dead, but was continued to be beaten?"

"Why are you so sure this person was killed?" Kimi narrowed her eyes from the corner.

Owen kept his gaze on the skeleton, not wanting to reveal the real reason he assumed this was a homicide... or his connection to it.

"The way the bones are arranged for one. Someone obviously did this."

"Could just be some kids having fun." Griffin shrugged. "Or... Atohi got a little busy with his hatchet again."

Sadie shot him a glance. "It's not our job to determine that." She looked at Owen. "Our job is to provide you with the facts. So, as I was saying, the fracture to the skull appears to be post-mortem because of the way the bone separated... *compared to...*" she shimmied down the Anarchy symbol and pointed to a long, thin bone. "This fracture on the rib bone."

Owen's heart skipped a beat.

"See how this fracture is smooth? And there's another on there."

Griffin and Kimi shuffled over. The cave was dead silent except for the *drip, drip, drip* echoing off the walls.

"These marks happened right around the time of death."

"A knife?"

"Possibly."

"What else can you tell just by looking?"

"I'll have to conduct a thorough analysis once we get them excavated before giving you anything else," she deflected.

"What about TOD?" He pushed.

"Not right now."

"What about the gender? Can you tell us that?"

She shifted her weight, considering what she should tell him, then crab walked to the skull. "I'll have to take measurements and analyze the pelvis, *but* men tend to have a squarer jaw line and thicker brow ridges than women, which is what I see here. My initial guess is a man."

A man. A spike of adrenaline shot through his body.

Sadie looked over her shoulder. "Okay, Griff, can you record the weather stats, and let's get pictures taken before we begin packing up." She turned to Owen. "I'm assuming you've done your own pictures and searched the area for any evidence?"

He nodded and took a step back, his mind reeling as he watched Dr. Sadie Hart begin to pack up pieces of something he knew was about to change his life.

~

Dusk settled on the mountain peaks, bright colors of orange and red fading into an indigo night sky where the stars were just beginning to twinkle. The woods, one big shadow in the dim glow of twilight before night fell.

Windows down, Owen inhaled the crisp fall air in an attempt to calm his racing thoughts. The information provided was too little—too nothing, really—to begin making accusations. Accusations that would turn the town upside down. Accusations that he'd go to the ends of the earth to prove, or disprove, for that matter. He was already spinning conspiracy theories, recalling years of gossip and hearsay, pulling back emotions that he'd tucked away for so long.

He was already counting down the hours until he could see Dr. Sadie Hart again... not only because he hadn't been able to get her off his mind since she'd stepped out of that dusty SUV, but because she held the answers to a black mark in his family's legacy.

He flicked on his turn signal and turned at the large, wooden sign that read *Ozark Outfitters*.

The road had been freshly graveled, the pits recently filled, and the trees and underbrush cut back from the road. It looked good—better—and made a difference, and would definitely make a difference on his bank account at the end of the month. But that was okay. It wasn't like he had much else to spend his money on, like a wife and kids.

He passed a truck packed with kayaks and high school kids, the music almost as loud as the laughter rolling out the windows. He wondered if the news of Brian Russell had leaked to the media yet. A Berry Springs senior murdered. The town would go ape shit, everyone looking at BSPD for answers.

Owen hung a left and began the descent down to the river. Another car, this one carrying a family with two beaming preschoolers in the backseat and an exhausted mom and dad up front.

Busy day.

Owen waved, then turned into the gravel parking lot, rolling to a stop next to a rack of canoes. He nodded at a trio of couples hovering next to the bathrooms before pushing through the front door of the large rock and log cabin that was the home to the Grayson family business. The business his father had started when Owen was in high school. The business Owen had helped run and operate, spending every single morning and night, until he left for the military.

The business his dad had tossed in the wind the moment his alcoholism took over.

Ozark Outfitters was exactly three country-road miles from his father's house and was nestled on a hill a few yards up from Queens river. His dad had purchased the cabin the year he retired from the Navy, and from that day, Owen had worked tirelessly alongside his father to renovate the building and turn it into the go-to tourist location for all things camping, fishing, canoeing, and kayaking. The business took off, growing year-over-year and became the number one destination for outdoor adventures in the area. The cabin had an equipment rental shop, clothing and supplies shop, and an organic farm-to-table restaurant—his idea. The newest addition was an upscale art shop featuring local artists from all over the state, also his idea. His father's little side-business had turned into an operation that brought in six-figures a year, with most of that coming in during tourist season.

The business was booming and had even been featured

in several national magazines and popular blogs. But the company's success was no match for the whiskey, apparently. When his dad started drinking morning to night, their business partner, an earth-loving hippie and self-proclaimed naturalist named Amos Abner had taken the wheel and turned it into what it was today.

And now, it was up to Owen to step in as owner... whether he liked it or not.

"Hey, Owen!" Amos called out from behind the cash register where two forty-something bikini-clad women were swapping dollar bills.

Owen made his way across the shop, making note of merchandise that needed to be restocked. He slid behind the counter, glancing up at the *dear Lord,* muttered from one of the women, a bit wobbly on her wedge flip flops. The friend winked, and licked her cherry-red lips. Cherry-red from makeup, or stained from the wine coolers they'd obviously been drinking all day, he wasn't sure.

He grinned. Amos laughed.

"Evening, ladies. Did you enjoy your day on the river?" He fought the drop of his gaze, a magnetic pull to the woman's left breast where a nipple was dangerously close to popping out. Not that she was aware of the potential nip-slip. Hell, he doubted if she'd notice if her entire top fell to the floor. As he contemplated whether he'd like to see that or not, she said—

"I don't think we've met. I'm Paula, and this here's Rainy."

"Owen Grayson. Nice to meet y'all."

"Did you say Grayson?" Paula's eyes popped as if she'd been injected with epinephrine. "As in, *Grayson?*"

Amos cut him a glance.

"That's right." He said, an unwarranted defensiveness creeping up.

"You're Les Grayson's son, aren't you?"

He nodded, ground his teeth.

Paula shot a glance to her friend, who's eyes had steeled like an iron rod.

"Well," she snorted. "We hung out with him at Frank's a few times." The nipple yanked her bag from the counter and grabbed her friend's arm who was shooting daggers into him. "Let's just say I hope you've got better manners than him." With that, they turned and stumbled out the front door.

Owen blew out a breath, braced himself on the counter and looked at Amos.

"Oh, don't let it bother you." Amos started across the shop.

"Don't fucking tell me dad started getting aggressive with women?"

Amos clicked the *Closed* sign, taking a second to word a response that wasn't going to make Owen's fist fly through the glass counter.

"It was pretty bad toward the end, Owen, I'm not going to lie to you. It started getting bad after your mom left him, but got real bad recently. Guy didn't even set foot in this building for two months. And then when Ray happened... that was the straw that broke the camel's back. But, to answer your question exactly, no, I don't think he roughed up women, just got pretty sauced up and a little loose with the tongue I think." He walked to the counter. "Frank came here once and talked to me about it. Said he had to kick Les out of the bar a few times. He'd cause such a scene, Frank started worrying about getting in trouble for over serving...

something you know he usually doesn't give a shit about. Ironically, that was the day before he got his third DWI that got him into this whole mess."

Owen shook his head. He'd only been back in Berry Springs two months and with each passing day it seemed he heard something else that embarrassed him about his dad.

Amos grabbed the broom and started sweeping. "You talked to him lately?"

"Yeah," he grumbled as he logged into the computer to check the day's sales. "Once. Quickly. Just enough for him to rattle off a list of things to send him."

A moment of silence ticked by.

"How much longer is he in?"

"Not long. The sixty days are about up. And he'll be on probation when he gets back." God, he couldn't believe the words were even coming out of his mouth. He couldn't believe his dad was in rehab, and it was even harder to believe that the man would get anything out of it.

As if reading his thoughts, Amos said, "Court-ordered rehab is a good thing, Owen. I honestly think that will have more of an impact on Les than if he went on his own accord... because honestly, son, I don't think he'd ever go on his own accord. Man's too stubborn."

One of the few characteristics he'd gotten from Les Grayson.

"How was the conversation when you guys spoke... if you don't mind me asking."

"There was no conversation. Just a list of shit I needed to send him."

Another heavy moment slid by.

"Owen, try not to be so hard on him. You're all he's got." He leaned on the broom. "The guy was in special forces for almost thirty years and was discharged when age started slowing him down. He was pulled from a life full of excitement and danger, and pushed into a life of nothing—the mundane day-to-day of small town living."

"Sounds fucking familiar, Amos."

"Yeah, I get it... because of your dad's poor decisions, you left a life you loved, and are back in Berry Springs to pick up the pieces. I get it. But do you know the difference between your situation and your dad's?"

Owen looked up.

"You can go back. You can get your life back after sorting out this mess."

Owen stilled as the words lingered in the air. Amos was right, but Owen couldn't help but wonder where that left him when the inevitable happened and he had to leave the military for good. What would he have to come home to?

"It's good you're part time BSPD. That was a good decision. Helps fill that void until you figure shit out. Wish your dad would've done that."

"No, dad used whiskey to fill that void."

"That he did," Amos said with a small chuckle. "That he did."

Owen's dad's whiskey drinking abilities were nothing less than legendary in Berry Springs. Until it wasn't.

"Anyway, you need help getting anything he needs?"

"No, I've been going through that pig sty he calls a house room by room since I've been back. Cleaning, organizing. I only just recently started sleeping in his bed."

"Hope you washed the sheets." Amos winked.

"Bleached."

Amos laughed. "Okay, well just let me know. That house is a wreck, isn't it. I'd do what I could when I'd stop by to check on him..."

"Thanks, Amos, seriously."

"Stop. I love your dad, and I love working here." He spread his arms, "Anything to do with beautiful Mother Nature, I'm happy as a bluebird on a spring morning."

Owen shifted his attention back to the computer. "Alright, to business. It looked busy today?"

"Oh hell yeah, the fall colors are almost at their peak. Everyone's coming out before the rain hits tomorrow—it'll blow the leaves off the trees."

Owen glanced outside as the last vehicle backed out of the parking lot. Ozark Outfitters was open before the sun came up, to accommodate early morning hunters and fishers, to dusk and sometimes longer during tourist season which stretched from around April to October in the mountains.

"I've been doing a lot of thinking about the business since I got back and I've got a few ideas I wanted to run by you..."

Amos's eyes twinkled. "Your ideas have proved to be very beneficial so far."

"How do you feel about events?"

"Like, an event venue?"

"Yeah. Just in the few months I've been here we've gotten several requests. Art shows, company parties, things like that. Could be a decent source of additional revenue."

Amos's smile reached his eyes. "I like that idea. Have considered it myself a few times over the years... but, you know, your dad..."

"I know." Owen's phone dinged. He glanced at the clock. "Shit. Hey, I've gotta go meet the boys."

Amos's face dropped as he stepped closer. "I heard about the bones."

"Yeah?" He wasn't surprised. Nothing was a secret in Berry Springs.

"Yeah." Amos stared at him saying everything by saying nothing at all.

"I'll let you know," Owen finally said.

"Please do. Ray's death never sat well with me."

Owen pulled his keys from his pocket. "Me either."

10

OWEN ROLLED TO a stop between two jacked-up duallys with American flags hanging from the beds. He scrubbed his hands over his face before grabbing his cell, wallet, and sliding his keys into his pocket.

A beer was exactly what he needed.

He made his way across the gravel parking lot glancing up at the stars twinkling in a clear, indigo sky. The cool, fall breeze carried a hint of BBQ, freshly burned leaves, and the whine of classic country music.

Owen pushed through the thick, wooden door of Frank's Bar, a local favorite and regular cop hangout. A former officer had turned the log cabin into a southern honky tonk bar where the beer was always ice-cold and the cowgirls piping hot. Cowboy hats and hot-rolled blonde hair circled around wooden tables scattered with pitchers of beer and the best BBQ in the state. Pool tables lined the back, just in front of a small stage primed for karaoke. The left side of the building housed a rock bar with a mirrored back.

It was his favorite bar, hands down.

"Grayson, over here."

Owen followed the shout of his old buddy, Detective Dean Walker, to a table in the back where Quinn, Aaron Knapp, Dean, and a tank of a man sat around two pitchers of beer and a basket of chicken strips. Dean was the sole reason Owen had accepted a part-time patrol gig at the station. Hell, Dean had practically begged him.

Owen sank into the one remaining seat.

"Owen, you know Wesley, right?"

The tank swallowed his sip of beer and turned. "Yeah, man, been awhile."

He recognized him instantly. A few years older than Owen, Wesley had enlisted in the military after graduation, just like he did. Rumor had it he'd built a successful gun manufacturing business and was recently engaged to a woman who analyzed bugs for a living.

"Good to see you, man." They shook hands.

"A *welcome back* is in order from what I hear," Wesley tipped up his glass.

Owen snorted. "Temporary."

"We'll see about that." Quinn grinned.

"Temporary's too bad." Wearing a black T-shirt and khaki pants with permanent stains at the knees, Aaron slapped him on the back. "I was gonna try to talk you into joining the SAR team. Kyle will be leaving us soon. Could always use a guy like you, especially after seeing you navigate the cave today."

Aaron didn't know how many times Owen had navigated that cave alone, and all the surrounding caves, during his last visit to Berry Springs.

"Like an old shoe," he said. "Hell, you and I probably explored that very cave together when we were kids."

Aaron's folks owned a lake house a few miles from his dad's cabin and despite their five year age difference, Owen and Aaron would meet up to explore the woods until the cow bells rang through the air reminding them to get home. Until Aaron's parents divorced and he moved across town, that is.

The good ol' days.

Aaron chuckled. "Remember how mad our folks would get when we'd come home covered in bat shit?"

"Looks like it never washed off." Owen nodded to Aaron's arms, a mismatch of black and red designs. "Damn dude, how many tattoos you got now?"

Aaron smiled proudly, as a parent would as they looked at their newborn son—although Aaron didn't have a newborn son. His wife left him before that ever happened. It was a typical small-town story of two high school sweethearts who decided to take the plunge before either of them knew what real commitment was.

Some days, Owen wondered if he even knew what real commitment was.

"I quit counting years ago. A few are pretty recent."

"Pamela never did like tattoos, did she?" Dean asked.

"Nope." Aaron grabbed his beer and scoffed, "Marriage. Who needs it? Anyway," he shifted, obviously ready to change the subject. "When you heading back to Louisiana?"

"Not soon enough."

Dean tilted his head to the side. "I think our boy here needs a few nights on the Buffalo river—a little reminder where he came from."

Wesley's brows tipped up. "Could use that myself. Boys trip. Beer, whiskey, fishing, canoeing. Hell yeah. I'll haul my boat down and we can spend some time on the lake. Get you back in the water. It's not the ocean, but still has plenty of bikinis."

Water sounded good, and bikinis not bad, either. Owen

missed the ocean. Over the last few months, he'd done nothing but work the beat, work at the outfitters, and work on his father's crumbling cabin. He should make some time for a little R&R.

"I'm sure they'll be plenty of damsels you can save on the lake."

The image of Sadie's curvy body and pink lips popped into his head... as it had a hundred times over the last hour. He cleared his throat and forced the image away.

"What can I get ya, sweetheart?" A gray-haired waitress wearing a colorful mini-skirt and tattoos to match slid an icy glass in front of him.

"This'll work, thanks."

"Anything to eat?"

"No, ma'am."

The waitress grinned, winked, then sauntered away as Quinn served him from the pitcher.

"You went into the Coast Guard, right?" Wesley leaned back and crossed his arms over his chest.

Owen took a deep sip, then nodded. "Rescue swimmer."

"No shit?"

"No shit."

Wesley chuckled. "You guys saved our asses once. It's a hell of a job, man. Never liked the water that much."

"This from the special ops marine." Dean popped a chicken strip into his mouth.

"Water's a different animal."

Yes, she is.

Aaron started chatting up a group of college-aged girls at the next table as Quinn's phone beeped. After checking the text, Quinn showed it to Dean, who then pulled out his own phone as the two began discussing whatever needed their attention.

Wesley sipped his beer, habitually ignoring the cop-talk. "Sorry about your dad, man."

Owen's jaw twitched. "Thanks."

A moment ticked by.

"Thing is... people don't understand." Wesley stared into his beer, his face darkening as he slid into memories, or perhaps nightmares. Owen knew the look because he'd seen it on his dad several times.

Wesley continued, "War messes you up. It's a mind fuck, man. We pledge ourselves to this country and then are given orders, and we're trained to execute those orders—no questions asked. It's the job, and I fucking loved every minute of it. But... once the bodies start piling up... and then nothing comes from the mission..." He shook his head. "They'll say it wasn't for nothing, of course, but you know. You know when shit goes sideways." He shrugged, sipped. "But, then, another mission comes, and goes off without a hitch, and you know you were a part of something that saved lives. Good and bad, I guess. It's an intense way to live." He snorted. *"Then* you get out and... it still has a hold of you."

"Christ, man," Dean blew out a breath and hollered at the waitress. "Can you get this guy a shot of Patron? Make it a double."

Wesley grinned and downed his beer. "Sorry."

"No shit, man... does anyone have a razor blade?" Quinn flagged the waitress and circled his finger in the air—shots all around.

Owen laughed, but the truth was, he understood. His military life had been different than most, especially those in special ops, but he'd seen his fair share of death. He knew it all too well... but did it turn him into a blubbering alcoholic who couldn't function in life? *Fuck, no.*

He was *not* his dad.

"What got you off on that tangent?" Quinn asked.

"Ah hell, just talking about his dad. Was just saying that I get it."

"Doesn't excuse it." Owen slowly spun his glass between his fingers.

"No. Agreed. I'm just saying... ah, hell, just get me that fucking shot."

They laughed, and on cue, four tequilas slid in front of them.

Ignoring the dressing, Owen tipped it back with the rest of the table.

Camaraderie. He didn't realize how much he'd missed it the last few months.

Quinn's phone beeped again. He checked it, blew out a breath and leaned back. "That was Jessica. She just got Brian's body and will start the autopsy tomorrow afternoon." Pause. "Gonna be hard to tell if any assault occurred considering the condition of his body."

The playful vibe of the table had turned on a dime.

"I bet it was the coyotes that got to him." Wesley scowled. "Damn cotes."

"He was ripped to shreds, no doubt about it." Quinn squeezed his face. "God, did you see his intestines and his—"

"*Dude.* I was gonna order some wings." Aaron scowled in disgust as he rejoined the conversation.

"Sorry."

"Two gunshot wounds, you say?"

Quinn nodded.

"And not from hunters, like you told the excavation crew." Owen sipped his beer.

"Well, that's going to be Crawly's job to determine that considering the body was found in his jurisdiction. But... no way in hell. No way in hell is it a coincidence that bullets hit the kid after he reported finding the bones in Crypts Cavern."

"Agreed."

"Crawly tell his folks yet?"

"Yep. After he and Tucker put the rope bridge over the ravine, they went to the kid's house."

"Did they have anything useful to say?" Dean mindlessly tapped his shot glass on the table.

"Not according to Crawly. They're shocked, of course. Can't imagine anyone doing this to their child on purpose."

"What about the other kid that found the bones? There were two, right?" Wesley asked, fully informed of the afternoon's events.

"Josh Penn. Clean. Both are good kids, good grades, never got any trouble." Quinn looked at Aaron. "Have you ever seen them out in the woods?"

"Not that I can recall, but, you know how many kids visit that cave? Hell, how many kids I have saved from that damn cave?"

"So... what?" Wesley said, getting back on point. "They call the bones in, you guys loop in the county police, and then this Brian kid goes back later by himself?"

"Yep, according to Josh, Brian texted him asking him to go back with him. Wanted to check it out again. Curiosity, I assume. Brian's truck was parked at the trailhead at the bottom of the mountain. No signs of break-in or any red flags. His phone was in his pocket, locked of course. Folks don't know the password so they're going to pull his phone records."

"So he goes back to explore the cave and gets gunned down." Wesley's eyebrows raised. "There's something in that cave that whoever killed Brian doesn't want to be found."

"We searched the room the body was in, and everywhere we could, when we checked it out. Took pictures before we called in forensics. Dean and I looked at the pictures again this afternoon. Nothing but rock and bones. Not to say that there's nothing else there, but shit, man, how many places are there to hide evidence in a damn cave? We don't even know where it ends."

"Well, there's something there that's being guarded. I'm going to find it." Owen's fists tightened around his beer.

"What about the people excavating the bones? Is Crawly assigning someone to watch over them?" Aaron asked.

"Don't think so, especially considering no foul play has been determined at this point. Nothing to suggest they're in any kind of danger. Truthfully, Brian really could have caught a few stray bullets. They're scheduled to be here overnight tonight, and leave tomorrow." Quinn sipped his beer. "I'll be out there first thing tomorrow."

"Oh well, that's good, because nothing bad happens in the night." Sarcasm colored Owen's tone. He didn't like the idea of Sadie and her team staying overnight in the woods alone, and it pissed him off that Crawly didn't give a shit. If Sadie had been alone? No fucking doubt that pervert would pitch a tent next to her. Pun intended.

"Hey, man, my hands are tied." Quinn shrugged. "Crawly's calling the shots."

"What about Deputy Tucker? Ask him to stay out there." Owen said.

Quinn raised his hands—not his jurisdiction.

Dean crossed his arms over his chest. "So we've got a dead teenager and a human skeleton with no ID, and someone who wanted to make some sort of stupid political statement with his bones. All we know is that the bones appear to be less than a year old, and belong to a male who was possibly stabbed in the ribs." Dean deadpanned to Owen, waiting for him to say something. He'd expected it. Dean knew Owen's family and all their issues.

"Thoughts, Owen?"

Owen glanced at his empty shot glass, willing it to refill itself. He didn't want to get into his conspiracy theories until he knew more about the bones.

Quinn looked at Wesley, then frowned as all eyes turned to him.

He sipped, exhaled. "You all know about what happened to my uncle, seven months ago." It was a statement, not a question. "The official report said he died spelunking in a cave around Devil's Cove, a few miles from Crypts Cavern." He shot Quinn a look, "Right?"

"That's right."

"But his body was never found."

Wesley cocked a brow. "I'm not sure I knew that little detail... his body was never found?"

Owen nodded at Quinn to pick up the story, who then said, "Seven months ago, we received a call from Amos Abner, the manager of Ozark Outfitters, saying that he was afraid that Ray, Owen's uncle, had gone missing—"

"Wait. Amos? Les's employee?"

"Right. According to Amos, Les, Owen's dad, had mentioned a few times that he hadn't heard from Ray in a few days and was worried about him. Said he'd gone out caving and that was it. This went on for a few more days, and Amos decided to drop us a call."

"Why didn't Les make the call?"

"Les... uh, wasn't in the best head space."

Owen cut in. "I didn't even know any of this at the time, by the way. My dad didn't even call to ask me if maybe I'd heard from Ray."

Quinn nodded. "So, we go out to the caves, and after a few days of searching, we found his backpack, headlamp, and rappelling ropes dangling down a crazy, narrow-ass hole in one of the caves. Goes down more than fifty feet. The rope was frayed at the bottom—the obvious assumption was that it popped, and he fell." Quinn shook his head. "To my knowledge, and everyone I spoke with, no one had ever attempted to rappel in that spot. Way too dangerous. The only way we know it goes down that far was because we had Kyle, the SAR guy, volunteer to go down and search for the body. Dude couldn't even squeeze down to where the rope ended. We found traces of Ray's blood along the narrow sides, which we assume he cut himself on the rocks, on the way down."

"Damn, dude. And no body? Nothing else?" Wesley frowned.

"Nope."

Owen picked up the story. "At that point, dad called and told me what had happened." He shook his head, his pulse quickening. "I was shocked."

"But Ray went caving all the time, or so I heard? It's dangerous shit."

Owen waited a second to respond. "It just doesn't add up." He clenched his jaw and spun the shot glass. "My uncle was adventurous, and yeah, a bit wild, but he wasn't stupid. He wouldn't go down in that hole. Hell, even I tried to go down it when I came back for the funeral. I couldn't get down as far as the end of his rope suggested he did." He paused. "And let's just assume for a second that Ray was stupid enough to go down it. He wouldn't have gone without someone there with him. Period."

A moment slid by.

"We even brought in an out-of-state survey crew," Quinn

said, "which didn't tell us much more about the cave than what we'd already had drawn up from years earlier. It's impossible to tell that far into the ground without being able to actually get there and take measurements. We couldn't find Ray's phone, so nothing came from that. No friends or family had seen him that morning. His house didn't turn up any clues, other than that he'd packed for a day in the woods. By all accounts, Ray Grayson had decided to go caving and fell to his death. Devil's Cove is technically in Berry Springs so we took the case, but worked closely with Crawly on it, considering the lines were so close. We had a lot of people on it." Quinn flickered a glance at Owen, sadness—or guilt, maybe—shining from his eyes. "We had his frayed rope and blood on the rocks, and a damn bottomless pit. McCord ruled it an accident and the case was closed."

Owen downed his beer, wiped his mouth with the back of his hand and said, "And now, there's a mysterious skeleton, who appears to have been murdered, found in a cave not two miles away from the cave where everyone assumes my uncle died."

"Just fucking say it, Owen. You think it's your uncle." Dean leaned forward.

"Yeah." His gaze leveled the table. "Yeah, I do."

"Y'all were close, weren't you?" Wesley asked.

Owen nodded, his stomach twisting. "He pretty much raised me while my dad was deployed, which was pretty much always. Hell, Ray was more of a father to me than my real dad. But, when Dad left the Navy and came home full time, I didn't see much of him anymore. Think there was kind of a rift or something."

"What? Like your dad was jealous of you and Ray's relationship?"

Owen shrugged. "Possibly. I'm sure he noticed I looked at Ray like a father." He chuckled. "And I know he always gave Ray shit for hitting on my mom. Guy was a hell of a flirt."

Aaron's phone dinged. After checking it, he chugged his beer and pushed away from the table. "Cows callin' me home." He looked at Owen. "Never believed Ray fell down that hole, either, for what it's worth. See you tomorrow morning?"

"Yep. Have fun with your herd."

"I've got to get on, too. Aaron, I'll walk out with you." Dean pulled a twenty from his wallet and slapped it on the table. "See you tomorrow."

Wesley snatched Dean's beer and chugged the rest. "Any idea when they'll have an ID on the bones?"

Quinn tapped his phone, checking to see if he had any new messages. "Not sure," then he glanced up and grinned at Owen. "That's assuming your girl's not paralyzed with fear in the corner of her camper."

"Your *girl*?" Wesley needled.

"If she was my girl, Crawly'd be missing a tooth right now."

"Whoa, heeeeey..." Wesley grinned while Quinn chuckled.

"He didn't hide it, did he? That perverted old bastard." Quinn laughed. "I swear to God, I could see his nasty old man boner from a mile away when he was watching her come down that ravine. *Correction*—while he was watching Owen *carry* her down the ravine."

"Okay someone fill me in here... on everything but Crawly's boner, you sick fucks."

Quinn sipped, still chuckling. "The forensic anthropologist we called in to excavate the bones. Hot as fuck, but crazy scared of heights, apparently."

"No shit?" Wesley smirked and turned to Owen. "Sounds like you don't need the lake to find your damsel in distress. You literally carried her down the ravine?"

"Oh, he wasn't complaining, trust me." Quinn was enjoying this way too much.

"Kind of like you weren't complaining about staring up at a boner for twenty minutes. Jealous, Colson?"

Quinn raised his eyebrows. "A little sensitive when it comes to the new girl, huh?"

"Okay so who is this chick?" Wesley asked.

"Name's Sadie Hart. Works for KT Crime Labs."

"You say *Sadie* Hart?"

"Yeah…" Owen frowned at Wesley's wide eyes, knowing he wasn't going to like what was about to come out of the man's mouth.

"Dude…" Wesley yanked out his phone, "*This* Sadie Hart?"

Owen looked down at the picture of a young couple dressed to the nines—a beautiful brunette in a red velvet gown, sparkling everywhere except for her eyes, standing next to an overly-tanned Ken Doll in a fancy tuxedo and black wingtips that Owen bet cost more than one of his paychecks. He looked like the type of guy who'd never had a spec of dirt under his manicured fingernails. Ken Doll was every guy Owen couldn't stand. His gaze lingered on Sadie —the forced smile, the rigid posture. It was complete opposite of the playful glimpses he'd seen from her in the woods, the passionate twinkle in her eye when he'd catch her watching him from a distance.

The headline read: *Billionaire beau and girlfriend split.*

Billionaire beau? He focused on the guy he already couldn't stand.

"Is that the kid who owns KT Crime Labs?" Quinn leaned over the table.

"Kid, well, he's our age, but yeah, his dad owns it. Only child. Total asshole. Rumor is, anyway."

"Let me see that." Quinn snatched the cell, skimmed the column, then glanced at Owen with a devilish smirk. "Maybe she needs a shoulder to cry on."

"Give her Crawly's boner, then," he snapped, with a bit too much emotion.

Laughter around the table.

Owen sipped to cool the heat rising up his neck. He felt pissed and shocked... like he really knew her or something. Like they had anything more than stolen glances. The chick was fresh off a breakup from a stuck-up billionaire brat. And if there were three things Owen wasn't, it was pretentious, spoiled, and a billionaire.

Owen was everything Sadie's type wasn't.

He set his drink down as conversation about the heir of KT Crime Labs turned to a buzzing chatter in his ears.

Maybe the flirty glances had meant nothing.

Maybe he was seeing things that weren't there.

Maybe Dr. Sadie Hart had no interest in him whatsoever.

He turned the sweating glass in between his fingers and pushed the twinge of disappointment aside.

Maybe that was for the best, because if the skeleton found in Crypts Cavern did belong to his uncle, Owen was going to spend every spare second looking for his uncle's killer, and the last thing he needed was a gold-digging acrophobic to distract him.

11

*W*INE.

She needed wine.

Sadie latched the door to the camper, and with the poor balance reflecting a day of manual labor and emotional toil, she shakily removed her ATAC boots which were covered in dirt, mud, some sort of black grime, and so much bat crap she'd considered tossing them into the ravine.

Careful to not transfer any of the nasty goo, she swiped the hair out of her face with the back of her hand and glanced at the clock—7:24 p.m.

Yes, definitely time for wine.

It was past six-thirty by the time they'd bagged up the bones and made it out of the cave—a task that should have taken half the time if not for the fact there was some obstacle to climb over, squeeze through, or slide under every step of the way... all while carrying a human skeleton. Griffin had left to take the bones to the crime lab, and insisted on coming back to stay overnight and help with the search for more bones tomorrow. He promised to be back by nine, with plenty of food to cook a, quote, "good ol' campfire dinner." She'd helped Kimi set up her tent, who had insisted on camping regardless of the dead teenage boy found yards away and haunted cavern. The girl was serious about her winning her bets. Sadie had to respect that.

As promised by Crawly, a rope bridge had been secured across the ravine, helping to decrease her panic level by about two percent.

She'd take it.

It had been a day filled with bumps, bruises, and unexpected challenges, and now, after the hike back to the clearing where they had to leave the camper, Sadie was officially exhausted.

After washing her hands, wrists, and forearms to the extent of a doctor going into surgery, she pulled a plastic cup from the cabinet and grabbed a box of red from her bag. Box traveled easier than bottle.

What. A. *Day.*

Her laptop dinged in the corner. She released a groan, fighting the urge to check it. If it was work, it could wait five damn minutes, or at least until her buzz kicked in. If it was someone else—another damn person—emailing her about her public break-up, well, they could wait until she was very, very drunk.

Her *billionaire beau.*

She snorted, shook her head.

To say it shocked her that her relationship had made the local news was an understatement. Although, the grandeur of it fit right in with the short, fleeting relationship she'd had with the KT Lab's owner's eccentric son.

She'd never forget the day he'd asked her out, four months earlier.

She'd just come in from the body farm, covered head-to-toe in dirt, and was making her way to the lab where she could spend the afternoon resurrecting cold cases from the dead.

Enter Evan Tedrick, his rich father, and four suits with matching Rolexes, walking down the hall like a firing squad blocking her pass. She'd avoided eye contact with a subtle nod, then slipped into the lab where moments later Evan had appeared with a smile and a charming charisma that awakened every sensor—and red flag—in her body, and two tickets to an exclusive art auction that drew the wealthiest from across the south.

She should have known right then.

She'd said yes—out of curiosity more than anything else —beginning a courtship filled with charity events, art shows, and exclusive dinners. She'd maxed out her credit card the first month buying cocktail dresses and heels she'd never wear again. She should have known she'd never fit into that world.

Sadie grew up in a family where her next meal depended on how many food stamps were available, daydreaming what it was like to have money. Not just *billion-aire* money, but enough to not have to worry about pesky things like food and medical bills. An only child to a construction worker and teacher, Sadie learned very early that if she was going to have anything worth having, she was going to have to get it herself. And so she did.

Sadie had started working when she was just fourteen, helping her father on construction sites for a few bucks a month. She got her hands dirty and learned the satisfaction —along with backbreaking pain—that came from a full day working in the hot southern sun. She liked it. Liked working outside. Liked hard work.

But it wasn't until the day that a backhoe dug up the skull of what turned out to be a fifteen-year-old girl who'd gone missing years earlier that Sadie knew exactly what she wanted to be when she grew up. Sadie became immersed in the story of the girl, and how the bones unraveled clues that led to finding the girl's killer—a homeless man who frequented the area before the land was sold. She'd even gone to the funeral, hiding in the back while watching as the family finally received the closure they'd so desperately needed.

It had touched her in a way she couldn't explain. The little girl had received the justice she deserved, while the family was finally able to lay their child's body to rest.

This new passion gave Sadie something solid to work for, a focus that didn't involve trying to drown out her parents' daily arguments about money. And when her mom and dad divorced when she was seventeen, Sadie's singular focus became a pursuit in forensic anthropology.

That focus paid off for Sadie, especially when she started working at KT Crime Labs.

And then she went and slept with the damn owner's son.

She'd tried—*really* tried—to fit into his world, but the truth was, Evan Tedrick was everything Sadie Hart wasn't. He was rich, entitled, sheltered, and one smooth operator when it came to women. Evan had swept her off her feet from date one, giving her glimpses into a life she'd only dreamed about as a child. But unfortunately, all the money in the world couldn't change one more thing Evan was— mind-numbingly pretentious.

Almost four months to the day of their first date, Sadie had broken up with Evan in the middle of the body farm after a heated argument about her not wanting to attend another awkward, suffocating, small-talk-laden, hoity-toity benefit with him.

It should surprise her that the blogs reported that *he*

broke up with *her*, but it didn't. That kind of money could buy any headline it wanted.

It could also buy a slew of reasons to fire someone.

She was crazy to think her days at KT Labs weren't numbered.

The thought sent her stomach dipping.

She took a deep gulp of wine, grabbed her laptop and decided to do the one thing that took her mind away from everything else. Work.

Two plastic cups later, Sadie glanced out the window at an orange light flicking through the trees in the distance. Her gaze shifted to her SUV parked under a tree. Griffin had made it back.

Dinner time.

She took another quick sip—the buzz giving her a much-needed burst of energy—then pulled on a clean pair of jeans, sweatshirt, and jogging shoes before stepping out of the camper, into the crisp autumn air.

Night had fallen. The woods were abuzz with chirping bugs, screaming cicadas, and the rustling of whatever animal was making their last rounds before nightfall. Or, perhaps, whatever animal was just beginning their evening hunt.

The thought made her uneasy as she clicked on her flashlight. She knew bears were common in the area, but had also heard stories of mountain lions, and aggressive coyotes—none of which she cared to come into contact with this evening.

The stars twinkled around a rising full moon shining through the thick canopy of trees. A breeze swept past her as she stepped onto the trail, wine in one hand, flashlight in the other, and the satellite phone tucked in her back pocket.

She blinked, allowing her eyes to adjust to the darkness.

Her stomach tickled as her shoes crunched along the dead leaves, each step taking her closer and closer to that damn ravine.

Her lip curled into a snarl, aggravated at herself for allowing a stupid fear to add to such a shit day. A quick pause, sip, then she picked up her pace, striding down the trail to the bridge. Griffin's voice followed by Kimi's laughter floated through the air as she gripped the rope railing. Her legs instantly feeling heavy, her knees weak.

Geez, Sadie. Get a freaking grip.

Another sip, and with her jaw clenched, Sadie stepped onto the bridge.

One foot in front of the other, one foot in front of the other...

Forcing her legs to move, anger spit like fire through her body as she pushed on, every step defiant at the fear coursing through her body.

If I fall, I fall. Admitting the worst-case scenario eased her. At least she wouldn't have to worry about losing her job anymore.

If I fall, I fall. Nothing I can do about it.

She repeated the mantra over and over until she crossed over onto the jagged rock that marked the other side of the cliff.

Thank *God.*

With that little victory, she walked down the trail, a bit lighter on her feet.

"Hey, Sade!"

Holding a can of beer and fire poker, Griffin pushed out of his folding chair next to a roaring campfire. A cooler and grocery bags littered the ground. He'd set up the campfire on a large flat rock a few yards from the mouth of Crypts Cavern. Dead leaves covered the ground, the moonlight reflecting off the rocks.

"Nice work on the fire."

"Thanks. Made a nice little pit in a crevice in the rocks. How do burgers sound?"

"Like freaking heaven." A self-proclaimed foodie, Sadie always could count on Griffin to get the food during late-night meetings, or to handle the cooking on overnight trips. He treated his food like he treated his women—passionate and open to experimentation.

"I'm going to make the Sadie Special—Swiss, bacon, topped with avocado." He turned and yelled over his shoulder. "As soon as slow-poke gets done setting up, I'll get started."

Sadie glanced back at Kimi, who was encircled in flashlights, unpacking her bag. Griffin's bright red tent sat a short distance away, nestled between two massive pine trees.

"You guys are really going to sleep out here?"

Griffin looked up like she was crazy. "A bet's a bet."

"Yeah, but—"

"Some kid caught some stray bullets by a drunk hunter. Not going to happen in the nighttime. Besides, I'm pretty sure Kimi'll wuss out, anyway."

Kimi walked up wearing a pair of tattered jeans, T-shirt, and a flannel jacket. "I'm not in the habit of backing down to boys."

"*Boys?*" Griffin pulled the poker from the fire and shot a look over his shoulder. "Who're you calling a *boy?*"

Kimi grinned and sank into a bright yellow folding chair.

Griffin tossed her a beer and turned back to the fire.

"There's more than enough room in the camper, guys. Really."

"I'm good. I've got bear spray—and garlic strung up in my tent."

Sadie forced a laugh although the idea of her team sleeping out in the open made her uneasy, to say the least. "Well, I'll leave the SAT cell with Griffin, then."

Griffin tipped up his can before taking a sip. "So... how're you doing?"

"Just peachy." She tilted her head back and looked up at the dark sky.

"No you're not."

Kimi popped open her beer. "Guy's an ass. Always thought you were too good for him, anyway."

"I'm too good for a billionaire heir?" Sadie's smirk didn't reach her eyes.

"Hey, money's not everything." A touch of defensiveness colored Griffin's tone. "And yeah, too good for that stuck up brat. Always got the vibe he looked down his little pointy nose at us, ya know?"

"Everyone looks down their nose at you." Kimi grinned.

"Oh, well, look who doesn't get dinner tonight."

Sadie smiled, watching them. It reminded her of two elementary kids with their first crushes. Innocent insults and slaps on the shoulders were as golden as a dozen roses.

"Speaking of, I'm starving, get moving." Kimi winked at Griffin as he huffed out a breath and began meal prep. She shifted her attention to Sadie. "So, what's the plan for tomorrow?"

Sadie sank into a chair. "I'm going to do another sweep of the Anarchy room, while you guys search the cave for any more bones. We'll start at daybreak, and if all goes well, we'll be out before the afternoon."

"That's good cause I think rain's coming tomorrow." That was the thing about changing seasons in the Ozarks—the weather was as unpredictable as the roads. "Perez said he'll start on the bones first thing in the morning, but if I know him, he'll get to it tonight." Griffin shook salt and pepper on the patties. "You know him, that guy's been known to never leave the lab."

"That's what happens when your wife leaves you for another woman. Guy buries himself in work. Hell, I don't blame him."

"Well, workaholic or not, I hope he gets us an ID ASAP."

"So, your initial read is kerf marks on the ribs, right?" Kimi asked.

Sadie nodded.

"So our dude gets shanked in the cave, dies, but the question I have is this: who waited until the guy decomposed into bare bones to use them as an art project?"

"Someone who didn't like him very much. My guess is, someone who frequents the caves."

"Or..." Griffin wiggled his eyebrows and glanced at Kimi. "The ghosts of Atohi's past did it."

"Oh, give me a freaking break. Stop talking about that damn ghost."

His eyebrows tipped up. "Hitting a nerve there? What? Don't believe in souls of spirits, the undead, goblins, witches, vampires, ghouls—"

Crack.

Their heads whipped toward the cave.

"What was that," Kimi whispered as Griffin dipped down and grabbed the bear spray.

"Atohi," Griffin whispered back with a grin. "He's pissed you don't believe in him."

"Shhh." Sadie picked up her flashlight as they sat in silence.

"Probably just a squirrel or coon," Kimi said softly, still staring into the inky darkness that surrounded them.

Another moment passed.

"It is kind of creepy out here isn't it?" Griffin said, his eyes locked on Kimi, whose gaze was fixed on the cave.

They waited in silence a good minute to make sure whatever critter made the sound was long gone. Sadie shook her head. "You guys are crazy for staying out here."

Griffin nudged Kimi, tearing her gaze away from the cave. "I'll back out if you're too scared."

"Please. A bet's a bet. I'm not scared."

"Since when did you become such a badass?"

"Since I watched Sadie make her way down that ravine." Kimi winked.

Griffin lifted a brow. "Oh, *no, no, no,* Miss Sadie here was only as strong as the man who helped her down."

"*Hey.*" Kimi swatted his arm as Sadie threw an empty beer can at him.

Griffin blocked the blows and laughed. "I'm just *joking.*"

"You know, Griff," a devilish grin crossed Sadie's face. "I think I left something in the cave, you know, right past that suuuuuper narrow pathway that you can barely squeeze through? Can you go grab it for me?"

He glared back.

Sadie chuckled.

Kimi, who'd picked up on Griffin's claustrophobia, laughed. "What a group we are. Motion sickness, fear of heights, and claustrophobia. If the guys come back tomorrow, they'll have their hands full."

"According to the sheriff, the SAR guys, Aaron and Kyle, will be here first thing in the morning to help us through the cave again. There and back. I don't know about everyone else." And wasn't about to admit how many times she'd wondered the exact thing.

"Ah hell, I've got no doubt the sheriff will be here, too. Guy hung onto your every word Sadie—although I'm not sure if it was because of your area of expertise or your bra size."

Griffin shook his head. "No, if anyone was interested in her bra size, it was Owen. Guy wouldn't leave your side."

Her stomach clenched. She sipped, and deflected. "Owen wouldn't leave my side because he was afraid I'd lock up like a total idiot on that ravine."

"No, I saw him watching you a few times. More than a few times." Kimi winked.

Sadie rolled her eyes, then looked down and shifted in her seat.

Truth was, she wasn't sure if she wanted to see the sizzling-hot rescue swimmer again. Truth was, she was embarrassed. And Sadie Hart did not do embarrassment well. Sadie wanted nothing more than to start over fresh tomorrow, confident, on-her-game. The real Sadie.

Then, get the heck out and face whatever was waiting for her back at the lab—vacant desk or not.

She stood. "Griffin get those burgers on the fire. I'll go get some more sticks."

"I'm going to heat some green beans with bacon, too. Sound good?"

"Like heaven."

"Try to find a hickory tree. There're tons around here."

"Yes, sir." Sadie smirked, then turned on her flash-light and stepped into the woods as Kimi and Griffin fell into their trademark flirty banter. Sweeping her light along the ground, Sadie made her way deeper and deeper into the woods until she spotted a soaring hickory tree with bright yellow-gold leaves a few yards away.

The voices faded behind her, the darkness engulfing her. She darted the flashlight round, the beam bouncing off the surrounding trees, then dissolving into the pitch-black just a few feet away.

A chill slid up her spine.

Get the sticks and get back.

She dipped down, grabbing an armful of sticks, twigs, and God knows what else. She hurriedly made her way back to the campsite, forcing herself to push away the warning bells in her head.

Just a bad day, she thought.

Tomorrow will be better.

12

OWEN CLICKED OFF his headlights as he rolled to a stop behind the excavation crew's camper. He glanced at the clock—9:44 p.m.—then at the dim light glowing through the thin curtain over a small window.

Sadie was awake... unless she slept with a light on, which considering the day's events, wouldn't surprise him. He turned off the engine, got out, and closed the door. Loud voices and laughter carried through the wind, scented with campfire smoke and hamburgers.

Owen recognized Griffin's boisterous laugh, followed by girly giggles. He pushed away the instant dart of possessiveness. He didn't get the vibe that Griffin and Sadie had anything on the side, but he couldn't help but wonder. Any man with a pair of balls would be crazy not to be attracted to Sadie, and even crazier to not make a move while being on an overnight trip. But more than that—why the hell was he feeling possessive of her, anyway? She wasn't his. Far from it.

And he was far from her type, he reminded himself as he stepped up to the camper and rapped on the door. He was there on a mission, and that mission did not include getting into Dr. Sadie Hart's pants.

When there was no answer, Owen knocked again.

He waited a moment, then glanced over his shoulder before peeking through the small slit of the curtain. On the floor lay a travel bag with clothes spilling out of the top, muddy pants next to muddy boots, a box of wine on the counter, and no Sadie. He found himself looking for another bag, wondering if Griffin, and Kimi for that matter, were shacking up in there as well.

Close quarters for a man and two women.

Lucky bastard.

After he was certain Sadie wasn't in the camper, Owen took off through the woods, following the voices and flickering light of campfire through the trees. He crossed the rope bridge Crawly had secured, testing it every few inches. The sheriff might have been in law enforcement for decades, but an outdoorsman, he was not.

The bridge held, and he stepped into the woods, taking a detour to the rock where Sadie had found Brian Russell's body. Although they'd canvassed the entire area, he wanted a second look. Alone. Keeping his light low, Owen stopped next to the brown, wilted grass where Brian's fluids had drained from his body sometime after death. He scanned the light to the red stains on the rock from where the kid had braced himself after taking two rounds to the chest, moments before falling to the dirt floor.

Brian Russell didn't die instantly.

Owen surveyed the surrounding woods, recalling the position the boy's body had been found, and the angle of the shots. Whoever had shot Brian had been close, and a decent shot. He scanned the trees, pesky obstacles that would have made any shot difficult. But whoever had done it, managed to land two kill shots, despite the thick coverage of trees.

His mind started to race. Who had experience with a gun, and was a hell of a shot? Military? Former officer, perhaps? Hell, just about every redneck in damn Berry Springs.

But who would kill a seventeen-year-old boy?

Someone with a lot to lose. And he knew in his gut that Crypts Cavern held the answers.

His gaze shifted to the campfire, a ball forming in his stomach.

Brian Russell had been murdered in cold blood... just like his uncle. And he had a feeling the nightmare wasn't over.

Owen picked his way through the woods, zeroing in on Sadie's laugh over the voices, a smooth, low escape of happiness sneaking out despite her serious, somewhat prickly demeanor. It was a soft, feminine laugh. The kind of laugh heard in a bedroom after an evening of too many drinks, and too little clothes.

"Hey—" Griffin's sharp tone halted the conversation as he spotted Owen's flashlight.

Owen stepped out of the tree line onto the rocky clearing that led to the cave, surprised they hadn't noticed his light already. Maybe they'd had more than one box of wine.

"Evening." His eyes locked on Sadie in her baggy, grey hoodie, skinny jeans with a sexy little tear above the knee, and running shoes, loosely laced. Her long, brown hair fell over her shoulders, tousled and wind-blown reflecting a day in the woods—or his bedroom, in his fantasy—and in her hands, a splay of playing cards.

The campfire sparkled in her eyes as she met his gaze. A small smile curved her pink lips.

Christ, she was gorgeous.

Her cheeks were flushed, from the fire or wine, he wasn't sure. But something deep down in him hoped it was the wine... because Owen guessed that if Sadie ever let her guard down, she'd be hell on wheels. All that pent up emotion would dissolve with the pure grain alcohol, leaving a reckless woman who didn't know how to handle the newfound emotional freedom of a hardcore buzz. Hell yeah, he wanted to see that.

Griffin blew out a breath, waving his spatula in the air. "Shit man. Glad you aren't a bear," Griffin chuckled. "Want some food?"

A guard dog, he was not. "No, thanks."

"Do bears carry flashlights?" Sadie asked with a smirk, earning her a flying bottle cap from across the fire.

Owen glanced around the campfire—empty plates stacked next to a cooler, a half-drunk bottle of wine, empty beer cans and bottles stuffed in a trash bag, jackets and a flannel blanket. A stack of dollars weighed down by an empty beer bottle sat on top of a small folding stool next to the fire.

No gun, or weapon of any kind whatsoever. Other than the spatula, of course.

Kimi was busy peeking at Griffin's cards he'd carelessly laid on his lap, while Sadie shifted toward Owen. "Didn't expect to see you tonight." The smile reached her eyes now.

"Just came by to check on you guys."

"You mean, to make sure Atohi and his men hadn't chopped us up?" Griffin grinned sliding a glance at Kimi.

"Or to make sure there isn't an inexperienced hunter lurking in the woods?" By the touch of sarcasm in her voice, he wondered if Sadie had heard his discussion with Crawly earlier. Did she know Brian was the one who called the bones in? Solidifying that there was a connection between his death and the skeleton? Owen glanced at the others. By the carefree look on Griffin and Kimi's faces, he assumed they didn't draw a connection. And that was good. He wasn't in the mood to field questions that he couldn't answer.

"Is there any news? On the boy?" Sadie continued her quest for more information.

"The autopsy will begin first thing tomorrow morning. We'll know more then."

"Do you think it's related to the bones found at the cave?" Kimi asked, earning a glance from Sadie.

"No." He lied. "Deer season just started up. A rogue bullet or two isn't hard to imagine. He wasn't wearing a vest or anything. Dark colors blend. But, like I said, we'll know more tomorrow morning."

"Who was he?"

"A local teenager."

"So terrible," Kimi shook her head.

"It is." Sadie said matter-of-factly, and obviously wanting to change the subject now, she continued, "But bottom-line, we've got a job to do here. Our minds need to be right."

"You sound like a third-grade basketball coach."

"You're playing cards like a third-grader," she replied with a quick wit. "You keep this up, you won't have any money to pay Kimi when she wins your bet tonight."

Kimi laughed. "Seriously. Have you ever even played poker before?"

As Griffin smarted back to Kimi, Sadie glanced up at Owen. "If you're looking to make some easy cash, pull up a chair."

"Here you go." Griffin stood, pulled his empty chair next

to Sadie, and motioned Owen to sit. "I've got another in my tent. Be right back."

Owen sat as Griffin pulled up another chair.

"Beer?"

"Thanks." After all, what's a campfire without beer? And by the looks of it, he needed a six pack to catch up with everyone else.

Griffin tossed him a can. He caught it mid-air and popped the top. "So, what's with the camper if you guys are sleeping in tents?"

"I like tents, believe it or not," Kimi said, grabbing another drink. "I camped a lot growing up. Always like a fun, little adventure. Minus the dead bodies and haunted caverns, of course."

"And I'm doing it because Kimi and I have a little wager on if she's going to be able to make it through the night."

He looked at Sadie. "And you?"

"Oh Sadie here will shack up wherever we won't." Griffin grinned and winked.

"Now that's not very nice." Sadie narrowed her eyes.

Owen titled his head to the side.

"Griffin here thinks I'm antisocial."

"Not all the time. Just the evenings especially. You need your alone time, I get it. Hell, after the day you had, I didn't even expect you to come out tonight."

Sadie's eyes focused on the fire as she shifted in her seat. Was Griffin talking about the ravine incident, or her name being splashed all over the gossip columns? Hell of a morning, either way, he guessed.

"Anyway," she said with a touch of attitude, then tossed her cards on the table. "Kimi, your deal. I've got one more game in me before I need to go seclude myself in a black

hole somewhere, away from all living organisms." She winked.

Kimi dealt the cards, and the game began.

Owen decided against telling them that he and his buddies spent every second of their free time playing cards. Owen was the best poker player on the base, hands down. It wasn't the money, or the bragging rights, it was the ability to read the hand across from him that made Owen love the game. The mind-fuck of it. The calculated risk and reward. Everyone had a tick, a tell, he just had to find it. And if he had to guess, this group had a lot of ticks. So, he decided to sit back and lose a few hands, taking some time learning his opponents before going in for the kill. By the crumpled twenties on the table, he estimated they were playing with around a hundred bucks. Enough to buy him a few more cans of paint for his father's deck.

Griffin pulled out the whiskey, and after the mandatory —apparently—pass around of shots, the games began.

Owen watched each player.

Griffin, typical macho-man, but this one had a major chip on his shoulder. Perhaps it was the fact that he was the intern and didn't like being low on the totem pole. If Owen had to guess, Griffin came from a household where his father worked full time and mother had dedicated her life to raising her children. Men ruled the roost, and the kid didn't like his current position in the group.

Kimi on the other hand, might as well have had a flashing light announcing her cards. Her face sparkled with each decent card she drew—a tell that Sadie had picked up on. Inexperienced at cards, yes, but based on how her leg settled against Griffin's, she was experienced with *his deck*, no doubt about it. Of the three, Kimi was drinking the least amount, and although she laughed and played along, Owen caught her gaze shifting to the woods, scanning from tree to tree as she had done on the ravine. What was she looking for, he wondered? It was a nervous tick that had nothing to do with cards.

The first game went to Sadie, with a pair of Kings. To Owen's surprise, Sadie was a damn good poker player. She was the type of woman to take her cards seriously—which was seriously *sexy*—and had no obvious tells. Sadie was smart, confident, and focused, with a killer calmness like a mountain lion waiting to strike—twice in a row, when she won the second hand, too.

Owen subtly watched her, hyper-aware of every movement, giggle, every shift of her body, each stolen glance pulling him deeper and deeper into intrigue.

To say that the woman he'd met in the woods was the same woman who dated billionaire brats surprised him, to say the least. *Woods* Sadie seemed like an uptight perfectionist with a touch of neurosis, who was dedicated to her job, and despite the fear of heights, seemed in her element being covered head-to-toe in dirt. His kind of woman—the dirt part, anyway. *Woods* Sadie didn't seem the type to sit in a man's shadow while spending hours in the beauty chair before attending her umpteenth charity event. No yapping, teacup sized dogs for her, no sir. He saw Sadie as someone who's best friend would be a burly German shepherd, complete with full obedience training.

The juxtaposition made him want to learn more about her. He didn't like being surprised, or knocked off his game, especially with a woman that looked like that. He didn't like how much she'd occupied his thoughts since he'd met her. He didn't like the little flutter of excitement he felt just sitting next to her.

He didn't like how many times he'd imagined her naked over the course of the last few minutes.

As time ticked on, he'd caught her glancing at him a few times, too, reminding him of the instant attraction the moment they'd met. Those damn eyes that seemed to burn a hole right through his skin.

Dr. Sadie Hart was a box full of surprises. A box of soft, silky feline curves that he'd like to crawl inside of and...

A *doctor*. What was he thinking? A doctor who dated rich kids would never have any interest in a military brat with a drunk as a father.

He sipped and drew another card—full house.

Owen looked up, catching Sadie smirking at him. She raised a brow.

He narrowed his eyes.

Alright then, time to drop the curtain. Like a hammer.

He rose the bet which was met by everyone but Sadie, who folded. Yep, she was onto him.

Smart little vixen.

"Okay show us your hand, Kimi."

Kimi laid down a pair of eights.

"Owen?"

Owen tossed the cards on the table and plucked the bills from under the bottle.

"Ah, *dammit,* man." Griffin tossed his cards into the air and grabbed the whiskey.

Sadie laughed and picked up her plastic cup. "On that note, I'm going to hit the sack, kids."

"Oh come on. One more game. I'm just getting warmed up."

"Sure you are."

Owen stood. "I'll walk you. Need to watch out for those flashlight-carrying bears."

She snorted a laugh—super cute—then shifted her attention to Griffin and Kimi who were already beginning a new game. "Sure you guys don't want the camper?"

"Nope. I'm good." Kimi winked.

"Alright, well, door's always open. Come in anytime."

"Will do."

"And you've got the SAT phone. We'll meet up first thing in the morning."

"Night, boss."

Owen clicked on his flashlight and motioned her ahead. They fell into step together into the woods, two yellow beams of light cutting through the darkness. A cloud drifted from the moon, casting deep shadows along the forest floor. A bit creepy, and beautiful, he thought.

"You're a hell of a poker player, Dr. Hart."

"You're a hell of a scammer, Grayson."

"Ah, caught that, huh?"

"You're not the only person who could read people around that campfire."

He grinned. "Well, I wasn't the only scammer around that fire. Your buddies seem to be pretty comfortable around each other."

"I've noticed. Can't say I'm surprised. Griff's something else. Good at what he does, though. He's going to make a great anthropologist, if he can learn to keep it in his pants, of course."

"Rules," Owen scoffed.

She tilted her head. "Have trouble with that yourself, huh?"

"Only while playing poker."

"Dodged a bullet, then."

"Bullet? No... more Mack truck."

"Or maybe more like your ego." She winked and stepped

over a rotted log. Owen lightly grabbed her elbow to help
her over.

"How did you get so good?" She asked.

"Keeping it in my pants or playing poker?"

She rolled her eyes.

"Well, I actually became very good on both points when
I entered the military. Played poker with my buddies during
the little spare time we had."

"And let me guess, you won every time."

"My name's on the wall. A plaque. Gold and shiny,
forever immortalizing Owen Grayston."

"Gray*ston*?"

"Yep. Fuckers. 'Scuse the language. I know they did it on
purpose." She laughed, and he fought a smile, then said,
"How about you? How'd you get so good?"

"I played with my dad and his buddies when I was a
little girl. Learned pretty quickly there was more to the
game than getting good cards."

"Pretty cool dad."

"Well, yes and no. He was in construction. I'd go to job
sites with him a lot, and the guys would play during lunch
breaks. I'd force myself into the group."

Dr. Sadie Hart grew up playing around construction
sites. Again, something else surprising about a woman who
dated billionaire assholes.

"What did your mom do?"

"Teacher and drove a school bus."

"Teaching is the most underrated job in our country.
And underpaid if you ask me."

She looked at him for a moment. "It is. I agree. But a
close second? Your job."

It caught him off guard, so he glanced down. Being in
the military paid shit, it was no secret, but like so many

other soldiers, he did it because he loved it. He loved being a part of something big. Being part of something that mattered, had a purpose, a world-wide presence. But as much as that, it was the constant challenge it provided. And when it came to saving someone's life? He'd experienced no greater high in his life.

Although being alone with Sadie Hart was quickly climbing the ranks.

He wasn't sure how to respond, just like he wasn't sure how to thank someone who paid for his meal, or gave him their first-class seat on an airplane.

"Why'd you go into the Coast Guard?"

He stiffened. "It's in my blood."

"You've got family in the Guard?"

"The Navy."

"Your dad?"

He nodded, feeling the tension lurking back up to his shoulders. God, he hated talking about his dad.

Their attention was pulled to a rustle in the distance. They stopped, swung their lights in the direction.

"That's where the body was found, isn't it?"

Owen nodded, scanning the dark woods. They stood in silence listening a moment. When Owen was sure they weren't being stalked by whatever animal was on the hunt, he shifted his light back to the trail. "Let's keep on."

Sadie scanned her light one more time before turning and falling into step next to him.

"You okay?"

"Yeah." Pause. "There's no way you think he was shot by accident, do you?" Her eyes narrowed as she stared at him, daring him to lie to her. Again.

"Why do you say that?"

"The location of the shots for one. Right in the chest.

The kid was shot down, Owen. And I heard Crawly tell you he was the kid who called about Crypts Cavern. He was killed the *same day,* nonetheless. Come *on."*

"Who says *nonetheless* in casual conversation?"

"Who's ill attempt at changing the conversation is as blatant as Kimi's poker face?"

"I can't get into the details with you, Sadie. But, just know that we're on it."

"I heard the conversation, Owen..." her words slipped away as they approached the bridge.

He looked at her and even through the darkness, saw her body tensing and that tongue of hers darting around her lips. If it wasn't a nervous tick, he'd be turned on.

"You crossed to get to the campfire, right?"

She nodded, her eyes focused on the bridge swaying in the breeze.

"So, just like that, again."

Gnawing on her lip now, she stepped forward and grabbed the edge of the rope, but stopped.

"Want me to go ahead of you?" He wanted to set the pace and avoid another lock-up situation like earlier.

"Sure." An ill attempt at sounding calm and casual.

"Okay, then just follow me. No big deal. Let's go."

He stepped onto the bridge, took a few steps and looked over his shoulder at Sadie death-gripping the rails. One foot on, one foot still on the rock. Below them, a black pit of jagged rocks. He didn't know if not being able to see the bottom made it better, or worse for her.

"It's go time... unless you want to go back to the cave and small-talk yourself to sleep."

After a quick breath, she stepped onto the bridge, her moves jerky and robotic.

"Good girl."

"What am I? A puppy?" She muttered as she made her way behind him.

He laughed and set the pace, slow and steady, careful to keep his steps sturdy because Sadie was shaking the thing enough for both of them.

"See? No big deal." They were about midway now. "This thing can hold us no problem. We tested it with about half our weight."

"You're an asshole, you know that?"

"Oh, well, Sadie and her dirty little mouth. This ravine sure does bring out your feisty side."

"Just keep moving."

The bridge swayed. He paused, allowing her a moment to gather herself, then pressed forward. He felt her finger-tips slide down his lower back, then settle into a fist-full of his T-shirt as she closed the inches between them. Goose-bumps flew over his skin at her touch, a reaction that took him by surprise. He slowed, enjoying the closeness of their bodies. Enjoying that he was her support system, a security blanket. There was a trust there, and he liked it.

He liked seeing Sadie Hart vulnerable.

With her practically attached to his back, they crossed the bridge.

"You did it."

She exhaled and shook her head. "Sorry. *Geez,* that is so ridiculous."

"Hey," he turned to her and lightly tipped up her chin with the tip of his finger. "Don't say another word about it. You crossed, that's all that matters. Don't make it bigger than you are."

Her eyes locked on his, and he trailed his finger along her jawline, memorizing every line of her beautiful face.

She shivered, then dropped her gaze. A moment lost.

"You cold?"

"No. Kind of warm actually." Then, she took a step back and turned away, the cool air cutting between them like a knife, severing the heat.

He watched her walk for a moment, her curves silhouetted against the orange beam of flashlight ahead of her. He would have kissed her if she hadn't turned away. Hell, he would have stripped her clothes off and had his way with her right there in the leaves if she hadn't turned away.

He forced away the thoughts, and caught up with her. He needed to get his head screwed back on. He had something important to ask her before she stole every bit of focus from him.

"To answer your question, yes, I came out here to check on you, but I also wanted to ask you something."

She walked for a few steps, as if her thoughts were a million miles away. After a moment, she looked over, the sparkle gone from her eye. The redness from her cheeks faded. Sadie Hart was a pro at covering her emotions.

It was like looking in the damn mirror.

"What do you need?"

"I want to understand how you get an ID from bones?"

"Well, there's a few different ways, but with the bones excavated yesterday, we've got almost a full set of teeth to examine." Her voice picked up, as if she were glad to be talking about work again. "Our forensic odontologist already has the bones. The first thing he'll do is compare the skeleton's teeth with dental records of missing persons in the area. If nothing hits there, we can trace the fillings which requires a lot more time." She cocked her head. "Why?"

"So, if you had a list of dental records ready to compare the teeth with, you could get an ID fairly quickly, right?"

"Right. Having a targeted list already is optimal."

"Well, I've got the dental records of someone I'd like you to look at. First."

"You do?"

"Yes... and I want you to tell me before anyone else. Okay?"

"Sheriff Crawly is my contact with this case."

"And I have a personal interest in this case."

She stopped in the middle of the trail and turned to him. "Indulge me. I like to know what I'm getting into, or have gotten into for that matter."

"I know the victim." There was a drop in his tone as he said *victim*.

"How so?"

"I believe you bagged up my uncle yesterday, who was reported dead seven months ago after reportedly going spelunking in a cave close to Crypts."

Her eyes widened. "I'm sorry to hear that."

"Me too. Can you help me or not?"

"Wait, what do you mean *reportedly* going spelunking?"

"His body was never found."

Her mouth dropped for a moment. "Wait, wouldn't he be in the missing person's index, then?"

"No." They started walking again. "The case was ruled an accident. Said he fell down a narrow hole."

"How long ago was this?"

"Seven months. You said you couldn't give a solid TOD yet, but does that at least align with what you suspect?"

After a moment, she nodded, then said, "Considering you think it's your uncle, if we can't get a solid ID from the dental records, would you be willing to submit a DNA—"

"Absolutely. I'll do whatever I need to do."

"Okay then. Email me your uncle's information and I'll

tell Dr. Perez to check those records first thing tomorrow morning."

"Thank you."

"Don't thank me yet. I'll make your uncle's dental records first priority but I can't tell you that I won't tell the sheriff the results. As I said, he is my contact here. I have no reason—"

"What do you think of Crawly?"

They stepped into the clearing. "Not much, to be honest."

"Not much when he can't take his eyes off your shirt?" He wasn't sure why he said it, or the sharp tone of it. Maybe it was the talk about his uncle, or the almost-kiss moment they'd just shared that had him off kilter a bit.

She shot him a look. "I work in a male-dominated field, Owen. Both as a forensic doctor and when I'm working directly with law enforcement, which is half my job. I'm used to guys who don't know how to sneak a peek, or hell, don't care to try to hide it."

"And that's okay?"

"No, it's not. I know how to handle myself."

He had no doubt she did, and didn't know what the fuck his problem was all of a sudden. They stopped at the front door of her camper.

"Don't let him get away with it."

"What do you want me to do, Owen? Spit in his face?"

"Just..." He wanted to tell her to stick with him, stay at his side. Why? So Crawly would back off. So, he could have her all to himself while she was here. So he could get to know her better. Feel the feeling he got when she grabbed onto his shirt. Protect her from whatever the hell was happening in that cave.

He needed to end this conversation.

"Just let me know as soon you as you hear about the dental records."

"I will." She rattled off her email for him to send the records. "I'll email Perez as soon as I get the records."

"Thank you."

She slid her hand onto the silver knob of the camper, but paused and turned back.

She stared at him with those big blue eyes and his heart gave a kick.

"Thank you," she whispered. "For today."

He swallowed the knot that had grabbed his throat. "You're welcome. Have a good night, Sadie."

She turned and disappeared into the camper. After waiting until he heard the lock click, he walked back to his truck and settled into the backseat to watch over Dr. Sadie Hart until the sun came up.

13

*G*RIFFIN AWOKE WITH a start.

He squeezed his eyes shut, ignoring the jack-hammer pounding in his head.

No way in hell it was morning already.

He groaned and pulled a fist-sized rock from under his sleeping bag that he apparently hadn't noticed when he'd crawled inside at... what the hell time was that?

He remembered Sadie and Owen leaving, then challenging Kimi to another game of cards, which ended in a game of quarters. The last memory was seeing the bottom of the whiskey bottle.

Wait... ... no, the last memory was of him begging for Kimi to come into the tent and give his air mattress a run for its money. She'd declined his invitation.

Shit.

Why was he awake? And buck naked?! He swallowed the cotton in his mouth as he searched for a water bottle when—

Snick.

His ears perked.

Another sound, this time a shuffling. Close by.

Shit, shit, shit. The last thing he needed at that moment was to come nose to nose with a black bear. Any other time, sure, but half-drunk, half-hungover, naked? Forget about it.

His thoughts jumped to Kimi again, surely asleep in her tent a few yards away. He needed to check on her. Was there such a thing as a *drunk* knight in shining armor? He was about to find out.

Griffin felt around for his bag, pulled it close and grabbed the small Ruger he always brought on campouts. He tapped his phone on, pulling the covers over his phone to block the light.

2:24 a.m.

Gross. The last time he'd been up at 2:30 in the morning was the night he'd graduated from college.

Gripping the hilt of his gun, Griffin slipped on a pair of sweatpants and crawled to the door of the tent. Inch by inch, silently unzipping the door, keeping his ears peeled.

Whatever had been moving outside moments earlier seemed to have stopped.

He grabbed his flashlight—keeping it off—and poked his head out, squinting to see through the dark night. No more full moon, no more stars. Clouds had rolled in, carrying with it the scent of rain. When he was certain no animal—or no human—was next to him, he crawled outside.

In a squat, Griffin took a moment to get his bearings. God it was dark. The eerie silence of mid-night in the woods added a major creep factor to his already disheveled state. He pushed to a stance as a sparkle of light caught his eye—a thin beam of a flashlight scanning the cave opening.

What the *hell?!*

Who the hell?

He looked at Kimi's tent, which was dark, then looked over his shoulder in the direction of Sadie's camper. No lights, and no way in hell would Sadie cross the footbridge alone, in the middle of the night, with no one awake to hear her scream if she fell. He knew how Sadie worked, and that woman did not take risks. Even calculated.

Whoever was shining the light couldn't be far from Kimi's tent.

Not good.

Griffin fought the urge to turn on his light and stealthily stepped across the rocks, bee-lining it to Kimi's tent while keeping an eye on the flashlight in the distance.

As he drew closer, a cloud drifted from the moon, illuminating the dark silhouette holding the light.

He frowned, taking in the short stature, fluid movements, lean build.

No. Way.

He looked at Kimi's tent, then back at the silhouette. He'd recognize those long legs anywhere.

Kimi?

He stopped and watched her for a moment. What would Kimi be doing wandering around at two-damn-thirty in the morning? Why hadn't she awakened him? Griffin darted behind a boulder as she turned and shined her light on his tent for a solid minute, before she stepped into the cave.

Stepped into the cave.

What. The. Fuck.

Kimi Haas was going into the haunted, treacherous cave at two-thirty in the morning. *Alone.*

He glanced back toward Sadie's camper, looking for any sign that she might be awake, and, for whatever reason, had arranged a late night canvass. Maybe he'd missed the memo. Hell, maybe he didn't remember getting it. But not a single light shone through the trees, not a single voice echoed in the distance.

He looked back at the cave.

What the hell was he supposed to do? Follow Kimi? Go get Sadie? Go back to bed?

He contemplated the last option, but shook his head. Something was going on here and he wanted to find out what it was. After a quick glance over the shoulder, he descended into the cave, his mind reeling. What was she doing? Where was she going? How well did he really know Kimi? What was she holding out on him, other than a roll on his blow up mattress?

Griffin followed the golden glow of Kimi's flashlight down the tunnel, across the log-bridge, and through the narrow opening that made his skin crawl.

The crazy woman was going back to the Anarchy room.

What the *hell*?

His pulse started to pick up as he followed her deeper and deeper into a cave where multiple people had lost their lives.

They shouldn't be in the cave without telling someone where they were.

It was stupid. Unsafe.

And Kimi wasn't stupid or unsafe.

Kimi was looking for *something*.

Something she wanted to keep a secret.

14

OWEN DRAINED THE last of his coffee and grabbed the wrinkled paper from the bed. He skimmed the list of things his father requested to be mailed to his suite at rehab. He'd put it off for two days now and at this point, he wondered if the package would even make it to his dad before he was released. Oh, well, he needed to get it done, anyway. And considering he was up and at 'em at six-thirty in the morning, he figured now was a good time to start.

After a sleepless night in his truck, he'd left the woods at the ass crack of dawn and headed home. Over the evening, not a peep from Sadie, and not a sound—or scream for that matter—from Griffin or Kimi in the distance. A storm had blown through sometime around four in the morning, and not even that had the lovebirds breaking their bets to stay overnight in the tents. Crazy kids. Crazy, horny kids.

He should be tired, but he was restless, edgy. He'd sent Sadie his uncle's dental records the moment he'd gotten home, hoping for answers by the end of the day. One could hope.

His dad's list of items was short—thank God. More clothes, books, his bible, and to Owen's surprise, a few old family pictures that included his mom.

Finding these pictures proved to be no easy task and during the search, he'd dived head first into a tornado of childhood memories. Apparently, his father had buried his sober life in dozens of beer boxes, hiding them in various places throughout the house. Closets, cabinets, the attic. It was as if he'd scattered the memories so each would fade away in their own time.

Owen came across a picture of his dad and his uncle, in swim trunks, with their arms around each other and a beer in each hand. They'd been close growing up, but just like everyone else in his dad's life, the relationship faded when Les joined the military at age eighteen.

Owen lifted a picture of his mother, sitting on a rock in the woods, with wildflowers in her hair. It had been months since he'd spoken with her. She had her own life, a new husband and new step-kids now. She'd left Les like he'd dumped everyone else.

Karma.

For the first time ever, Owen *felt* for his dad. Les had lost his wife, his brother, and retired from a life-long Navy all within a few years.

Talk about life changes.

Owen's gaze shifted back to the picture of his uncle, a protective arm around his dad.

Was it possible he really fell to his death in that cave? Did he die instantly? Suffer? Was he really that stupid to go caving alone? Who had he talked to that day? Was his uncle involved in some sort of secret Anarchist cult?

Someone had to know something.

Over the last few hours, he kept reminding himself that

it wasn't confirmed—yet—that the skeleton belonged to Ray, or that the marks on the ribs were indeed proof of something nefarious. Although, Sadie seemed sure, and she didn't come off as the type to throw around pesky little details about potential homicides unless she was certain.

Deep in thought, he glanced out the window at the fog beginning to settle above the lake. It was a cool, dark, gray morning. No sunrise today.

Fitting.

Owen slipped the pictures into a Ziplock bag and placed the box back onto the top shelf of his dad's closet. As he turned, he noticed a small box tucked in the back. This one missing the layer of dust that the others had gathered.

He grabbed it and pulled it down.

Ray

The name written on the top was scribbled in his dad's shaky cursive.

Ray

Frowning, Owen settled onto the bed and removed the lid. The box was filled with things that belonged to his uncle. After the funeral, his dad and Amos had packed up Ray's house, shoved everything into a storage unit where it remained today. Except for this box, apparently.

Carefully, Owen unpacked the items one by one as more memories hit home. There was an old pair of hiking boots, ratted flannel shirt, a few T-shirts—one with *Cave Dweller* written across the front, another with *Born to Spelunk*—a few random lighters, knick knacks, and a small velvet satchel. Owen pulled the little strings and tipped the bag over.

A tarnished outdoor watch with a bright orange band, a peace-sign earring—Owen laughed, remembering Ray sporting the gold stud in the 90's—and a silver band with a heart hammered across the top.

Owen's brow drew together as he turned it over in his fingers. He didn't recognize it. He slipped it on, the small ring catching on his knuckle.

No way this would have fit his uncle. A woman, yes.

He looked around the room, as if the walls were going to tell him who the ring belonged to.

Why was it in his uncle's things?

Perhaps a gift for someone that never was received? Or, a gift returned?

A low rumble of thunder sounded in the distance.

He held the ring up to the lamp and titled his head, peering at the inside of the band.

PEG

Peg?

His mind raced thinking of all the women Ray had brought to the house, or talked about during an evening of drinking. More than Owen could count. But one thing was the same with all the women—they were all blonde, beautiful, and no-strings-attached. No way in hell his non-committal uncle would buy a *ring* for one of them.

Right?

Owen ran his fingers across the heart etched in the center.

Was it possible Ray had given this ring to someone, and she had given it back?

Why?

How long ago?

Peg.

He slipped the ring into his pocket, grabbed his coffee from the dresser, clicked off the light, and added one more thing to his to-do list today.

Figure out who the hell Peg is.

~

"Morning!"

Sadie turned as the SAR guys, Aaron and Kyle, stepped out of the tree line, a grin on their alert, ready-for-the-day faces that carried a touch of sarcasm as if they knew her team wasn't looking forward to another day covered in bat feces.

Behind her, Griffin huffed out a snort while Kimi had yet to emerge from her tent.

The dull, bleak morning promised rain ahead. It was a damp, overcast sixty degrees, and according to the cuss words being mumbled behind her, too early for caving.

"How was last night?" Aaron asked, earning another grunt from Griffin.

"Aside from the rain, it was good."

"Those tents hold up?"

Griffin nodded. "Not a drop."

"Good. Supposed to get some more this afternoon sometime. We'll need to be packed up by then so the water doesn't catch us in the cave. That storm dropped a few inches north of us last night."

"Bad storms coming," Kyle echoed as he dug though his pack, his first words of the day.

Fantastic. She'd be towing the camper on roads as narrow as a toothpick in the rain. Maybe they could get out before it started up. She clapped her hands together, "Well, let's get on it then."

"We'll check the ropes in the cave and will holler when we're ready."

"Sounds good." As they walked away, Sadie spied the empty whiskey bottle next to Griffin's tent. She grinned. "So, got a little *turned up* last night, huh?"

Griffin groaned as he lowered himself onto the rocks to tie his boots. "Well, something definitely turned up last night."

She frowned. "What do you mean?"

Griffin glanced over his shoulder as Kimi emerged from the tent. He turned back and lowered his voice. "Uh, we need to talk."

Something in his tone had her stepping closer. "What? We need to *talk*?" She flickered a gaze to Kimi. "About Kimi? What's going on?"

Another quick glance behind him, "Can't get into it right now, but Kimi went on a little spelunking adventure last night."

Sadie kneeled down, pretending to tie her shoe. "She went into the cave?"

"Yep. I followed her in. She went to the Anarchy room. Don't know what she was doing or why, but I eventually came back out and went back to my tent. She was in there for a few hours then came back out and—"

"Morning, guys." Kimi stepped up, shrugging into her pack. Dressed in khaki pants, a red hoodie with a jacket over it, and her hair in a messy ponytail, Kimi looked like she'd gotten about as much sleep as Griffin.

"Morning." Sadie glanced at Griffin, who was avoiding eye contact with his high school crush.

She stood, staring at Kimi a moment, waiting to see if she'd get the same "we need to talk" look that Griffin had given her. But there was nothing. If anything, Kimi was also avoiding eye contact. Maybe a lover's spat? Maybe Kimi wanted to get out of the rain? Or, maybe Kimi needed to get away from Griffin's epic snoring? Or, was it something less innocent?

Griffin stood, breaking the tension. "So what time do you think we'll get out of here today?"

She stared at him a moment trying to figure out what the heck was going on. "Uh, well, before the storms hit. We'll be out of here by lunch, hopefully sooner." She glanced at Kimi again. The tension was as thick as the humidity from the impending rain.

Just then, Sheriff Crawly stepped out of the woods. "Mornin'."

Sadie instinctively stiffened as their eyes met. She held his gaze, forcing his focus to stay on her face rather than her breasts. "Morning, Sheriff."

"Looks like I just made it." He narrowed his eyes and glanced at the cave entrance where Aaron and Kyle had just stepped inside.

Lucky her.

Crawly shifted his attention back to Sadie. "Ready for another day in the cave?"

"Always ready."

"I'll bet you are." The sexual innuendo thick. What an ass.

"Will anyone else be joining us today?"

Crawly flickered a glance to the woods. "Not sure. Haven't spoken with Colson or Tucker yet this morning. Regardless, let's get a move on."

She looked past him into the woods, hoping to see Owen's tall, thick body stepping onto the rocks. The almost-kiss the night before had kept her up until the early morning hours, kicking herself in the ass for not allowing it. When he'd given her that look, all she could think was that kissing Owen was potentially another bad decision that could end up like her latest bad decision—in a humiliating, gut-wrenching, job-threatening tornado of a mess.

She was questioning herself now, her choices, her decisions, and she hated that.

What the hell was wrong with her?

She'd awoken with her stomach in knots with regret. She'd missed an opportunity to kiss a man that gave her butterflies every time he looked at her. An opportunity to forget everything and just be *happy,* if only for a moment.

An opportunity of maybe something more.

Owen's email with the dental records was blank, other than the attachment. Bruised ego, perhaps?

Geez, she'd really screwed that up. Nothing she could do about it now.

With that thought, she joined Griffin, Kimi, Crawly, Aaron, and Kyle at the head of the cave.

Aaron checked everyone's packs. "Alright, so today will be a little different as I understand the objective is to search for more bones, correct?"

Sadie nodded. "I'd like to start in the Anarchy room again and work our way back out. My team will split up and search assigned quadrants. Anything we find, we'll bag up and take back to the lab with us this afternoon."

"Sounds like a plan." Aaron glanced at his watch. "It's almost seven now. We'll work until ten, take a break, then start back up at eleven. Finish up by one or so. Sound good?"

Nods around the group, and after falling into line, they descended into the cave with Aaron leading, Kimi then Griffin, then Sadie followed by Kyle and Crawly.

Griffin and Kimi split off to their respective quadrants, while Aaron led Sadie back to the Anarchy room. After setting up her lights, he retreated to a nearby tunnel to do his own exploring.

Sadie focused on the drum of the drips around her as

she unpacked her tools and got to work, wanting more than ever to put this job behind her and get home to a warm bath and nice bottle of red. Bottle, not box.

Just a few hours, she thought, just a few more hours and she'd be out of Crypts Cavern forever.

15

GRIFFIN GLANCED OVER his shoulder as he grabbed the satellite phone from his tent. Once the team had dispersed, Griffin had snuck back out to do a little investigative work of his own. He walked to the tree line and dialed the number.

"This is Paul."

"Paul, hey it's Griffin."

"Hey, man. Hey... aren't you supposed to be in a cave somewhere?"

"Yeah, I am. Calling you on the SAT phone."

"How's it going? Man, did you miss out last night. Amber got on stage and sang."

Griffin laughed. "Damn dude, how many shots did you feed her beforehand?"

"Only two. Keepin' it classy."

"I'll bet. How was she?"

"You mean on stage or later at my house?"

"Yeah, right..."

Paul laughed. "Just joking. She sang—drumroll please—

Respect. Butchered the hell out of it but it didn't matter because no one was listening to her, or looking at her face for that matter."

Griffin chuckled. Every Tuesday evening, he, Paul and a few others from work went to a hole-in-the-wall bar for fifty-cent pints and cheesy karaoke. Amber, a new addition to the group, had a newly-bare ring-finger and a chest the size of two watermelons. A good combination for any happy hour. And although he would have loved to have been there, he was way too wrapped up in his rapidly developing feelings for a certain midnight sleuth.

"Sorry I missed it. Hey, I need a favor."

"Okay."

"You know Kimi Haas?"

"Yeah. New girl, right?"

"Yeah. She came with us on this trip, and..." he paused, realizing he hadn't planned how to approach this. "Well, I want to know what you can tell me about her?"

"Other than that she's hot?"

"You really need to get laid, bro."

"Workin' on it."

"I mean from an HR perspective. What's in her file?"

"I can't just go around revealing employee's personal files, Griff."

"You run the HR department. You can do whatever you want."

"But the question is, will I?"

Griffin rolled his eyes and shook his head. "God, you're pathetic. Fine. Twenty bucks."

This proposition was met with boisterous laughter.

"Fifty."

"Dude I could get fired for this."

"One hundred and I won't tell everyone about the time you peed yourself on my couch."

"Done. And I bought you a new couch, you asshole."

"Damn right you did. Pull up her file."

"Okay, hang on."

A few clicks later... "Okay, what do you want to know?"

"First, what was her last job?"

"Let's see, she worked at a coffee shop during college, then interned at a private lab over in Texas before moving here."

"What about her background check. Anything there?"

A second passed. "Ahhh, *very* interesting... seems our gal has sticky fingers."

Griffin's eyebrows lifted.

"Looks like she got caught shoplifting in college."

"No way."

"Yep, I've got the police report. She claims she stood at the checkout line for twenty minutes, and after asking for someone to check her out—the manager of the store said she yelled at him—no one did, so Kimi just straight up walked out with the merchandise."

Yelling, anger, and irrational decisions didn't sound like the Kimi he screwed to oblivion in the janitor's closet. Well, maybe irrational decisions.

"What did she steal?"

"*Gross.* Pre-menstrual relief pills." He enunciated each word as if it were a different language. "*Extra*-strength."

Yelling and anger didn't sound like Kimi... unless Kimi had PMS.

"Crazy women. Okay, what else?"

"Nothing else on her record."

"What about her personal life? What do you have there?"

"Let me look at the interview notes."

A minute ticked by.

"Well this is interesting. Says here her folks died when she was little. She moved in with her grandma—only child. Then, granny passed and she was shuffled to one of her older cousin's houses. Left at eighteen. Attended, like, four different junior high and high schools while she lived with her cousin, who moved a lot for work apparently. That had to have sucked."

Griffin chewed on his cheek. Carefree, lighthearted Kimi had quite a rocky past. Maybe it was all a facade.

"What else?"

"Her credit's good... oh, wow... well her high school life might have sucked but her college sure didn't."

"What do you mean?"

"Every penny of it was paid for."

"What? By who?"

"By the government. Looks like Kimi's thirty-one percent Native American."

Native American?

He turned and looked at the cave, rumored to be haunted by Indians.

Owen pushed through the front doors of *Ozark Outfitters* and flicked on the open sign. Amos always got to work at dawn to assist early morning fishers and kayakers, but the store and cafe didn't open until eight-thirty in the morning.

"Mornin', Owen!"

"Morning, Ms. Doris. How are you on this fine morning?"

"Busier than moth in a mitten, son. George called in this

morning. Runnin' a bit late. Something about gout." She shook her head. "So now I've gotta get everything in the kitchen ready."

George was the cafe's main chef—with bad feet, apparently. Ms. Doris was the cafe's one and only waitress, and part-time pastry chef.

"What can I help with?"

"Get the coffee started. Lord knows I need a cup, and," she tilted her head to the side. "Based on those circles under your eyes, you might need a shot yourself."

"It's a little early for shots."

"It's never too early for shots, son."

Owen grinned as he followed Doris Brimley back to the kitchen, her generous hips swaying the bright, multi-colored muumuu dress underneath an apron that read *Will Cook for Wine*. Per usual, her long gray hair was pulled into a bun, not a single strand missing. Owen had yet to see the woman without a pair of red reading glasses perched on the top of her head. Come to think of it, he'd never seen her wear them over her eyes.

Les had hired the retired school teacher and legendary baketress years earlier. Ms. Doris was a workhorse, arriving every morning twenty minutes early and not leaving until the last customer was "fed, fat, and happy", as she always said. Over the years, Doris had taken an interest in Owen's personal life every time he came into town, and had even started sending him cards during the holidays. It was the only mail he ever received while at the base. She'd become somewhat of a mother figure to him, always asking about his health, telling him he needed to eat more, find a good woman.

Settle down.

Owen had grown to love and respect the woman, and wanted to do whatever he could to keep things as normal as possible for her while his dad was "away."

"Where's Amos?" He asked as they rounded the corner into the kitchen.

"Not sure. Haven't seen him this morning, don't guess."

Owen frowned. "But there's a few folks fishing on the river this morning."

"He must be here, then. Just ain't made it into the shop. Grab the French Roast, will ya? It's a French kind of day."

Owen did as he was told and began scooping grains into the maker. He pressed the coffee to brew, then turned to face two dark, hooded eyes boring into him.

With her hands fisted on her hips, Ms. Doris narrowed her eyes. "You know I'm not good at beating around the bush or sugar-coating anything that doesn't have gluten. So, I'll just come out with it. I heard about the bones found in Crypts Cavern. Are they Ray's?"

The waitress had served Ray more than a hundred flapjacks over the years, and Owen knew they'd been friendly. Although, he hadn't expected to be bombarded with her speculation first thing in the morning.

"Okay" He inhaled deeply. "Since we're not bullshitting here... I don't know if it's Ray or not, but I've got someone looking into it."

Doris took a deep breath, nodded. "Good. Glad you didn't let it drop. Never did make sense. Not like Ray to be that irresponsible."

"Seems to be the general consensus."

"Not general enough for Chief McCord to call it an accident and close the case."

"Can't argue with you there." He reached into his pocket

and fingered the small, gold ring. "Hey, let me ask you something."

"Anything, son."

"Do you know anyone named Peg?"

"Peg?"

"Yeah. Peg."

"Like Peggy?"

"Maybe."

Deep in thought, Doris bit her lip. "Peg... peg... Peggy... *ah,* yes, the lunch lady at the elementary school. Peggy Herbowitz."

"Peggy Herbowitz," he repeated. "Doesn't ring a bell."

"Probably because she died eight years ago. Heart attack. Right there in the middle of the damn lunch room, can you believe it? Poor kids saw it all."

He blew out a breath. Not his Peg.

"Why you asking?"

"Oh, nothing—"

"Don't you dare *oh, nothing* me, my dear. Why are you asking?

Owen glanced out the window where a blue truck packed with canoes was backing into the parking lot. He looked back at Doris, took a step forward, and lowered his voice.

"I'm asking because of Ray... do you know if he knew anyone named Peg? Or perhaps the initials, *P EG?*"

"Ray?"

He nodded.

Her furry brows knitted together. "Well, let me think... you know Ray had a lot of... *friends* that were female, right?"

"I do." Which made the fact that he had a ring with the name of one even more interesting.

"That was one of the things that always bothered me about the man. Ray was good looking, charming, with an ass as ripe as a Georgia peach—"

Owen scowled.

Doris winked. "Sorry. Anyway, never did understand why that guy wouldn't settle down. Instead, he just slept his way around town." She snorted. "Weren't for that, he'd would've made a good husband." She chuckled, "Or, hell, what do I know? I married three and look where that's got me. Anyway, a Peg or Peggy could have just been one of his many conquests."

Owen nodded and glanced out the window again, where Amos was walking up the hill from the river.

Doris followed his gaze. "Well, there he is now. Told you he was around somewhere." The coffee pot dinged simultaneously with the front door. "You go get the folks who just walked in, I'll bring you some coffee."

"Thanks, Ms. Doris."

"Hey, Owen?"

Owen stopped, turned. "Yeah?"

"You could learn a lesson from Ray, you know."

"Never go caving alone?"

"No. Don't die alone."

The words lingered in the air like lead weight.

"Go get those customers, I'll be right there, son."

Owen walked into the shop still contemplating Doris's blunt advice. Truth was, when he was at the base, having a family life never entered his mind. Hell, having a serious relationship never even entered his mind. He was always busy and the few times he wasn't, Owen either played cards with the guys, or went to the bar where he rarely went home alone, celebrating every woman who kept their strings in their pockets. They all did. It was life on the base, and it wasn't half bad.

But there was something about being back home. Something about his small, country hometown that made the thought of having the comfort, friendship, trust, and partnership with a ball and chain creep into his mind more than ever before. Something about the way he watched men open the doors for their wives of fifty years—the respect, routine. Something about the kids playing in the river while their parents stole the few moments of alone-time with a kiss.

Something about being in his father's house that had made his stomach clench. Is that what life would be like without a woman? Without a strong woman to handle life's ups and downs? There was no energy to the house, no vibrancy, no femininity. No love. Just empty beer bottles and three inches of dust.

Since he'd been back, he'd catch himself thinking of his life in ways he never had before.

And it threw him the fuck off. God, he needed to get back to life on the ocean, where things were simpler.

But first, he needed coffee.

"Morning." He greeted two men in overalls and fishing vests as they searched the tackle tower.

"Morning," the first man said.

"Good morning for fishing."

"Yes, sir," the man replied. "Rain last night stirred the fish up. They'll be biting like crazy before the next round hits."

Owen looked out the window. "Storms coming again today?"

"'Cording to Dan the Weatherman, yep. Supposed to start up later this afternoon and through the night."

He thought of Sadie as he slid behind the front counter.

"We'll take these, and a ride down to Crawdad's Point."

"No problem. I'll have Amos take y'all down as soon as he gets up from the river. Should be just a sec."

As Owen rang up the fishing tackle, the older man cleared his throat. "Sorry about your daddy, son."

He sniffed. "Thanks."

"He's a good guy. Who cares if the man drinks? He served our goddamned country. Let him do what he wants."

Owen forced a half-smile. "That'll be twenty-six-seventy, sir."

After bagging up their loot, he watched the men take a seat on a bench outside.

He's a good guy.

"Here's your coffee, son." Doris padded across the shop.

"Thank you."

"You let me know when they ID those bones, alright?"

He nodded, and glanced at the clock.

"Go."

He tilted his head. "Where?"

"To whoever the woman is that's got you all off kilter."

He narrowed his eyes.

"Oh, now, don't give me that. I saw the look on your face when I told you not to die alone. You thought of someone." She slid a hip onto the counter. "Owen, ever consider the fact that you might be back in Berry Springs for a reason? That everything happens for a reason. Sometimes, when your world gets thrown upside down, there's a reason for it. Be open to seeing why." She stood. "Go. And you let me know if you need anything, okay?"

"No, Ms. Doris, I'll stay until—"

"*Git.*" An oven dinged from the kitchen. "That'll be the biscuits." She started across the store. "Talk soon, son."

As Owen slid behind the wheel of his pickup truck, Doris's words echoed in his head.

Everything happens for a reason...

He thought of Sadie, and a zing of nerves swept over him.

Dammit, what the hell was this girl doing to him?

16

*W*HAT FELT LIKE hours of sifting through rocks and bat crap later, Sadie sat back on her heels, grabbed a water from her pack and chugged half the bottle.

She stretched her neck from side to side. Her back was in knots, her head hurt, and her stomach felt as hollow as the cave she was in.

She'd found a distal phalanx of what she assumed to be the middle finger of their Anarchy skeleton, and a colorless, beady five-inch millipede that shaved ten years off her life. Other than those two surprises, nothing.

It had been quiet all morning in the cave, other than her carousel of thoughts dominated by a certain rescue swimmer. No matter how many times she'd pushed his face and that tall, muscular body out of her mind, he'd found his way back, not five minutes later.

Some thoughts gave her butterflies, some made her sick. Why didn't she kiss him? Did he know about her nasty billionaire beau breakup? Did he care? Or, heck, maybe she'd misread the whole thing and maybe Owen Grayson wasn't interested in her at all. Maybe she was just one of many women that swooned over him. Wouldn't surprise her.

With that thought, her stomach soured for the umpteenth time.

She lifted the bottle to her lips for another sip—

"Heck of a way to spend a morning."

The water slipped from her hands, tumbling onto her lap and splashing everywhere. She swallowed the knot in her throat and waited until her heart started beating again before saying, "Especially now that I'm wet." She turned as Owen slid through the tiny opening in the cave wall and lowered himself into the room.

He landed with a thud. Two-hundred plus pounds of muscle usually did. The dim light of her flashlights caught the strong curves of his face, the small smile on his lips. The five-o'clock shadow that was darker than the day before. The crazy-sexy rugged handsomeness.

Sour gone, butterflies back.

"Good lord, you scared me."

"Sorry," he grinned. Wearing an olive green pair of tactical pants, and a gray T-shirt that stretched in all the right places, Owen walked across the rocks and squatted down next to her. He pulled a red bandana from his back pocket and hovered the fabric just above her lap.

She cocked a brow.

His smiled widened. "Here you go."

Taking a mental inventory of herself, Sadie took the bandana and wiped herself down. Her hair was pulled back in a messy ponytail, grime covered her KT Labs T-shirt and jeans, and undoubtedly, her face, too. She probably looked like a train wreck.

"I didn't expect to see you today."

Owen simply smiled, then said, "Find anything?"

"A distal phalanx."

"Sounds ominous."

"Not nearly as ominous as the bugs I've found."

"Creepy crawlers in caves."

"Understatement of the day."

"I'm assuming a distal... whatever... is a bone?"

She wiggled her fingers. "Part of the middle finger."

"A very important one, then."

She laughed, feeling a rush of pep all of a sudden. Happy. Excited. Owen's mere presence had brought a lightness into the dark room. The energy had shifted, and she liked it.

Shit, she liked him. Really, really, really liked *him*.

"Does the finger belong to our skeleton?"

"I'm assuming, but I won't know for sure until I get a better look at the lab."

"Have you heard back on the ID yet?"

"Not as of six this morning."

"Not long after I left."

She cocked her head. "Left?"

"Yeah. I slept in my truck last night."

"What?"

"What?"

"Why?" Her eyes rounded... *no way in hell did he—*

"Just testing out my backseat." He winked.

...*stay the night just to make sure she was safe.* Her mouth dropped. This six-foot-something military man slept in the backseat of his truck just to watch over her.

As if she needed any more reason to fall head over heels for this guy.

"You didn't have to do that. Geez, why didn't you let me know, or hell, you could have slept in the camper or something." The moment the words came out, she felt a flush on her cheeks. And she knew why he didn't. Because she'd sent him mixed messages when she'd pulled away from him.

"Trust me, I thought about it," he said with a devilish grin. "But then I thought anti-social women probably aren't fans of strangers barging into their sleeping quarters."

She was at a loss for words. This guy had witnessed her paralyzed with fear within the first few hours of meeting her, and helped her through it, not once, but twice. Then, he'd voluntarily stayed the night in the middle of freaking nowhere to make sure she was safe.

"Thank you doesn't feel like enough... but... thank you." She wanted to grab him and kiss him right there, but—

He gave a swift nod, then changed the subject. "When do you think you'll hear back from Perez?"

She tore her gaze away from him, otherwise, not a single word he said was going to register through her shock. Shock of him, shock of her emotions.

Shit, Sadie, pull it together.

"I'm not sure. What time is it?"

"Close to eleven."

"Wow, really? Geez, no wonder why I'm so hungry. He might know something by now, especially considering he already has your uncle's dental records." She glanced toward the cave entrance. "Were Griff and Kimi still in the cave when you came through?"

"Saw Griffin outside, not Kimi. By the way, the kid looks like the walking dead."

She frowned. "Yeah, I know. I think he and Kimi stayed up late last night. Did you hear or see them?"

"Nope, not a thing. Honestly, I expected them to come knocking on your door at some point."

"Me, too. But, they didn't." Her thoughts went to Griffin's

story about Kimi sneaking around last night. She wanted to get the whole story.

"Okay, let's head out. I'll see if I've got anything from Perez."

"Ladies first."

"You just want to stare at my butt as I try to squeeze through this hole again." She smirked, turned and placed her hands on the rock wall.

He leaned into her ear, his breath warm against her skin, "Anything wrong with that?"

A ripple of goosebumps flew over her skin as she turned her head to the side.

His hand swept down her arm, grabbed her hand, and gave a little tug. She turned around, butterflies bursting in her stomach. His eyes twinkled behind a flicker of a flame that confirmed he was feeling the exact same thing she was. He pulled her closer, interlacing his fingers with hers.

Her heart started to pound.

With his other hand, he trailed his finger down her cheek, paralyzing her where she stood. The tip of his finger lifted her chin, and without a word, he pressed his lips to hers.

Shivers ran over her cool skin as his tongue found hers, gentle at first... until his hand wrapped to the back of her head, entangled in her hair. Her thoughts evaporated, her knees weakened as he took her with his mouth, commanding, greedy.

Unapologetically.

"Sadie?" A distant voice behind them.

Owen slowly pulled away, leaving her spinning and her lungs depleted of air. She opened her eyes, focusing on the man in front of her, his eyes rounded, his chest rising and falling heavily.

Yeah, she felt it, too.

She opened her mouth to say something—anything—but was a frozen mess of surprise, lust, desire—*shock.*

"Hey? Sadie!"

Kimi's voice yanked her from her daze. "Yeah?" She yelled back through the rocks, her voice cracking like a prepubescent boy.

"Lunch is ready!"

"Okay!... Coming..." she whispered breathlessly.

He grinned.

She smiled back, her heart like a jackhammer.

"Need help in there?" Kimi's voice called out, getting closer.

Sadie whipped around to face the rocks. "No! I'm on my way." She took a deep breath, slid her toes into the first foothold, then the next, then felt Owen's strong hands around her waist as he helped her the rest of the way.

Dammit.

She had it *bad.*

Forty-five minutes and a stomach full of sausage veggie frittata later, Sadie and Kimi helped Griffin secure the remaining food and trash as Owen and Crawly finished their plates.

The afternoon had brought dense, steel-gray cloud cover and cooler temperatures. It had sprinkled at some point during the morning, leaving a shiny gleam over the rocks.

"You feeling okay?" Sadie frowned, noticing Griffin's skin was still as pale as earlier this morning.

Griffin glanced over his shoulder. "Yeah, just tired is all."

"You look like crap." Kimi grinned and stuffed a water bottle into her bag.

"Thanks."

"Why don't you go in your tent for a bit and lay down." Sadie took the trash from his hands. "We covered a lot of ground this morning. We'll finish up within a few hours. Just come back out when you're ready."

"I might just do that. Thanks, boss."

"Good. I'm going to check email in the camper for a quick sec, I'll be back."

"Sounds good." Griffin grabbed the SAT phone from his bag and tossed it to her. "In case I fall asleep." He winked.

"Try. Really, you look like a zombie."

Sadie met Owen, who had been chatting with Crawly, at the tree line and they both set into the woods.

"Where's Aaron and Kyle?"

"Ran into town for lunch. They'll be back in an hour. And I'll say, they missed out. Who makes frittatas at a campsite? That's what those things were called, right?"

She laughed. "Yes. And Griff does. He loves to cook. Never breakfast though. He hates mornings, so, we always do brunch for lunch, then a kick-ass dinner."

"Not exactly roughing it."

"Apart from the ravine and bridge made of dental floss? No."

He smiled. "Joking about it is the first step, you know."

"So is having a bodyguard around all the time. I still can't believe you stayed in your truck last night."

He looked at her with a twinkle in his eye. "Maybe tonight I'll make it into the camper."

"We're leaving in a few hours." She glanced at him. He kept his gaze forward. Stone cold, except for a twitch in his jaw.

"You live, what? Two hours away?"

"An hour and a half," she quickly spat out. Desperate, much?

"Not too bad."

They walked in silence a moment, both thinking about the kiss, and contemplating where to go from there.

"When do you go back to Louisiana?"

Owen kicked a rock from the path. "Pretty soon. Gotta shore up some family stuff then I'm gone." He cleared his throat. "But not today." He looked at her. "Let me take you to dinner before I leave."

Her heart skipped a beat. She looked at him and smiled. "Yeah?"

"Yeah."

She nodded. "Okay, but you're coming to my neck of the woods this time."

"As you wish."

They stepped to the bridge and crossed together with the same intimacy as the night before, but this time, she let her fingers linger on his muscular back before gripping the back of his T-shirt, and to her shock, forgot to have a panic attack.

They walked the short distance to the camper in comfortable small talk, and Sadie couldn't remember the last time she'd enjoyed a man's company so much. Maybe, in the most ironic twist of all ironic twists, the fact that he'd already seen her at her worst gave them a comfort level that usually took months, if not years, to obtain. He'd been there for her—multiple times—already. And she wanted to prove to him that she could be there for him, too.

"Welcome," she said as they walked up to her camper. "To my humble abode."

"Wow what a beaut," he said as they stepped inside.

"Not bad, huh? The lab just got it this year."

"Nice. And yeah, a heck of a lot better than the back seat of my extended cab."

"Now you're just rubbing it in." Sadie pulled her laptop from the counter, sank into the small couch and powered it up. She clicked on her email as Owen tinkered with some bells and whistles she didn't even know were there.

Loading, loading, loading...

With each new email she was reminded how much work she had to do and how behind she was.

"Ah. Okay, here's an email from Dr. Perez." Owen walked over as she scanned the message. "Damn, it just tells me to call him. Geez, okay. Grab the SAT phone from my bag, will you?"

Owen tossed her the phone and began pacing. Sadie dialed the number.

"Perez here."

"Hey, it's Sadie."

"Sadie, hey, how's the dig going?"

"Found a part of a finger this morning, but that's it. Got your email asking me to call. Have you been able to analyze the teeth yet?"

"I have, and I've got your results."

"Wow, great. Give it to me."

"The teeth on the skull match the dental records of Ray Grayson, the records you sent over this morning."

Her eyes shot to Owen, and she nodded—*it's him.*

"Okay, thank you so much Dr.—"

"But there's something else..."

Perez's tone had her back straightening.

The doctor continued, "There were a few loose teeth you provided as well."

"That's right."

"Four to be exact. So, three matched the skull, as well as Ray's records."

"Three?"

"That's right. The fourth tooth is a left, second premolar. Both of Ray's were still attached. So, I scanned the tooth and ran it through the system, with no hits. Then, just for giggles, I ran a quick check to see if any of our cold case files within a thirty-mile radius of Crypts Cavern noted missing a left, second premolar—not expecting much. And bingo."

"Bingo?"

"Case number 7370. The woman that was found dumped in Otter Lake a few months ago. Her body was found fully intact, only missing a left, second premolar—"

"Yes, I know the case well. The tooth is missing from a presumed blow to the head, based on the fractured maxilla..." Her voice trailed off as she stared at Owen, who was laser-focused on her.

"Exactly. Thought that would interest you."

"It does, yes, very much. Thank you, Dr. Perez."

"Not a problem. You made my job a lot easier by sending over those dental records, so really, I should thank you."

"No problem. Let me know if you find anything else."

"Will do."

Sadie clicked off the phone. "I'm so sorry, Owen."

He nodded and ran his fingers through his hair. "Thanks. I should be surprised but I'm not. I always knew it didn't add up. I knew it was him, in my gut." He began pacing. "You've still got to officially report that you believe it was a homicide, right?"

"Yes. And I can't do that until I get back to the lab. Will be a few days."

He stopped, turned to her, his eyes as cold as steel. "But you are certain, Sadie, aren't you? I could see it in your eyes when you said it. You're certain, aren't you? You're certain my uncle was murdered."

She slowly inhaled and nodded.

He nodded, his thoughts running overtime. He didn't tear up, didn't need a second to gather himself. No, Owen was not the type of man to wallow in misery. Owen was a man of action.

"Okay... this changes everything, then. We've got to reopen the case."

She lightly grabbed his arm. "There's something else... There was another bone found mixed with your uncle's."

"*What*? From someone else? Someone else's bone?"

"Yes. A tooth."

"*Who?*"

"Well, we don't know. But what we do know is the bone is possibly—very possibly—linked to a cold case that I've been working on."

"A homicide."

"Exactly."

"Tell me everything."

She grabbed her computer as Owen slid next to her.

Her fingers flew over the keyboard. "Dr. Perez linked the tooth found with your uncle to cold case 7370. Ah, here it is." She clicked open the file. "7370—this case number was assigned to a body found buried in a shallow grave next to Otter Lake five months ago."

"Five months ago?"

"Yes."

"Two months after my uncle went missing, or was killed, I guess."

"Exactly, and the ME estimated she'd been deceased around two months. The body was in pretty bad shape when it was found, decomposed. Completely unrecognizable. I analyzed the bones personally and determined the body belonged to a Caucasian woman, mid-forties. Long story short, an identity was never discovered, and the case went cold."

"My uncle was forty-three." Owen pushed off the couch and began pacing, again. "Is that all you know about her?"

"Other than her stature and height, yes, that's all I could tell. No dental records to compare, and no fillings or implants or anything like that to trace. I've got her on a list to analyze her isotopes, but that takes a lot of time, and there's kinks—"

"Isotopes?"

She waved her hand in the air. "Not now. Anyway, she had a fracture on her skull just above the missing tooth that suggests foul play."

"Whoever killed my uncle killed her, too. In Crypts Cavern."

"It's possible, Owen."

A moment slid by. "Wait... did they send the case file to you to review?"

"Who?"

"The police. This would have been before I started on the force."

Her eyes popped. "Yes, they did. Oh my God, good thinking." She clicked through a few more files. "Here it is." Owen hovered over her. "Blah, blah, blah. No one reported missing. No trace evidence at scene, of course... oh... *wait....*"

"What?"

"Apparently someone called in an anonymous tip that Lieutenant Colson noted may, or may not be related. Said they'd seen a woman hitchhiking and sleeping in various places all over town."

"A homeless woman."

"That's what this person said. And it might make sense considering no one has come forward with any information. Especially in a small town like this. If one of their own went missing, they'd be all over it. Anyway, the reports say that woman was last seen down county road 3228..."

"They interviewed someone about it." Owen leaned in. "Holy shit."

"What?"

"Katrina Silva."

"Who's Katrina Silva?"

"That's Ray's ex-girlfriend."

17

"*R*AY'S EX-GIRLFRIEND?"

"Yep."

"How long ago?"

"A few years... before she re-married."

"Do you know her?" Sadie climbed into the front seat of Owen's truck. Owen jogged around, slid behind the steering wheel and started the engine.

"Kat. Everyone around town calls her Kat. Fitting, really."

Sadie noticed a hint of disdain as he said her name. "Fitting, how so?"

"Kat's just..." Rocks spun from his tires as he backed up. "She's one of those women, ya know? Sneaky. Been married three times and dated every man with a pulse and savings account in town. She's the type of girl to underhand you in a game of pool. Cheat her way through life with a wink, smile, and fake boobs like a pair of bowling balls..."

"And Ray and her dated?"

"Yeah, not for very long." He turned onto the narrow dirt

road that led them out of no man's land. "Shocked me, to be honest. She's the absolute opposite of his type."

"What's his type?"

"Earthy, hippie, kind soul. Not a whiskey guzzling gold digger who had a throat as wide as the Mississippi."

Sadie cocked an eyebrow. "You speaking from experience, hot rod?"

"Uh, no. I've heard the stories. Trust me, you hang around town long enough, you will, too." He paused, then glanced at her with a grin tugging at his lips. "Hot rod. I like it."

"Well, I'm happy to know that the top of your checklist isn't bowling-ball-boobs and a wide throat."

A full grin now. "Nope. I like my women independent and au naturale. Someone who enjoys getting their hands on big bones is a bonus."

She rolled her eyes and laughed. "Subtle, Owen."

He winked. "Witty sexual innuendos are one of my main talents."

"Impressive." Sadie shook her head and returned to the subject. "Okay, so Ray dated Bowling Ball Throat, then what happened?"

"The expected. After the lust wore off, he said he couldn't stand her, and they never spoke again."

"So he was just in it for the sex?"

Owen shrugged. "Maybe."

"So, let's lay this thing out. A teenage boy, Brian Russell, finds a human skeleton in Crypts Cavern, calls it in—"

"And winds up dead."

"Ah, you're finally admitting it. Good. So there is no question it's related. That whoever killed him didn't want him going back into that cave."

Owen cut her a glance. "Which is why I want you guys

out of there as soon as possible. Which is why I stayed the night last night."

"Why didn't you just come clean when we talked about it? I told you I heard the conversation between you and Crawly."

"You didn't need to know all the facts."

"Well, between your uncle and my cold case, we're in this thing together now, *Rod,* so you better start being open with me."

"Rod sounds like someone with a handlebar mustache, playing pool at two in the afternoon in some hole-in-the-wall bar with a box of cigarettes rolled up in the sleeve of his discount Hanes undershirt that he thinks passes as a traditional T-shirt."

"You missed the plastic rebel flag wallet chained to his belt loop."

"Nice. Anyway, it's not Rod. It's *Hot Rod.*"

"It'll be *Rod* as long as you keep shit from me, okay?"

"I didn't keep shit from you, just didn't openly tell you the facts."

"Semantics. *Anyway,* so the kid who finds your uncle gets shot, then we find a rogue tooth mixed in with your uncle's body. The tooth belongs to an unidentified homeless woman who was last seen walking down the only dirt road that leads to big-throated Kat Silva's house, who happens to be the former girlfriend of your uncle."

"Exactly. And we know *all* the same things now, Sadie. I won't keep from you; you won't keep from me. Got it? My family's involved now. This is serious."

"All my cases are serious to me." She held up her pinky, and as he wrapped his around hers, he kissed the top of her hand. Warmth spread over her body. He smiled, winked, and released her pinky leaving her feeling like a little girl who wanted just one more lick from the lollipop.

Sprinkles dotted the windshield as she peered out the window at the manicured pastures and freshly painted wooden fence line. "Are you sure Kat's not going to mind us just dropping in like this?"

"Well, it's official police business, isn't it? She'll just have to get over the inconvenience."

"All this land is hers?"

"Yep."

"Kat's got a lot of money. It costs a lot to keep land up and running like this."

"You have a lot of land?"

She snorted. "About eight hundred square feet."

"An investment property?" He asked sarcastically.

"An apartment. No, no land, but it's not a stretch to imagine... and look, horses." Sadie counted ten horses grazing in the field.

They came to a large iron mailbox at the end of a freshly paved driveway that led to a large, colonial style mansion.

"Hope the new husband made her sign a prenup," Owen muttered as he rolled to a stop next to the curved front steps. He turned off the engine. "Here goes the first step in finding out what really happened to my uncle."

They pushed out of the truck, scaled the steps and rang the doorbell. A moment slid by before a woman in a fifties-era maid uniform opened the massive wooden door.

"Hello, there. How may I help y'all."

"Hi, I'm Officer Owen Grayson with the BSPD, and this is Dr. Sadie Hart. I was hoping to speak with Katrina, if she's here?"

The maid's polite smile faded to concern. "Um, just a moment, let me see if she's available. Please... come in."

Owen and Sadie stepped inside as the maid scurried off.

Sadie let out a low whistle as she looked around the massive marble foyer. A double staircase flanked the sides, leading up to a second floor just below the biggest chandelier she'd ever seen. "Maybe I should do some throat stretches."

"I can help with that," he smirked.

"Mrs. Silva will be down in just a minute. Let me show you to the sunroom."

As the maid led them through the house, Sadie whispered, "If she's married, she didn't change her name."

"Never has." Owen whispered back. "Probably didn't want to deal with all the paperwork when the marriage fell through."

Sadie laughed.

"Can I get you some tea?"

"No, thank you." They replied in unison.

"Okay, please have a seat. Mrs. Silva will be right down."

Sadie sat on the edge of a Victorian-style antique couch as Owen remained standing next to sweeping windows that overlooked the fields. The mint and cream colored room had a dated, antique feel with multiple ticking grandfather clocks, a mismatch of old paintings, and hundreds of knickknacks covering the surfaces.

"Well, well, well..."

Sadie turned toward a sugary-sweet voice at the doorway.

"When I woke up this morning, I sure as hell didn't expect one of BSPD's finest to grace me with his presence this afternoon."

Katrina—Kat—sauntered into the room, sparkling with platinum blonde hair and a starched white jumpsuit that glowed against faux tanned skin. Fire-engine red lips curled behind a puff of smoke streaming from the Marlboro hanging out of her mouth.

True to her nickname, the blonde's eyes skimmed Owen like a *Kat* about to pounce on her prey. Then, she cast a quick once-over to Sadie before returning to her interest. The woman knew who she had power over—men.

"To what do I owe this pleasure?" Kat exhaled a steady stream of smoke into the room and flicked the cigarette against a gold ashtray.

Kat remained standing with Owen, making Sadie feel like a little kid that had been cast aside on the couch. On purpose? No doubt in hell.

"Mrs. Silva, my name is Owen Grayson, and this is Dr. Sadie Hart—"

A perfectly-pointy eyebrow raised. *"Doctor?"*

Sadie stood and released a *what-the-hell* snort, earning her a lightning-quick *stop-it* glance from Owen.

Owen continued, "We're here to speak with you about the woman who was found trespassing on your land seven months ago. Do you remember this?"

Kat took a long drag from her cigarette. "I do. She'd been hanging out on our land for a few days. I'd catch her petting the horses from time to time. Fired a few warning shots into the air one night..." she batted her long, black eyelashes. "But that's not illegal is it?"

Her question was met with silence.

She smiled, laughed, the faint smell of whiskey on her breath. Something was off with that woman, and it wasn't just her left breast, which was considerably larger than her right. "It bothered me, but it wasn't until the day she was screaming like a maniac that I called the cops."

"Screaming?" Owen looked at Sadie, and she gave a subtle shake of her head—this wasn't in the file.

"Yeah, damn lunatic. I grabbed my gun and went out on the front porch, told her to get out. Crazy bitch kept running toward the house, so," she flippantly raised her eyebrows. "I pointed my gun at her and told her I'd shoot. That stopped her in her tracks."

"What was she screaming?"

"She was hysterical. Couldn't make out a word. Well, something about calling the cops. Oh, and she kept screaming something about a flag."

"A flag?"

"Yep. A flag."

"What kind of flag?"

"That I don't know. Anyway, that was it. Once I told her I was going to shoot her ass, she started backing away. I went back into the house, and when I looked out the window a minute later, she was gone. Never saw her again."

Sadie glanced at Owen.

"Did you recognize her?" He asked.

"Nope."

"Did you say anything to her other than telling her to get away?"

"Hell no. I'm not in the habit of conversing with homeless people."

"Not without your shotgun, huh?" Sadie asked, not bothering to hide the attitude in her voice.

"That's right," Kat sneered back.

Owen took a step forward to defuse the heating tension between two women that were as different as oil and water. Well, cheap whiskey and boxed wine.

"Why did you presume the woman was homeless?"

"She carried one of those stupid hiking backpacks on her all the time. You know, those really long ones that look like you're carrying a twin-sized bed on your back? Had all sorts of things hanging off the sides. She just seemed dirty, you know?"

"Can you describe her to me?"

"Ah hell, that was so long ago. But I remember she had brown, *dirty* hair," a flicker of a glance to Sadie's brown hair. "And was short, I remember that. Real skinny."

"Did you ever see her with anyone?"

"No."

"What about your husband?"

"What about my husband?"

"Would he have noticed anything that you might have missed?"

A chuckle laced with disrespect. "No. My husband wouldn't have noticed anything I missed, Officer."

"Why so sure?"

"Because my husband is never home. He travels eighty-five percent of the time for work. I did the math." She grinned. "So, no, he wouldn't be able to help you any more than I can."

"Must be lonely," Sadie said.

"Not really," Kat replied.

"Mrs. Silva, do you have security cameras on the grounds?"

"Of course," she said as if it would be crazy not to with a house as magnificent as hers.

"Were they up and running during the time the woman was on your land?"

Kat shrugged. "Don't know why they wouldn't have been."

Sadie flickered a glance at Owen. She didn't remember reading anything about security camera footage in the case file.

"Do you know if the tapes have already been reviewed?" Owen asked.

"Don't know. Come to think of it... not sure if they even asked about that last time."

"Do you remember who spoke with you about the woman?"

"Yeah, Sheriff Crawly."

Sadie's eyebrows raised as she looked at Owen.

"I'd love to take a look at those tapes, if you don't mind."

Kat took another drag as if deciding whether to help them or not. She concentrated on Owen while blowing out a string of smoke. "Was sorry to hear about your uncle."

"Thank you."

"Shouldn't have gone caving alone, you know. But he always was a careless guy."

Owen's eyes flashed with anger.

The smile that curved on the woman's red lips made Sadie want to slap her.

"Thought that whole mess was behind me, but seems Ray's just as popular now as he was when he was alive."

"What do you mean?" Sadie asked.

"You're not the first person to come asking about him."

"Who?" Owen's voice was as cold as ice.

"That deputy. What's his name? Deputy Tucker. That's it. Odd guy if you ask me. Heard he got discharged from the military for getting in a fight with his superior or some-thing." She snorted, "Real American hero."

Sadie's eyes rounded as the image of Deputy Tucker's hiking pack flashed through her head—with a patch of a large American Flag sewn onto the front pocket.

18

"S IT."

Kimi shot him a look that would send most men's balls shriveling to the size of grapes.

But he didn't care.

He wanted answers, and he wanted them now.

Griffin waited until Kimi sat on the folding chair he'd dragged into the cave, just out of the rain. After a few seconds of staring him down, she conceded.

"Thank you. Now." Instead of taking the seat next to her, Griffin opted to stand. He had a feeling he needed to exercise every bit of authority he had in him with this conversation.

"What were you doing last night?"

Kimi's eyes rounded. Bingo.

"How..."

"I need you to tell me what's going on. Right *now*."

She stared at him, scrambling to put together a sentence.

"I saw, Kimi. I followed you into the cave. What the hell were you doing?"

Kimi closed her eyes. "Oh, my God." She pushed out the chair. Well, that didn't last long.

He watched her wheels turn. She'd been caught, and she knew it. No way to sweet-talk—or lick for that matter—her way out of this one.

Kimi heaved out a sigh and crossed her arms over her chest.

Dammit she was cute when she was pissed.

"Fine. Yes, I did go into the cave in the middle of the night, alone. But it wasn't anything to do with the skeleton we're excavating, or the kid that was shot, or anything like that. I *promise."*

"What, then? What were you looking for?"

"My God," she laughed a humorless laugh and scrubbed her hands over her face. "This is so fucking embarrassing."

"Hey." He closed the inches between them. "Listen. I know... what we have isn't exactly a relationship, but it's me, Kimi. The dude you've seen every inch of. You know me, and I know you. Don't be embarrassed. Of anything."

Kimi blew out an exhale and nodded. It was the first time he'd seen her vulnerable.

A minute stretched between them with nothing but the buzz of the rain on the rocks outside. He waited patiently for her to open up to him in the only way she hadn't already.

"The legend of Atohi..." she said, finally.

"Yeah?"

"I'm a many-times removed descendant of him."

He blinked, giving the words a moment to process.

"Yeah. See? You think I'm crazy now. It's crazy, huh?" Her big eyes looked up at him and he saw something else he'd never seen before—insecurity.

"No. No, no, no... just... keep going." He said it calmly, urging her to continue. As he stared back at her now, he saw

it. Clear as day. The flawless, naturally tanned skin. Dark eyes punctuated by black hair as soft as silk. He should have seen it. He should have put the pieces of the puzzle together.

"Okay." Another deep breath. "So, your story of the legend isn't exactly accurate." She shifted her weight. "It's true that a man butchered his family in here, in Crypts Cavern... but not everyone. His daughter got out. That man was my great-great-grandpa, and the girl who escaped was my great-grandma." She paused, staring at him, waiting for some sort of reaction. When he didn't give one, she continued, "So, when I heard you and Sadie were being called to this cave, I had to come. Why? I don't know, I wanted to see it. I've never actually been inside. I wanted to finally face this horrible past that haunts my family... My name, Kimi, means 'secret' in Algonquin. That's the tribe I'm a descendant of. And the curse?" She shook her head. "Evil, horrible things have happened to my bloodline since Atohi killed himself in this damn cave. Do you know both my parents died in a car accident? Two of my cousins—a house fire. The list goes on." She paused again, mindlessly kicked a rock. "My granny told me she believes that the reason that we're cursed is that Atohi never received a proper burial. Once he does, the curse will be released. I thought maybe if I came here, maybe if I face it, maybe it would go away or something. Or hell, maybe I'd find his bones and give him the burial he deserves. That's why I asked you to ask Sadie to let me tag along. This is why I wanted to come so badly."

"Kimi," before he could talk himself out of it, he reached out and grabbed her hands. "Why didn't you say something?"

"It's embarrassing, Griffin. It's something I've removed myself from. Something I didn't want you, of all people to know." She looked away, and he swore he saw the glint of a tear in her eye. "I think I'm cursed, Griffin. My life is cursed... and everyone in it." ·

He pulled her in for a hug and kissed her on the forehead. "You're not cursed, Kimi. We all create our own paths, our own destinies. You've got a shitty past. So what? It doesn't have to define you, or your future."

A sniffle confirmed that she was crying. "No, Griffin, you don't understand. Tragedy swirls around me like a vicious, unstoppable force of pure evil. Anyone in my life is cursed."

Thunder rumbled in the distance as the rain began to pick up.

"Don't worry, Kimi." His gaze shifted to the storm outside the cave. "We're all going to make it out of here just fine."

Owen hit a patch of mud, sliding to a stop inches behind Crawly's bumper, which was parked next to Kyle's Subaru. He'd spent the entire drive—until reception dropped—on the phone with Lieutenant Colson, updating him on Dr. Perez's findings of the extra tooth that connected to her cold case, the visit with Kat, and the desperate screams about a flag. He demanded they put a BOLO out for Tucker and bring him in for questioning, and threaten Kat with a warrant if she didn't turn over her security tapes immediately. The two hung up agreeing to an immediate meeting with Chief McCord to discuss developments—just as soon as he saw Sadie and her team safely out of the woods.

"Tucker's not here. I didn't see him this morning either." Sadie squinted to see through the rain as she looked around the small clearing.

"I want you guys to pack up and hit the road," Owen

said, his tone deep, words clipped as if he was giving orders to one of his men. The man had switched from Mr. Charming to all-cop somewhere over the last twenty minutes.

She glanced at the puddles forming in the potholes. It wasn't just the rain, she knew, it was that he didn't want Sadie anywhere close to the cave, to Deputy Tucker, or to Sheriff Crawly. The longer she and her team stayed near that cave, the longer they were in danger.

"What are you going to say to Crawly when you see him?"

"Nothing. And you're not either. Not until we get more information, or talk to Tucker. And not before I get another look in that cave for whatever the hell Tucker is hiding in there. Brian Russell went back to the cave to look for something. I'm going to find it. For all we know, Crawly's an accomplice here."

Sadie nodded. It made no sense why Crawly didn't add the confrontation between Kat and Jane Doe in the police report. *Jane Doe* had been the name assigned to the homeless woman over the course of Owen's conversation with Lieutenant Colson.

"What about the Anarchy angle?"

Owen turned off his headlights and pulled out his keys. Although it was mid-afternoon, the storm that was blowing in cast a deep gray shadow over the woods. "The guy was discharged from the National Guard. That'll give anyone pent-up anger." He reached back and pulled out a pack of plastic pullover raincoats. He tossed her one—bright yellow. "Sadie, whoever killed my uncle and Brian Russell also killed our Jane Doe—you said it yourself. Her skull indicated blunt force trauma, and the woman was buried in a shallow grave for Christ's sake. Why their bodies were separated, I don't know. But I'm going to find out. In the meantime? You're getting out of these woods."

"Owen, I haven't even completed my search yet, there could be more—"

"You're done, Sadie."

She heaved out a breath and slipped on the raincoat.

After checking the gun he kept in an ankle holster, Owen pushed open the door. Rain pelted the interior of the car. She nodded to the extra raincoat on the console. "Raincoat?"

"No. Too confining. Let's go."

Sadie pulled up the hood and jumped out, the rain pounding her shoulders despite the thick trees overhead. She grabbed her pack from the camper, and then they stepped into the woods, the rain too heavy, too loud, to allow for any sort of conversation.

They reached the rope bridge and without a word, he stepped in front, and reached for her hand. Together, they crossed—a comfortable rhythm, a comfortable intimacy. Then, he grabbed her hand and led her through the woods, his steely eyes scanning the surrounding woods every few seconds.

Sadie frowned as the cave came into view—not a single bag, pack, water bottle, person. Nothing.

"Where is everyone?" A feeling of dread washed over her as they stepped onto the boulder, the rain splashing off the rocks, soaking the bottom of her pants.

Owen looked around. "There's their stuff. At the mouth of the cave."

"Let's go."

As they reached the entrance, a light bounced off the dark wall inside.

"Sadie!" Griffin emerged from the tunnel, his face and body covered in mud and grime. "Boy am I glad to see you."

Sadie dipped into the cave, out of the rain. "Geez, you're covered."

"I've been exploring deeper into the cave the last hour." His breath was short, eyes hyper.

"Where is everyone?"

"Kimi's searching the other side of this hill, looking for anything we missed. Aaron and Kyle split off a while ago. Crawly was still here when I went back in the cave. Is he not at the camper?"

"No." Frowning, she glanced at Owen, who was scanning the dense forest lining the cave.

"Sadie, I've got to tell you something..." Griffin's eyes twinkled with excitement.

She tilted her head, every instinct in her body on high alert now. Why exactly, she wasn't sure.

"I think I might've found the murder weapon."

"*What?*"

Griffin nodded feverishly. "Yeah. In the lake, just outside of the Anarchy room. My light sparked off something in the water, on a rock ledge. I got as close as I could and, it's a knife, Sadie."

"What makes you think it's the murder weapon? It could be anyone's—"

"It has an Anarchy symbol etched in the hilt."

Owen's neck snapped toward the back of the cave. "Are you sure?"

"Yes. There's no way I could reach it though..."

"Take me."

"Okay. Just give me one minute. Let me splash this bat shit out of my eyes real quick. It's burning like a bitch."

As Griffin stepped outside, Sadie turned to Owen.

"Oh my God, Owen. That's why whoever shot Brian Russell didn't want him going back into the cave."

He stepped past her. "I'm not waiting. I'll head back and meet you guys back there."

She glanced at Griffin who was squatted by a puddle splashing rainwater on his face, then turned back to Owen. "No. Wait. Griff will be just a sec—"

Pop! Pop, pop!

Sadie spun around just as Griffin's body slumped over and rolled down the rocks.

19

"*G* RIFF!*" SADIE LUNGED forward, but was yanked back, sending her stumbling onto the rocks.

"*Stop.*"

Her eyes popped to Owen. "What? *Griffin's been shot!*" Her voice pitched. "You have to—"

"You have to *stay here.*"

"*No!*" She struggled against him but was pushed to the ground.

"Whoever shot him probably wants to pick us off one by one as we come out of the cave, *Sadie.* You. Stay. *Here.*"

He didn't wait for her to argue, instead he pulled his gun, chambered a bullet and with both hands gripping the hilt, he nimbly bounced from rock to rock, and pressed himself against the side of the cave.

Sadie shifted to a crouch, her pulse roaring in her ears.

Griffin had been shot.

Chest heaving, she focused on Griffin's limp body barely visible just beyond a boulder, a mixture of ice-cold terror and disbelief clashing together like a stun gun in her head.

Someone *shot* Griffin.

She couldn't just sit there and wait for Owen to *approve* her to move. They had to get help. They had to call 911.

Sadie watched Owen slide behind the shadow of the entrance of the cave, his head tilted toward the trees, scanning the hill above.

Sadie crept forward, willing her heartbeat to slow so she could hear anything other than the *thump, thump, thump* of her heartbeat in her ears.

Just then, Owen darted out of the cave.

Sadie froze and watched him hurl himself over the boulder.

She waited, holding her breath.

No gunshots.

"Griffin!"

The faint scream of Kimi's voice had Sadie scrambling over the rocks and out the cave.

"Sadie!"

Sadie turned to see Kimi practically sliding down the hill in a mad panic.

"What happened? Oh, my *God,* what *happened?"*

"I don't know!" Sadie yelled back as she ran to the boulder where Owen was hovered over Griffin, sprawled out on the rocks, his skin waxy-pale against a pool of blood spreading across his T-shirt. Another puddle below his thigh.

"Owen, is he alive?" She squeaked out.

"Sadie," Owen said with a chilling calmness as he ripped open Griffin's shirt. "I need you to call 911 on your SAT phone immediately. Kimi, the flannel shirt around your waist, I need you to shred it and make a tourniquet for his leg, can you do that?"

Tears rolled down Kimi's face as she yanked the shirt from her waist.

Sadie spun on her heel and sprinted to the pack she'd left in the cave as Crawly jogged out from the tree line, his eyes wide with shock.

"Hey, whoa, is everyone okay?"

The next hour was a blur.

The paramedics made it in record time and rushed Griffin to the hospital, moments before Sadie had heard them say *"he's not breathing."*

Lieutenant Colson had dragged Sheriff Crawly away—not in cuffs, but not happy.

It seemed the whole town had shown up. BSPD officers, state police, medics, and a few other people that looked like they'd caught a ride to catch the action. Sadie, Owen, and Kimi had given official statements, then Sadie and Kimi had been asked to step aside as the officers searched for bullet casings and any trace evidence.

The rain continued, a restless force hellbent on making everyone's job harder. Deep red blood snaked through the puddles, encircling a blood-stained rock where Griffin's body had laid.

It was horrific.

Owen seamlessly stepped into his role as police officer, but as Sadie watched him from a distance, she realized he was so much more than that. Owen ran the show. There was a calm, authoritative demeanor to him that everyone responded to, even the Lieutenant, and she knew she was seeing shades of his time spent in the military.

Still no signs of Deputy Tucker.

"Where're you going?" Sadie grabbed her pack and fell into step next to Owen as he stepped into the cave.

"To find my uncle's murder weapon."

"Right now?" She struggled to keep up with his stride on

the slick rocks.

"Yeah."

"What about everything else? How's Griffin? Have you heard?"

He shook his head, slowing as the cave closed in around them. "He's a tough kid. Healthy. Young. He's got a better shot than most."

"Owen, don't patronize me, I heard them say he wasn't breathing as they strapped him down."

"Doesn't mean he's not going to make it. You can't think like that, Sadie." He grabbed her hand and helped her through a group of thick stalagmites.

"You act like you know where you're going."

"Griffin said the knife was on a ledge just below the water, somewhere past the Anarchy room." Owen squeezed through a narrow crevice, then helped her through.

"That doesn't pinpoint where to look." Why was she trying to talk him out of this?

"I'll find it... Goddammit." His voice trailed off as they looked at the small river of water rushing along the bottom of the rotted tree trunk bridge. It was at least two inches higher than it had been that morning.

"Quickly," he said. "Let's go." He helped her across, and through the next narrow passage until they reached the Grand Room. The roar of the waterfall almost deafening.

Sadie's mouth gaped. "Whoa."

Owen shined his light along the rippling black water. "It's risen about a foot since this morning." He turned to her. "Go back. Tell the sheriff what I'm doing."

"First, don't act like you didn't tell someone you were coming in here. You're not that irresponsible. Second, *no.* I'm coming. I haven't finished my job yet. I'll finish up while you look for the knife. All bases covered."

His jaw twitched as he stared at her.

"I'm not going back. I'll finish my search with or without you."

He nodded, as if deciding something, and if she knew Owen, it was that he'd rather keep an eye on her himself, than leave her fate to the group outside.

"Fine. The water's not going to rise quickly enough within the next hour to trap us in. *But* that doesn't mean we don't need to hustle, you stubborn, little..."

"Shhh." She grinned and pressed her finger to his lips.

He nipped. "Okay, let's get at it. Ladies first."

Sadie stepped onto the wooden footbridge that lined the far wall of the Grand Room, making a mental mark of the height of the water. Not that it mattered. The waters were rising and there was nothing they could do about it. Like Owen said, they needed to hustle.

They crossed the bridge, shining their lights into the water just below them, looking for the ledge that Griffin was so sure held the knife that killed Owen's uncle.

"I can tell you one thing," she raised her voice over the rushing water. "Griff wouldn't have hung out on this bridge long enough to spot a knife in the water, I promise you that. He's claustrophobic. Doesn't like to be trapped."

"Okay, let's keep going."

They stepped onto the rock floor, and made their way to the opening that led to the Anarchy room.

"I'm going to address the elephant in the room," she said, forcing out the thoughts that had been swirling in her head over the last hour.

Owen glanced over his shoulder with a cocked eyebrow.

"It can't be a coincidence that Griffin was shot right after he found the knife."

"No, I don't think it's a coincidence at all." He swept his light along the walls.

"Then, it had to have been someone around. Someone in our group. Someone watching him in the cave." The thought sent a shiver up her spine.

"These woods go on for miles and miles, Sadie. Crypts Cavern is legendary, a damn tourist attraction. Hundreds of people hike around here. There's nothing keeping anyone from walking up on us."

"True. But it goes back to the timing... Griffin found a knife, and either whoever shot him saw him find it, or Griffin told someone about it before he told us. Whether that person is the person who tried to kill him or not, they must've told whoever did." She looked at Owen for validation of her sick thought, or maybe hoping for the opposite.

He nodded. "Agreed."

"Has Lieutenant Colson found Deputy Tucker?"

"Has the day off. They're looking for him."

"What was Crawly doing in the woods when Griffin got shot?"

"Taking a shit. Offered to take us there to prove it."

"Gross. Really? That's what he said he was doing?"

"Yep."

"Who shits in the woods?"

Owen cast a confused look over his shoulder. "Every man who's ever grown up in the woods. And I'm guessing Colson sent someone to verify."

"That's disgusting. I hope he wiped with poison ivy."

"Doubt he wiped at all."

"*Gross.* That still doesn't cross him off the list, in my opinion."

"Crawly didn't shoot Griffin."

"Why are you so sure?"

"Griffin was shot by someone on the far side of the cave, in the opposite direction that Crawly came from."

"How do you know that?"

"The angle of his body. How he fell. Where the shots were on his body. There's a clear path with line of sight to the right of the mouth of the cave. They'll confirm it with the autopsy of Brian, too."

"Did you search the path?"

"Colson and his team are. This rain, though..."

"I know..."

"Crawly doesn't have anything to do with this."

"Why so sure?"

"Colson confronted him about everything. Crawly admitted that he didn't include Kat's comments about Jane Doe's hysterics because, frankly, he didn't believe her. Says Kat was so drunk she could barely stand when he got there. Took note of the trespassing and moved on."

"That's why he didn't bother to ask about cameras."

"Right. He got a call about some kids pushing someone off Devil's Cove and left her with her drunk ass to go take care of more important things, in his words. Never entered his mind again."

Sadie wondered how many times officers blew off what appeared to be small disturbances, that were actually a huge clue in another case. All the time, she bet.

"Why did Tucker visit her today asking about your uncle?"

"We'll find out as soon as we find him. Alright, so there's the Anarchy room." Owen shined the light on the narrow opening at the end of the tunnel, then swept it to the passageway to the left. "Griffin either searched inside the room, or explored further this way. I'm assuming the water runs out that way."

"I'll take the room. You take the tunnel."

"Thought you'd say that." He winked. "Alright, finish up looking for bones first, then look for the knife." He glanced at his watch. "I'll meet you in the Anarchy room in twenty minutes. Don't leave there. We need to hustle."

She nodded, then Owen lifted her over the rock wall and helped her squeeze through the tiny opening.

"You good?" He hollered through the opening.

"Yep."

"Alright. Twenty minutes. I'll be back."

"I'm counting on it." Sadie set down her pack, positioned her extra light in the corner, and looked around. Fast-moving streams of water ran down the walls of the room—water that hadn't been there earlier in the day. Her stomach dipped with nerves. *We need to hustle* was an understatement. Sadie pulled out her tools, rolled up her sleeves and got to work sifting through the only corner of the room she hadn't searched that morning. She heard movement outside the room, a few grunts echoing against the rock wall where Owen was exploring the passageway.

Sadie kneeled lower and switched angles, flashing her light along the corner of the room. Her hand slipped and squelched into nasty black goo up her wrist. She frowned, cocked her head, hearing a faint whistle of wind along a small crack where the rock met the floor of the cave. She lowered further, scooping away the goop with one hand as she shined the light with the other. Slowly, a gap became visible. Sadie flattened to her stomach, twisted her neck, and repositioned the flashlight to shine into the gap.

The beam reflected off grimy ivory.

"Holy shit." She shimmied forward until her forehead was pressed against the rock. "That's a freaking bone."

20

OWEN GLANCED AT his watch as he squeezed through another crevice in the rock wall. Ten more minutes.

He shifted the headlamp he'd slid on and looked around. After getting through a hold so tight, he wasn't sure if he could get back out, the cave had opened up to a four by four tunnel with a small river of rushing water running along the side. He'd noted a constant flow of air coming from the end of the tunnel, indicating that there was an entry-point to the cave that they didn't know about.

But someone else did.

Regardless, he didn't have time to look for that now. He needed to find that damn knife and get Sadie out of the cave and out of these Godforsaken woods.

Owen hunched over and made his way down the tunnel which narrowed into a *V* that was too tight to push his body through, which meant Griffin couldn't either—claustrophobia or not. So, he turned and started from the beginning, shinning his light into the water.

A fish—so translucent that he could almost see through

it—skirted past him. He cocked his head and looked at the spot where the water ran under the rocks.

"Must lead to the lake…" he muttered into the silence. "And that's a damn decent current".

Following his gut, he crab-walked to the rock wall and shined his light in the far corner—the beam sparkling off the tip of a knife on the far side of the rushing water.

Bingo. Whoever killed his uncle tossed the knife in the lake and the current caught it. All secrets come to light, indeed.

He positioned his light on a rock, rolled up his sleeves and lowered down to his stomach. The river was about six feet wide, with the knife sitting on an underwater ledge just out of his reach. Definitely easy to miss.

Dammit, dammit, dammit.

He grit his teeth and repositioned, stretching farther until the skin under his arm felt like it was about to tear. Ice-cold water rushed against his chest as he hung as far over as he could without falling in.

No luck.

Son of a bitch.

He pushed to a stance and looked around. For what? A Reacher grabber to magically appear?

Well… *fuck.*

He sighed. Only one option left.

After another quick check of the time, Owen stripped down to his boxer-briefs, opting to keep them on. No telling what might come up from the depths below, ready to nibble on his junk.

He popped his neck from side to side. "Alright, it's go time."

Another exhale steeling himself for the frigid, black water, before he lowered himself down.

"Son of a..." It felt like shards of glass piercing his skin.

Owen had been in colder water in the ocean, but this was a damn close second.

Anchoring one hand on the rock wall, he kicked his way over to the ledge, reached down, and slid the cold metal out from the ledge. Just as Griffin had said, the letter A, enclosed in a circle, decorated the hilt of a six-inch, smooth blade hunting knife. He turned, kicked over to the ledge, and pulled himself out. After securing the knife in his pack, Owen pulled on his clothes.

Time was ticking.

He quickly made his way back to Sadie, squeezing through the tiny opening and sliding down the slide of the Anarchy room. He turned, and his eyebrows popped up.

"Whoa."

With nearly every inch of her face, neck, and arms covered in mud, Sadie grinned from ear to ear. "Found another bone."

"Really?"

"Yep," she nodded to the clear bag sitting on top of her pack. "A tibia—leg—bone. Human, no doubt about it. Very, very old. Definitely not your uncle or from anyone recent. Check it out."

"Where was it?"

"In the corner, over there. There's a gap in the wall that was buried under a crapload of well, crap and mud. It leads to what appears to be a tiny room, more like a coffin, really. It was in there."

Owen kneeled down and looked at the small crevice in the rock. "Good find, Dr. Hart."

"Thanks. Did you get it?"

"Yep."

"The knife? You did?" She pushed to her feet, slipping a moment before catching herself.

"Yep."

"Oh my God, that's fantastic, Owen."

"Let's head back."

"You read my thoughts." Sadie placed the bone in her pack, then made her way to the rock wall and grabbed onto the hand holds. "Grab my light in the corner will you..."

"Yes, ma'am." Owen jogged across the rocks and bent down to pick up her flashlight when—

"Shit!"

He spun around as Sadie slid down the wall and hit the ground with a *thud.*

"Ow! Shit! My foot." she spurted out.

Fuck.

Owen crossed the room in two steps, fell to his knees, and the moment he saw her foot, he knew.

Twisted at a ninety-degree angle, the bottom half of her leg looked like a number 7. Her ankle, trapped between two rocks, was undoubtedly broken... in several places if he had to guess.

"Shit."

"Owen," tears fell down her flushed, panic-stricken face. "Oh, my God, it hurts." She squeezed her eyes shut and rocked back and forth in pain, as much as she could, anyway.

"Get it out, Owen," she begged between her teeth. "Get it out."

"I will." He ground his teeth and clamped one hand over the toes, and one over the heel—no budge.

Shit.

"Okay, Sadie, I need you to look at me."

She opened her eyes, releasing more tears down her cheeks.

"You're going to be okay, but your ankle is broken."

"Thanks for the newsflash, Dr. Grayson."

She was a strong woman to crack a joke while her foot dangled like a piece of meat. "I'm going to unwedge it—"

"Go slow," she whined, slamming her eyes shut again.

"Do your breathing, okay? Focus on the breaths, in, out, in, out."

She started breathing in a rhythm that reminded him of those eighties sex-education films they'd made him watch in junior high school.

Once her trembling lessened, he started working her foot out, little by little, inch by inch. After five minutes of torturing her, he sat back. No way in hell was "slow and gentle" going to cut it. He was going to have to yank it out.

"Okay, this isn't working."

"You can't get it out?" Her eyes shot open, sweat now mixing with the tears wetting her face. "Like, you have to cut it *off?*" Her voice pitched.

"No." He couldn't hide his chuckle. "No, this isn't 127 Hours. No, I'm going to get your foot out, but, baby, it's gonna hurt." He swiped the tears from her face. "I need you to be strong, okay?"

She nodded, jutted out her chin and sniffed the tears away.

His heart kicked.

"Okay, on three, okay?"

She nodded feverishly, strength reflecting in her clenched jaw.

"One..." He gripped both ends of her foot. "Two... *three.*"

Her scream vibrated off the walls as he yanked her foot free from the grip of the cave floor. The surge of adrenaline only lasted until she caught a glimpse of her limp ankle... and passed out cold.

Fuck.

Twenty minutes of fanning and administering water later, Sadie was finally able to sit upright without turning a shade of green Owen had seen on rookies' faces during their first helo ride in a thunderstorm.

"A little better?" He helped lift her head off his lap— pleased with himself that he'd been able to fight the boner that had been threatening to peak.

She groggily sat up. "Besides feeling like my leg has been run over by a school bus? Sure."

"The ibuprofen should kick in shortly. I gave you half the bottle."

"What?"

"Just joking, but definitely enough to dull the pain and help the swelling." He glanced down at the cantaloupe that was once her ankle.

"Well, yeehaw," she muttered.

He smiled, then took a deep breath, and frowned as he looked at her. It was time—beyond time. "Sadie, we've got to get out of here."

She nodded. "I know."

During the handful of minutes he wasn't thinking about sex while she'd regained her composure on his lap, he'd decided that the only way they were going to make it out of the cave was if he carried her. There was nothing available to build a travois to drag her out, and even if there were, he wouldn't be able to get her through the narrow passage ways. Nope, Sadie Hart was going to have to deal with dangling over his shoulder for the next ten minutes... after he got her over the damn steep wall of the Anarchy room first.

He grabbed her shoulders as she attempted to stand. "No. There's no way you can walk."

"I can bounce."

"As much as I'd like to see that, no. Bouncing on one foot through a dark, slick cave is a great way to break your other ankle."

"Good point. So... what now?"

He opened his arms. "Hot Rod at your service."

"You're *kidding.*"

"No, ma'am."

"Owen. You cannot *carry* me."

"Well now you're just insulting me." He positioned himself behind her.

"But—"

"Giddy up, baby. No time to argue. Not another word about it." He rubbed his palms together. "Okay, we've got to get you over the wall first. You've got this."

As Sadie turned to face the wall, he checked the time— *shit*—then slid his forearms under her armpits and lifted her off the ground.

She steadied herself on one foot, fighting the pain that was surely shooting through her body. After a quick inhale, she nodded. "Let's get this shit done."

God, he was beginning to love this woman.

"Okay, I'm going to put you on my shoulders, lift you, and you'll pull yourself up and over. Be careful not to hit your ankle when you go through the opening. Cause, you know—"

"It's broken. Got it."

"Then, just slowly slide down using the hand holds and land on your good foot."

"Obviously."

He grinned. "It's flat on the other side so we shouldn't have a repeat." He kneeled down, gripped her hands above his head, and guided her onto his shoulders. A few grunts and girly curse words, she was secured around his neck. An onslaught of inappropriate comments came to mind, but he bit his lip. Not the time.

"Lift on three. One, two, three."

Sadie gripped the opening as he lifted her into the air, then pulled herself into the opening. After a slow push, Sadie was through the opening and on the other side.

Obstacle one, complete.

With a single jump, Owen was through the opening and sliding down the other side.

"Uh... Owen..."

The tone of her voice sent a chill up his spine. He hit the cave floor with a thud and turned around.

"... ... Well. Shit."

Owen scratched his head as he looked at the bridge that ran alongside the lake, now halfway underwater. The thirty-plus minutes of tending to Sadie had set them back. He shifted his gaze to the waterfall roaring down the cave wall. The lake would continue to rise as long as the rain kept up.

Obstacle two...

He turned to Sadie, who's eyes had grown to the size of her ankle. "Well, at least you won't get wet." He kneeled down to pick her up.

"Wait."

"What?"

"You can't cross that bridge carrying me. Thing was half rotted as is. It won't hold."

Truth was, he was worried about the same thing.

"We don't really have a choice, do we? It's either cross or stay here for the night. We're not trapped *yet.*"

The words were like a cattle prod to her system. "Cross," she demanded.

"Thought you might say that. Bottoms up." He stuck the flashlight in his mouth, reached down, pulled his Glock from his ankle holster and slid it into his belt. He swooped her over his shoulder, her hand dangling just above his crotch. Under normal circumstances...

"Ow," she interrupted his thoughts.

"Sorry." He muttered around the flashlight. "Hold on."

Owen took a moment to shift his weight, then stepped onto the bridge. Icy water seeped into his boots, hitting at the knee. He clenched his jaw and bit back a curse. Wet clothes? Fine. Soaked boots? Not fine. The roar of the waterfall drowned out Sadie's labored breath as he slowly put one foot in front of the other, knowing that one slip, one bad plank, and he'd be in a rising, pitch-black lake with someone who couldn't swim, or even tread water, for that matter.

He pressed forward, testing each plank before releasing the three-hundred-plus pounds of he and Sadie combined.

Finally, they crossed to the other side. He shined the light with his free hand.

"Holy *shit,*" Sadie exhaled in his ear, the relief evident in her voice.

"My thoughts exactly. How you doing?"

"Dandy. Just get me out of here."

"Your wish is my command, dear."

With a bit more speed, Owen made his way through the tunnel, and rounded the corner to the narrow passageway that led to the home stretch.

"I'm going to set you up on this ledge, then I'll squeeze through, then pull you down."

"What ledge?"

"To your left. You'll straddle those stalagmites."

She looked up at the tree-trunk looking structures. "Impressive."

"You think those are impressive, you should see—"

"God, you're perverted."

He laughed. "Gotta make light of a bad situation. Okay, on three, I'll lift."

"Okay."

"One, two, three." The last word came out as a grunt as he hoisted her into the air. She pulled herself up as he hovered beneath her.

"Got it?"

She nodded, out of breath.

"Okay, I'm coming around."

"Owen... um... ... where's the log?"

He squeezed through the passageway. "What?"

He followed her gaze to the small river of water rushing between two boulders, where the log had once been.

"Well..." he fisted his hands on his hips. "Now we're trapped."

21

SADIE BLINKED, STARING at the white caps of water rushing over their only hope of escape.

Yes, they were stuck.

She looked at Owen. A forced smile pulled across his lips. "Hey, it could be worse."

"How?"

He shrugged. "You could be trapped in here alone."

Well, he had a point there.

She watched him look past the river, then back toward the Grand Room, assessing their next move. Her heart started to pound as her mind began to catch up with the reality of what was happening. They were trapped. In a haunted cave out in the middle of nowhere. For how long? Did they have enough water? Food?

Holy *shit*—light? Did they have enough battery in their flashlights?

How would she hear how Griffin was doing? If he'd even survived?

Did Owen have enough pain meds so that she wouldn't gnaw a hole through her leg?

Dear Lord, where was she going to pee?

Her lungs began to constrict with panic. She needed to get to the hospital to check on Griff... she needed medical attention herself... she needed a shower—

"Stop."

Owen's voice shook her from her impending panic attack.

"Take a deep breath. Everyone knows where we are. They'll come looking for us shortly, see that the bridge is down and know we're trapped. Regardless, the storms will stop tonight and the water will recede quickly. We'll be out of here by morning."

Morning. Holy. Shit.

A solid minute of silence passed between them as they stared at the water.

"Okay," she took a deep breath. "So what now?"

"Well, we get to the highest level possible, which is in front of the Anarchy room. We'll hunker down there and wait until we can hike out."

"Cross the bridge again?"

"That's right." He skimmed the platform she was perched on. "Stay right there," he winked. "I'm coming around."

"Not the time for jokes, Owen." She rolled her eyes as he shimmied his way through the passage below her.

Once around, Owen lifted his arms, a smile on his face that seemed to help diffuse the anxiety coursing through her veins. The guy was made to deal with difficult situations. The guy was a born leader. She bet he had that same calming effect on every person he'd saved from perishing in the ocean.

"Alright princess, come here."

She slid into his arms, and with a grunt, he hoisted her over his shoulder.

"I don't think many princes carry their princesses like this." They took off down the tunnel, in the direction they'd just come from.

"Sure they do. Haven't you watched any medieval movies before?"

"Those men are apes and the women are complacent whores who are part of their harem."

"If the shoe fits."

She slapped his back, then quickly gripped him again as they stepped onto the bridge. She watched the black water swaying beneath her with each step Owen took, motion sickness beginning to wave over her body. How deep was the water? What lurked under the depths below? To avoid vomiting all over her knight in shining armor's back, Sadie closed her eyes—and her mouth—the rest of the short journey over the bridge.

The roar of the waterfall started to fade, and she opened her eyes as Owen set her on the cave floor in the middle of a flat, raised platform next to the Anarchy room. The lake stretched in front of them, still, a black mirror reflecting the beam of their lights. God, it was dark.

"How you doing?"

She leaned against the rock wall. "A bit better now that we're over the bridge." She smiled, "You, me, and bridges."

"A winning combination. I'll be right back."

She watched him disappear into the blackness, his flashlight pointed to the ground. After a few *bangs*, he returned carrying two long sticks.

"What are those for?"

"A splint for your ankle."

Of all the people to get stuck in a cave with, she lucked

out with a search and rescue expert. A heart-stoppingly handsome dreamboat with a body like a tank, search and rescue expert.

"Where did you get sticks?"

"The bridge." He positioned the flashlight where it shined next to them, illuminating the small space.

"You removed a plank from an already rotting bridge that's our only hope for getting out of here?"

A smile curved his lips. "Yep." He grabbed his pack, unzipped, and pulled out a ball of cord. She watched him as he quickly, smoothly, efficiently used his knife to chop and smooth the wood, then place the slats on either side of her ankle. He was laser focused, his hands steady, confident, as he cut the cord and secured the slats against her leg.

"Thank you," she said as he pulled the last cord tightly with his teeth.

"I've got a half bottle of ibuprofen left. We'll be able to stay on top of your pain, and the splint will help with the pain, too."

"Do you think it's bad?"

"I think you'll get to keep it," he smiled. "But, yeah, you're going to have a cast for sure."

"Dammit." She blew out a breath and leaned her head against the wall.

"It's going to suck, but it will heal completely, and with this splint, you might not have to have surgery. I did."

"You did? Have to have surgery?"

"Yep. Broke my ankle in two spots playing football. Healed, and here I am now, able to carry Dr. Sadie Hart over my shoulder with no more than a grunt."

She smiled. "I don't think that's only because of a nicely healed ankle."

"No?"

"No. You've got cannons for arms."

"All the better to carry you with, dear. So, let's get some food and water in you..." He searched through his pack, obviously uncomfortable with compliments. Which surprised her. Any guy that looked like that probably received more winks and whistles in one day than she got in her entire life. He had every right to have an ego the size of Texas, but he didn't. And that was quickly becoming one of her favorite things about him.

Owen pulled out an energy bar and a canteen of water and handed it to her.

"I've got a pack, too, you know?"

He grinned. "Let me guess, makeup and toilet paper?"

She tossed it to him. "Take a look."

"Alright." He unzipped her pack and began pulling out her own little survival kit.

"Antibacterial hand wipes—good job—water... a *compass?*" His voice raised with surprise.

"Yes... I know how to use it. Ass."

He chuckled and kept going. "Granola bars, a first-aid kit, girly-scented bug spray, a knife—nice work—lighter..." Then he pulled out a small, pink tube and cocked a brow.

"Every woman needs her lip gloss."

"*Makeup.*"

"Lip gloss is *not* makeup."

"Tell that to the makeup section at Wal-Mart."

"You spend a lot of time in the makeup section at Wal-Mart, Owen?"

"It's next to the condoms. Okay, what else... overpriced sunscreen that is *not* waterproof, and... a *Blow Pop?*" He raised the large, confetti-colored lollipop. "What are you? Eight?"

"Hey, it's a sucker *and* piece of gum. Talk about a winning combination."

"This thing is as big as a baseball." He examined it. "Cherry?"

"The best."

"Well, if the town's blood sugar drops, I know where to look."

She rolled her eyes and snatched it from his hand. "As a matter of fact, I could go for a blow pop right now..."

"I'm going to ignore the million comments that are rolling around in my head right now."

She unwrapped the lollipop and stuck it in her mouth. "Because you're a gentleman?"

"Exactly." A smile spread across his face as she slid the sucker to the side of her cheek. "You look like a squirrel."

She grinned, knowing how distorted the massive sucker made her face look as she smiled.

He laughed.

"Okay, what's in your pack, big shot?"

"Besides my secret stash of Wal-Mart makeup?"

"Right."

Owen grabbed his pack. "And besides the cord—*that you didn't have*—to splint your ankle?"

Her eyebrow tipped up.

"Just saying, your girly pack could use some work." He started emptying his own bag. "Let's see. The normal—water, food, bug spray, SPF, a knife, first aid kit, tarp, fire starters—"

"Fire?" Hope sparked.

"Already thought about it. Nothing dry enough in here to light. Sorry." He continued, "A tent..."

"You've got a tent in that pack?"

"That's not all, darling Sadie…" He pulled out a blue roll the size of his fist. "An insulated sleeping bag."

"That's a sleeping bag?"

"Yep. And believe me, you're going to be thanking me for this later. What else? Extra bullets, a compass, map, cell phone that of course doesn't work out here, a few multi-tools, whistle, extra flashlight—"

"Batteries?"

"No."

"Damn."

"And, last but not least, most importantly," He pulled out a brown bottle. "A pint of Tennessee's finest."

"Whiskey?"

He nodded.

"Whiskey is part of your *survival* pack?"

"Whiskey should be a part of everyone's survival pack. Good whiskey, anyway." He unscrewed the cap and took a swig. "Ahh, yep, can't leave home without it." He offered it to her.

Sadie stared at the amber-colored liquid, debating. Was it a good idea to drink alcohol while being trapped underground with a man that made her stomach do flip-flops?

Yep.

She grabbed the bottle and tipped it up. After sucking in a breath and blinking away the tears from the burn, she nodded. "Not bad."

"See? Told ya." He took it back, took another swig. "This beauty can clean wounds if you need it, too. Multi-purpose."

Her face dropped. "Maybe we should have used it on Griffin."

"Not those kinds of wounds." Owen sat down beside her, leaning his back against the wall and crossing his legs at the ankles.

"God, I hope he's okay," she whispered.

A minute of silence slid between them as Sadie looked at the cave around them. Her racing mind evaporated as acceptance of temporary defeat took over. She was trapped in a damn cave with a broken ankle and there was nothing she could do about it. She couldn't help Griffin, couldn't console Kimi who she assumed went back into town with Lieutenant Colson, couldn't get back to the lab to help Owen solve the mystery of his murdered uncle. Hell, she couldn't even walk by herself.

On an exhale, she leaned her head back and muttered, "What a freaking week."

"A dead body, a skeleton, and wounded buddy'll do that to you... and getting trapped in a cave."

"And having my name splashed all over the damn news." The words slipped out before she could catch herself. She looked over at him when he didn't respond.

"You know, don't you?"

"The boys told me."

"*Everyone* knows?"

"Hey, it's not everyday someone from the Ozarks makes the gossip columns."

"Oh my *God*." She shook her head. "Un-freaking-believable. Crawly and Colson must think I'm an incompetent gold-digging, media-loving..."

"They don't think you're incompetent." He winked.

She slapped his arm. "But gold-digging and media-loving, huh?

"I'm just joking."

"I have no doubt they think I'm incompetent. After watching me freeze-up because of damn heights? I saw the way they looked at me after. Their opinion of me totally changed."

"They're just thick-headed good ol' boys. Not used to working with a beautiful woman who's smarter than they are."

"If you're patronizing me, keep it up. I don't care."

He turned his face to her, inches from her nose. "I don't patronize, Sadie. And I don't lie." His gaze slid down to her lips, lingered.

Blush heated her cheeks. She tore her eyes away and looked down.

"So... what did happen between you and your *billionaire beau?*"

"Oh you saw that headline, huh? Nice." Of course he did. "My *billionaire beau* wasn't for me. Contrary to what the gossips said, I left him, believe it or not. My friends thought I was crazy." She laughed. "But no amount of money in the world could make me fit into his lifestyle. I tried. God, believe me I tried, but at the end of the day, it just wasn't me. I dig in the dirt and analyze bones for a living, not spend my days planning dinner parties. It just wasn't for me."

Owen shifted next to her.

"What? This surprises you?"

"I thought every woman wanted golden flutes filled with five-thousand dollar champagne."

"Every woman wants a man who can make a splint out of a rotted footbridge."

His lip curled up before taking another sip of whiskey.

"What about you?"

"What about me, what?"

"Making splints for any other women in your life?"

"Not lately."

So, Owen was single. And that made her happy. Very happy.

"Been pretty busy since I've been back in Berry Springs."

He looked at her and grinned, "Otherwise, you know, splints, ropes, handcuffs—I'd be using my entire arsenal."

She grinned. "Player."

He laughed out loud at this. "Nope. That is one characteristic that dear daddy—or my uncle for that matter—didn't pass onto me."

"Come from a long line of ladies men?"

"Yes, ma'am."

"Bet that's tough on your mom."

"It was. That's why she left my dad after his second hiccup."

"I'm sorry to hear that."

He shrugged. "She's down in Mexico, married, living on the water. Happy."

A moment ticked by.

"So, why exactly are you back here in Berry Springs?"

Owen shifted again—a nervous, or uncomfortable tick, apparently.

"My dad."

"Something happen?"

"You could say that." He grabbed the whiskey and took a deep sip. She took it from him and did the same, settling in for the story she could tell was coming.

"My dad... is in a court-ordered rehab program." He glanced at her. "So, trust me, I know all about the feeling of being gossiped about."

"I'm so sorry." She touched his arm. "You left your job to come back and deal with it?"

He nodded. "Dad has a business, a house, bills that I found out he'd stopped paying... life goes on whether he's here or not. Someone had to take care of everything."

She paused, "You didn't *have* to."

He grunted.

"You're a good son."

He glanced down for a moment before saying, "You know the kicker of it is? I didn't even hesitate. When Amos called me, I put in my notice five minutes later. All these years dad wasn't around, but the minute he really needed my help, I didn't hesitate. The guy would have come back to absolutely nothing. The bank was threatening to take his home, car, business. Everything."

"Gone all those years? Where was he?"

"Navy. Gone almost all my childhood."

"That must've been tough."

"No, it was tough when he got out. That's when everything went to shit. 'Scuse my language. It was like he... it was like he just became a different person. Like he was completely lost without the military in his life anymore."

She saw the pain in his eyes... but there was more. A thinly veiled sympathy.

"When does he get back?"

"Soon."

"And then you're going back? To Louisiana?"

Dead silence dragged by before he finally looked at her. "That's the plan."

She bit her lip and nodded. "Figured." The thought made her stomach sink and also reminded her that she needed to pull back on the flurry of emotions this guy invoked in her. He was leaving, heck, *she* was leaving, and chances were they were never going to see each other again.

What an idiot she'd been to even think otherwise. On that thought, she attempted to shift away from him, when a bolt of fire shot up her leg. A groan escaped as she squeezed her face in pain.

"Whoa, whoa, don't move like that. Where are you going? What do you need?"

She waited until the lump of pain dissolved in her throat. "Nothing, just repositioning."

"Here." He shifted behind her, one leg on either side and positioned the packs around them. "Lean back." His warm arms flanked her sides as she leaned into him, the back of her head settling onto his chest. He unwrapped the tarp from his pack, shook it out and tossed it over her. She was immediately engulfed in warmth. Comfort. A tornado of emotions.

"Better?"

"Yes." Was she better? Or was she more confused than ever?

She felt this heartbeat through his T-shirt, matching hers that had picked up the moment they'd touched.

Silence settled around them as they inhaled and exhaled together, the sexual tension shooting like electricity between them.

The light touch of his finger had her jerking as he swept a strand of hair away from her face, and tucked it behind her ear. Goosebumps flew over her skin. Next, a subtle movement behind her, followed by his warm breath along her ear lobe.

Her heart skipped a beat.

She closed her eyes, his lips like a feather against her skin.

His fingers began to slowly trace the top of her thighs as he kissed the sensitive spot just below her ear.

Oh, my God.

His kiss on her body sent a storm through her, a desire, a heat she hadn't felt, maybe ever.

Her hands found his, and she turned her head, angling so they were face to face. Her eyes met his, a fire through the dim light, and without allowing herself to think—to talk herself out of it—she sealed her lips against his.

Butterflies burst in her stomach as he kissed her back with an intensity of throwing caution to the wind, letting go, and releasing what was happening between them. No, she'd never felt like this before. She never wanted anyone so badly in her entire life.

She grabbed his shirt, demanding him closer. On her.

Owen slid out from behind her, careful to avoid her leg.

"Crush it. I don't care," she whispered between kisses.

He grinned before pressing his mouth onto her again. This kiss was different, less soft and sensual, more frenzied. Greedy.

Commanding.

She frantically tugged his shirt over his head. Her fingers danced over his flesh, rippled, tan, swollen with muscles that only came from hours swimming in rough water. Owen Grayson was the sexiest man she'd ever seen in her life. He leaned her back, guiding her head onto the pack he'd repositioned. She wanted to leap on top of him, rip his clothes off, devour every inch of his hard body, but—her *damn ankle*. Well that wasn't going to stop her. Hell, a hurricane wouldn't have stopped her.

Propping himself up on one elbow, he leaned into her, answering her demand for his lips to be on her while using his other hand to explore under her T-shirt. He pulled down the top of her bra and rolled her erect nipple in-between his fingers. Lightning shot through her body. Her shirt was pulled off, followed by her bra. He took her in his mouth, licking, kissing, sucking her nipple, a soft groan between kisses.

"Owen..." she fumbled with his belt, but he moved out of touch, down her stomach, kissing her navel.

She ran her fingers through his dark hair, her skin sizzling against the cool rock below her.

Dammit, if she could only move!

He looked up from her stomach, the intensity in his eyes sending a shiver down her spine.

"I want you, Sadie. I want every inch of you," his voice gravelly as he undid her pants.

She desperately gripped his head. "Come *here*."

The corner of his lip curled with a subtle shake of his head as he unzipped her.

"Owen, I can't..." she whispered desperately, willing her leg to heal in that very moment. "I want to...*Dammit,* Owen, I can't *move*."

"You don't have to," he said as he slowly, carefully, pulled her pants down to her knees, straddling her one good leg.

His finger trailed her barely-there lace and mesh panties, the white color glowing through the darkness. He grinned and looked up at her. "See-through."

She met his smirk, thanking her lucky stars that she'd forgotten to do laundry and the sexy panties were the only thing available as she was packing for the trip. "I'm not all bones and dirt, Owen."

"No," he leaned down and blew his warm breath through the mesh. "No, you're not."

His fingers felt like silk against her skin as he pulled the teeny straps down, exposing her to him. The rush of cold air between her legs did her in, sending a wave of tingles across the delicate skin.

She was wet, ready, desperate, and the man hadn't even touched her yet.

He reached up and rubbed her nipple as his face disappeared below, his mouth kissing her inner thighs, the crease of her legs, until finally, he enclosed over her.

She closed her eyes and inhaled deeply, every bit of her focus rushed below. His tongue slid warm, silky between her folds, tasting, teasing, until settling onto her clit.

Her hands wrapped into fists as the sensation overtook her—small, wet circles, caressing the tiny, swollen bud.

She put her hands on his head, feeling the slow rocking of his head, back and forth, while his mouth worked her below, devouring the most intimate part of her.

His hands left her breast and slid into her, one finger, two, matching the rhythm as he licked back and forth over her clit.

Tiny prickles spread over her skin, the warmth funneling between her legs. Her mouth went dry, her muscles tensed in tiny spasms like fireworks exploding through her system.

He pressed harder into her, licked faster. Greedy. Frantic.

She squeezed her face, gripping at the rock below her, grasping at anything to anchor her.

"Owen..."

Another finger.

Faster. Wetter.

"Owen..." She squeaked his name as the orgasm ripped through her, wave after wave, an explosion so intense that tears filled her eyes.

Her muscles fell limp, lead weight attached to her body. She inhaled deeply and opened her eyes, meeting the gaze of a man that appeared to be as satisfied as she was.

"Owen, that was..."

He kissed her thigh, slowly tracing her wetness with his fingers.

"Good," he said. "How's your ankle?"

"What ankle?"

He grinned, leaned up, and grabbed the tarp that had

been tossed to the side. She stared at him as he covered her up, looking at him in an entirely new light. His touch was soft, gentle, as he took care of her, completely okay that they didn't have sex. Or, that he didn't even get off, for that matter. He was content. Happy, as if he enjoyed pleasing her more than anything else. She was staring at, yes, the perfect man.

Once she was secured in warmth, he slid behind her and pulled her to him. "Now, try to get some sleep," he whispered in her ear. "It's going to be a long night."

$\mathcal{O}$WEN LOOKED DOWN at Sadie sleeping in his arms, the heavy rise and fall of her chest in perfect rhythm with the *drip, drip, drip* echoing behind them. She'd been out cold for three hours, and he'd spent the last three hours fighting the desire to wake her up for round two.

The turn of events had not only surprised the hell out of him, but shaken him to his core. And not just because he'd been strong enough to withhold sex, but because of the connection he'd felt when he kissed her, when he'd felt her skin beneath him, when he'd slipped into the most intimate part of her body.

It was the first time he'd had foreplay without a grand finale in the end. Hell, it was the first time he'd remained dressed next to a half-naked woman. It was the first time, he thought about *her,* instead of him.

He wanted to tell Sadie in his own way that he might not be a billionaire beau, but he could give the fucker a run for his money. The overwhelming desire he'd had to make Sadie happy—more than anything else—both caught him off guard and excited him. He'd never felt that way about anyone. Ever.

It was all about her, and to his utter shock—it was *HOT. AS. FUCK,* and only made him want her even more. And although he wasn't quite ready to admit it, he knew it wasn't just because of that face, those curves, or those damn see-through panties.

He'd been infatuated with Sadie Hart since he first laid eyes on her in the woods.

She was smart, beautiful, tough, funny, with enough attitude in her to make things interesting.

She was perfect for him. They fit.

He took his hundredth deep breath, the thought still knocking him off kilter.

What time was it? The rain had stopped. He knew because the lake had stopped rising, but not before engulfing the bridge. If they weren't trapped before, they sure as hell were now. The roar of the waterfall had turned into a calm, white noise over the last hour which meant the water would recede quickly. They'd be out soon enough.

His gaze shifted to the narrow tunnel on the far side of the Anarchy room, as it had every minute for the last three hours. When Sadie had fallen asleep, he'd shifted the flashlight to shine outward, a dull beam fading into the water ahead and reflecting off the tunnel. That was the only light. One stream of yellow in a massive room of black. There was an entry point into the cave somewhere down that tunnel, and the thought made him uneasy.

Had someone really been watching Griffin?

Had someone used that tunnel to kill his uncle?

His thoughts drifted to Deputy Tucker. The guy was former military, which certainly didn't mean he wasn't a cold-blooded killer, but Owen couldn't wrap his head around the *why* of it. As far as he knew, Tucker had no connection with Ray, his dad, or anyone who had anything to do with Owen's family. Furthermore, if Tucker did kill Ray, where did the venom come from to mess with the dead man's bones afterward? Someone hated his uncle bad enough to not only leave his body to rot in the cave, but come back after the fact and desecrate his bones.

Anarchy.

Whoever killed Ray and Jane Doe was someone who despised authority, conformity. Someone who played by their own rules. Someone who probably had a criminal record. None of that matched up with Deputy Tucker. Hell, the guy didn't take a piss without Crawly's approval. No, this was someone with a lot of anger.

Someone who had something out for his uncle.

Who?

Who checked all those boxes?

And who would kill an innocent kid, and innocent homeless woman on top of it? What was Ray's connection to Jane Doe?

And who the fuck was Peg?

He thought of their conversation with Kat.

A flag.

Jane Doe had been hysterically screaming something about a flag.

The American flag stitched on Deputy Tucker's pack? Possibly. It made sense. But, still, it didn't sit well with him.

He imagined the Anarchy symbol in his mind. Anarchists had flags. Shit, they proudly displayed flags.

He frowned, recalling the few times that he'd seen them.

Red and black, the colors split diagonally across the flag.

Red. Black.

His eyes widened.

Red. Black.

His spine straightened, remembering meeting the boys at Frank's the night before. Lieutenant Quinn Colson, Detective Dean Walker, Wesley Cross and Aaron Knapp... with a fresh black and red tattoo peeking out from his shirt sleeve. He closed his eyes and pulled his memory, recalling the slant in the blocks of black and red. The fucking anarchy flag—right there on Aaron's goddamn shoulder.

No. Fucking. Way.

Aaron Knapp.

Owen's pulse kicked up, heat rising up his neck as the realization gripped hold. *No way.* No way was this right. No way Aaron would kill his uncle. Owen *knew* Aaron. He knew his family. Shit, he'd gone to the guy's wedding when he'd married little Pam Ellen Granger right out of high school.

His blood froze ice-cold.

Pamela Ellen Granger.

P.E.G.

Son of a bitch.

Ray had a ring he'd intended to give to Aaron Knapp's ex-wife.

Holy shit.

His attention was pulled to a ripple in the inky-black water, a circle of small waves spreading over the once-still lake.

Knowing they were hidden behind the light beam, he slowly picked up the Glock he'd kept at his hip for the last three hours, watching over Sadie while she slept.

Something was in the water.

Something was coming straight toward them.

Owen narrowed his eyes, feeling a tingle of adrenaline. It was the same feeling he got before something big was about to happen.

The ripples faded, the dripping in the background like the steady beat of a war drum in the distance.

Holding his breath, he stealthily slid out from under Sadie, using their packs to prop her up. He paused, focused on her breathing again until he confirmed she was still asleep.

Gripping his gun, he clenched his jaw as he stepped in front of Sadie, guarding his precious territory.

The slightest shuffle had his head turning to the left, focusing on the far corner of the lake, shrouded in blackness. He considered moving the light, but didn't want to alert whatever—or whoever—was lurking in the shadows.

He closed his eyes, allowing his senses to adjust to the darkness. He listened to the waterfall in the distance, the drips. Felt the still air around him, the heavy, wet humidity cool against his warm skin.

His eyes opened at the faint sounds of steps along the ledge of the lake—where he couldn't see a damn thing.

He turned, re-positioned so he was in front of Sadie again, then shifted his weight to his toes.

It's go time.

Sadie moved behind him, momentarily breaking his concentration just as a barely-visible outline emerged from the darkness. Too close to get a shot off, Owen lunged forward and felt the whoosh of a blade inches from his cheek. He gripped the hilt of his gun and whipped it against his attacker's face.

"*Owen!*" Sadie's yell was followed by a frantic strobe light of flashes until she finally settled the light on his attacker.

Aaron Knapp.

Holy. Shit.

He took a swing, connecting with Aaron's jaw, sending

him stumbling backward. Owen pointed his gun between Aaron's eyes.

Blood dripped from his former friend's mouth as Aaron's gaze shifted to Sadie and a devilish grin cracked his face, showing two teeth missing.

"Just like your fucking good-for-nothing playboy uncle."

"What the *fuck* are you doing, Aaron?"

"Give me the fucking knife."

"The knife you used to kill my uncle?"

Aaron's eyes flared with rage. "Your fucking uncle cheated with my wife for *years,* Owen! Right under my nose. We were supposed to be friends." He spat blood. "He *ruined* me and Pam."

Sadie's pulse roared in her ears as she frantically searched through her pack for her knife. She needed some kind of protection. Something to help Owen if he needed it. Her foot throbbed as she pulled herself up to a seated position, then pulled her good leg to her chest, ready to push up as soon as she found her damn knife.

She wasn't just going to sit there watching.

"You didn't have to kill him for it," Owen snarled and spat, the black outline of his tall, thick body tensed and poised like a snake about to strike. His shadow stretched along the cave floor stopping just in front of Aaron, climbing to his feet, dressed head-to-toe in diving gear. Blood dripped down the front of his wet suit.

"Your piece-of-shit uncle got what he deserved. He and that skank he had with him."

The tooth—case 7370. "Who was she?" Sadie asked calmly behind him, trying to distract him.

"Some homeless bitch he'd picked up and befriended. I didn't expect him to show up with her. Bitch got away from me, but I got her in the end. Collateral damage, but hell, I did society a favor getting her off the streets."

"Was Brian Russell collateral damage, Aaron?" Owen's voice was as cold as ice.

"And Griffin?" Sadie asked, her tone meeting Owen's.

Aaron's eyes skirted between them, then settled on Owen. "Toss your gun in the lake."

Without a second of hesitation, Owen tossed the gun.

Aaron nodded, his shoulders relaxing, and it was then that Sadie knew why Owen tossed the gun. He could take that skinny rat with one hand tied behind his back.

"I want that fucking knife."

"Sadie," Owen said, his voice deep and chilling, "I need you to get the knife out of my bag."

Her eyes widened. *"No,* Owen..." It was the only piece of evidence they had.

"Do it."

She grabbed his pack, keeping her eye on Aaron, shifting his weight back and forth on the rocks like a cagey inmate. Sadie pulled the knife from Owen's bag.

"I've got it."

"Stay there."

Keeping his eyes locked on Aaron, Owen slowly backed up, and took it from her hands.

"You get your knife, and no one gets hurt here, Aaron. We'll all get out of here and never speak of it again. *Fuck,* Aaron, we went to fucking grade school together for Christ's sake."

"The knife, Owen."

"I'm going to toss it in the middle, between you and me." Owen tossed the knife, the tip of the blade sparking in the light. It clattered on the rock floor, tumbling just inches from the lake.

Sadie noticed the tremble in Aaron's hand as he crept forward.

Sadie gripped her knife and held her breath.

One step, two, three—

Owen lunged forward, barreling into Aaron like a bull, knocking him into the air.

Sadie scrambled up the wall, knife in hand, wobbling on one foot.

Owen and Aaron's silhouette faded into a swirling black mass as they wrestled on the cave floor.

Her stomach turned to liquid as she heard the pop of bone crunching, followed by the sparkle of blood splattering on the shiny rock walls. Aaron scrambled to his feet and lunged for Owen with the knife in his hand.

"*Owen!*" Sadie began scrambling across the rocks.

"*No,* Sadie." Owen twisted his head, a flash of panic in his eye.

Aaron seized the moment of distraction and barreled into Owen, waving the knife. The next few seconds were a blur. The splash of Owen's body hitting the water, followed by the flash of a body lunging toward her, the glint of light reflecting off the blade slashing inches from her chest. Sadie threw her body backward, her head slamming into the side of the cave. Stars burst in her eyes as her stomach rolled. Her vision wavered, the dark silhouette standing over her with a knife in his hand.

Her gaze drifted to the water, still and black as death. Where was Owen? Oh God, had he drowned?

Tears welled in her eyes as Aaron leaned down in front of her, the blood from his mouth dripping down the side of her face. A wicked smile cracked his face, his eyes wild, feral. She flinched as he reached around and grabbed a fist-full of her hair, pulling tiny strands out as he squeezed. Her fingers desperately searched for her knife that had fallen from her hands sometime during her stumble backward.

She opened her mouth to speak but was cut off when Aaron yanked her head back, exposing her neck to him.

He raised the knife and pressed the cold steel to her skin.

"Too bad, really, you're not half bad to look at."

Everything stopped—her thudding heart, the roar of panic in her ears. She was going to die. But she was going to die fighting.

She swept her good leg along the rocks, knocking him off balance. As she scrambled to pull herself up, Aaron lunged forward and raised the knife just as Owen barreled into him from the side.

Aaron flew back, the knife tumbling from his hand, his head bouncing off the rock floor. Sadie watched his limp body roll into the water.

"*Sadie...*" Owen fell to his knees next to her. "Are you okay?"

Blood speckled Owen's face... but that was nothing compared to the river of blood covering his side. "*Owen*, oh, my God..." she grabbed the flashlight. "Owen, you're bleeding badly."

He frowned—as if just noticing it—and glanced down at his arm where a deep gash ran across his bicep. She grabbed his good shoulder, and gently turned him to the light. Blood ran down his arm, dripping from his fingertips.

"Well. Shit," he said.

"Owen," panic swept through her as she inspected the wound. It was bad. Puffy flesh lined a deep *V that cut to the bone.* "This is beyond needing stitches. And you're losing a lot of blood. A lot."

Her heart picked up speed again, racing with a different kind of fear.

He calmly assessed, then stepped past her and grabbed his pack with his good arm and tossed it to her.

"Can you grab my bandana out of the side pocket?"

Her hands trembled as she fumbled with the pack.

"Here."

"I'm going to need you to help tie this off." He nodded to the wound.

"A tourniquet?"

"Exactly."

Sadie pushed up to her knees as he kneeled down next to her. Owen had just been in a life-or-death fistfight and had his bicep sliced in half, but was as calm as she'd ever seen him. It was a remarkable thing to see and inspired her to suck it up and man up.

"Loop it just above the wound," he instructed. "And tie it off. As hard as you can. Use your teeth."

She nodded and wrapped the fabric, ignoring the dip in her stomach as the blood oozed out.

"Tighter," he said through his teeth.

She looked at him, noticing a flush on his cheeks. "Tighter? Are you sure?"

"Yes. As tight as you can."

She blew out a quick breath and using all the energy she had, pulled the fabric tighter.

"Good job. Now hand me the whiskey."

She unscrewed the lid and handed it to him.

After three solid chugs—she smiled—he lowered to a sit, blew out a breath, and looked at her.

"So that happened..."

"I can't believe…" she positioned herself in front of him as he seemed to take a second to get his bearings. "I'm worried about you, Owen. That needs medical assistance, like, *now.*"

"Can't believe the fucker got me."

Sadie looked at the water, still as glass, and imagined Aaron's body floating through the darkness, disappearing into the depths of hell. "You won the fight, though."

"Fucking *Aaron.*" He shook his head, grabbed the whiskey then took another sip. "Okay," he looked around the cave. "You're right. We've got to get out of here."

She looked down at her ankle. "… A broken ankle and severed arm."

"A winning combination." He winked in his ever-calming nature, then shifted his gaze to the water and seemed to decide something.

"Can you get my tarp and duct tape, please?"

She dumped his pack and separated the items. "Now what?"

"Take the knife and cut a square out of the tarp, about two feet long and a foot wide."

She did it quickly and efficiently, knowing that time was of the essence.

"Now, we've got to wrap up my cut, over the tourniquet, and secure it with duct tape."

He watched her as she did it—not to ensure it was done correctly, but staring into her eyes, making her heart skip a beat.

She finished. "What do you think?"

"I think I want a kiss."

A grin tugged at her lips as she leaned forward and kissed him, a soft, sensual kiss.

"Better than the whiskey." He winked. "Okay, do another

layer of tape... who the hell knows what tiny organisms and bacteria are in this water."

"Water?"

"How do you think we're getting out of here?"

"We're *swimming* out?"

"Yes, ma'am."

She looked at her ankle. "I can't... I mean, I won't be able to—"

"I'll carry you."

She laughed. "You're kidding."

"Sadie, I'm a rescue swimmer. This is kind of what I do."

"But not with *one* arm!"

"At least it's my left. Lucked out there. We'll have to work together. You'll use your arms in the water, and I'll use my legs. We work together."

"No, Owen, no. There's got to be another way."

"*Sadie.*"

His tone had her snapping to attention.

"Here's the deal. One, the sooner we get you to a doctor, the less likely you'll have to have surgery."

"I don't care about my damn ankle."

"I'm not done. Two, you did a great job with this tourniquet and have slowed the bleeding significantly, but, the longer the lower half of my arm goes without blood, the greater the chance I'll have to have it amputated. And, I've kind of become attached to the little guy."

Her stomach fell to her feet. "Amputated?"

"Yep. With no blood flow, the tissue dies. I'd say we've got a handful of hours before that begins to happen, and this water isn't going to recede before then."

She stared at his arm. That was it. There were no more options.

She set her jaw and nodded. "Swim it is, then. Let's get going."

He smiled, leaned forward and kissed her on the forehead. "Good girl. Alright, let's pack up. I've got a waterproof bag to wrap the SAT cell in."

They gathered the packs, her slithering along the rocks like a snake, and him like a bird with his wings clipped. They were a hell of a team.

"How did Aaron get the jump on us? There's no way he crossed that bridge. We would have heard him coming."

"He came from the opposite side of the cave, where I found the knife. There's an exit point somewhere down there. He snuck in, and under the rocks through the water. Fifty bucks that's how he knew Griffin found the knife."

She slid on her pack and helped Owen into his. "Did you know Ray was having an affair with Aaron's wife?"

"No." Owen looked down for a moment. "He wouldn't have told anyone. That's how he lived his life."

"Jane Doe must have gotten away during the scuffle, but not before Aaron got a solid hit on her. And I'm guessing that's what she was so hysterical about when she ran to Kat's house. Kat wasn't drunk. Her story was true."

He turned to her. "We don't have time to play detective now, we've got to get a move on."

She nodded. "So which way are we going to go?"

"We're not exactly in the shape for new explorations, so, we go back the way we came. Through the lake, then we'll have to swim across where the log is down."

Her stomach tickled with nerves.

Owen grabbed her chin, and with a twinkle in his eyes said, "You've got this. Just like the ravine. I've got you, and you've got me. We can do this. *Together.*" He turned and squatted. "I can't lift you over my shoulder, so you'll have to get on my back."

Sadie slid onto his back, and after a grunt, Owen was up and making his way across the rocks to the bridge, now completely under water. In a slow fluid movement, he squatted down and Sadie released her weight on her good foot.

Owen scooted to the ledge and dangled his legs into the water. "You'll hook your right arm around me, and will flow behind me, at my side. Hang on, and use your other arm like hell to push us through. I'll kick and use my right arm. Only use your upper body. Got it?"

She nodded.

"There's an undercurrent we're going to have to fight. You use your arms to keep us straight, okay?"

"Okay." She scooted to the edge and wrapped her arm around him, careful to avoid hitting his wound.

"Okay. Bottoms up."

He put the flashlight between his teeth, slid into the lake, pulling her with him.

Sadie gasped as the icy water flowed over her. They dipped initially, the water coming over her chin. Then, she felt his legs kicking and with one arm, Sadie grit her teeth and pushed through the water. Inch by inch, they swam through the blackness, water splashing into her eyes with each stroke.

"Current's picking up here," Owen yelled out.

Sadie pushed harder, gasping for air.

"Good girl, you're doing good. Almost there."

Finally, they reached the far side of the lake. Sadie pulled herself onto the ledge, then Owen came up beside her and spat out the flashlight. Her chest was heaving, he was barely breathing heavily.

"You okay?"

She nodded, her teeth chattering. "Let's get the hell out of here."

"Music to my ears." He turned his back to her. "Your chariot awaits, darling."

She was lifted into the air as her arms wrapped around his shoulders. He was warm, strong, safe, her knight in shining armor. And it was that moment that Sadie knew, without a shadow of a doubt, that she could fall crazy, head-over-heels in love with this man.

Hell, maybe she already had.

With a steady pace, they made their way through the cave. No breaks, no breathers, in a comfortable rhythm they'd already established during journey number one. Minutes later, they reached the small river—the last obstacle before the homestretch.

Using the same technique as before, Owen lowered into the water, and together, they swam the short distance to the other side.

Exhilaration burst through her as she pulled herself onto the ledge.

"We did it!"

"Don't count your chickens till they hatch, darling. Let's get out of the cave, call in the cavalry, then I'm going to rip your clothes off, pin you against the rocks..."

Sadie grabbed his sopping wet-shirt. "Why wait?"

"Because my arm might get cut off."

She gasped and released. "Shit. That's right. Okay, let's go."

He laughed. "Let's go."

A few long minutes later, they reached the exit. The rain had slowed but was still coming down. Not a soul was waiting for them. Not a single person.

"The phone won't connect inside the cave. We've got to go outside." She kissed the back of his neck as they stepped past the cave entrance, into the sprinkles of rain. "You freaking did it, Owen." A smile slid across her face, "You did—"

A flash of movement beside them—

"*Owen!*"

Aaron leapt out from behind a boulder, a bloody knife in his hand. As Owen whipped around, Sadie's weight shifted, sending her tumbling off his back and onto the wet ground. Owen dipped to catch her, but slipped on the rocks and went down on his left arm.

"*Owen!* Aaron, *no!*"

The knife cut through the air above Owen's head—

Pop!

Aaron's eyes popped as he locked up and tumbled to the ground, a red dot spreading over his chest.

Owen jumped up, shielding Sadie, shock and confusion washed over his face... until the dark silhouette stepped out of the tree line.

"Dad," he slowly breathed out.

23

2 weeks later...

*H*OLDING HER BRIEFCASE in one hand and a coffee in the other, Sadie hobbled through the lab doors. She was welcomed by a wall of cold air and a buzz of conversation from a group of interns, each dressed in crisp white lab coats huddled around a silver table in the back.

"Sadie!" Kimi crossed the room, an ear-to-ear smile over her face, her body vibrating with excitement like a miniature poodle. "Every single bone is accounted for. Can you *believe* this?"

"You double-checked?" She skimmed the lab.

"Three times." Kimi's gaze shifted to the bottom of Sadie's dress. She grinned, then bent down and popped something off the hem. "Tag's still on."

"Dammit. Thanks."

"Oh, come on. You look good in dresses."

"I hate wearing dresses. But I'm not cutting off the

bottom of another pair of pants just to fit around this damn boot."

"I'll admit, the walking cast distracts, but you still look pretty. And it's a good day to look pretty. Are you all set with your presentation?"

The presentation that had taken her all night to put together? Hardly. Her stomach tickled with nerves. "Is the boss here, yet?"

On cue, the lab door opened and Sadie's boss, Ronnie Sharp, followed by Allan Tedrick—the owner of KT Labs, and the father of her last failed relationship—stepped into the lab.

Her breath stopped as a hush fell over the room.

"Oh, my God..." Kimi whispered as the suits made their way across the lab. "Did you know he was coming?"

"No..." she swallowed the lump in her throat.

"Dr. Hart, good to see you again." Allan smiled and stuck out his hand.

"Mr. Tedrick, sir, good to see you, as well," she forced herself to yank her shoulders back and look him square in the eye. The guy put his pants on just like everyone else... except her. She required a twelve inch bellbottom.

"I hear you've been digging up quite a few bones lately."

"They just... fall into my lap, sir." She fought an inward eye roll.

Her boss shot her a look that told her he didn't realize the big boss would be joining them. He stepped forward to exude his authority. "Let's step into the conference room."

Sadie grabbed her folders from her briefcase and cast Kimi a quick look before following the suits into a small office that they'd turned into a conference room.

Her boss sat, Tedrick remained standing. "Sadie, tell us what you've got so far on the Crypts Cavern cases."

"Yes, sir." Willing her nerves away, she walked to the head of the table as Kimi slid into a plastic chair.

"As you know, my team and I were called to Crypts Cavern to excavate human remains found by two Berry Springs teenagers. I've determined that the markings found on the lower ribs were, indeed, kerf marks, made peri-mortem, indicating a homicide. Mixed in with the bones, I found a tooth, which happened to match cold case 7370. As you may remember, 7370 belongs to a woman found buried in a shallow grave in the Ozark mountains about five months ago. Although I didn't excavate the bones person-ally, her case is part of my cold case project that I'm working on—"

"Which is getting a lot of visibility with the board," Ronnie included.

She nodded, knowing that the pressure had been turned up the moment Allan Tedrick took interest in the fact his lab was assigning a team to reopen cold cases.

"We know now that her name was Shauna Winters, a free-spirit backpacking through the mountains, who was murdered alongside Ray Grayson, by a search and rescue expert named Aaron Knapp." She looked at her notes that she'd gone over with Lieutenant Colson ahead of her presentation. "Although the media has put its own flare on it, it was determined by local authorities that Mr. Grayson had picked Shauna up on his way for a hike, where they ran into Aaron Knapp. Aaron had recently found out his wife and Ray had been having an affair, and had followed Ray and Shauna into the cave where he confronted, then killed Ray. Shauna got away during the scuffle, but unfortunately Aaron found her on his way out and forced her into his truck where he then murdered and dumped her body."

"How do they know this?"

"Security cameras from a woman named Kat Silva's house. Deputy Tucker, with the Carroll County police had the tapes pulled after questioning her about the last time she'd seen Ray. Apparently, he'd linked the bones found in the cave to Mr. Grayson early on, just like Owen did, and was conducting his own investigation on the side. Aaron covered his tracks by placing Ray's pack in another cave, along with a smear of his blood, making it appear that Mr. Grayson died in an unfortunate spelunking accident, then burying Shauna's body. He took care of everything, except the knife he lost in the cave. The knife he used to kill Ray. The knife he was worried Brian Russell would find if he went back into the cave."

A moment passed as everyone took a moment to digest the events of the last few weeks.

"Shauna White's family called the lab personally, you know," Tedrick said. "To thank us for providing closure to the nightmare they'd been living the last seven months."

Sadie nodded. She'd seen their interview on the local news, where they'd thanked local law enforcement and mentioned the lab several times. Apparently, Shauna had been fired from her job and decided to take some time 'finding herself' and backpack through the mountains. Shauna had been gone for weeks when Ray found her.

"Alright, so we've got Ray Grayson and Shauna White... now onto the third set of bones," her boss said, to move things along.

Sadie shuffled through her papers. "While I was conducting my last search in the cave, I found another bone buried deep in a crevice." She glanced at Kimi, who's spine was as straight as a board. "When we determined that this bone didn't belong to Ray Grayson or cold case 7370, Kimi and I went back to the location and discovered that just beyond the crevice was a small room—"

"A tomb," Kimi corrected, her tone peaked with excitement.

Sadie nodded and grinned, "Complete with a full skeleton. We excavated the remains, and…" she slid a stack of photos across the table. "I have determined that the bones belong to a male, mid-fifties, estimated TOD to be more than three hundred years ago." She lifted a photo of the skull, "I took facial and cranial measurements, and you can see here… the almond shape of the orbital bones, high cheek bones, and wide, round face, are consistent with Native American features. But it wasn't until I ran an isotope scan and discovered elevated levels of C4-plants, most notably maize, that I can officially assess that we are looking at a Native American male."

"Which also fits with the TOD estimate," Kimi added. "Native Americans lived on that land during that time."

"The legend of Atohi lives," Allan Tedrick said, a gleam in his eyes. This story would get more press than his son's breakup.

"Or, dies, however you choose to look at it," Kimi said with a smile. "The legend says that once his body receives a proper burial, the curse on his bloodline dies."

Sadie smiled, watching the excitement radiate from Kimi. At Kimi's request, they kept the fact that she was part of that bloodline out of the details, but she had been working day and night on the case, earning her plenty of pats on the back for her work. Allan Tedrick had taken notice.

"There are rumors that descendants of Atohi still live in the area," Sadie said. "If we find them, I'd like to release the bones to them, sir."

Allan nodded. "Nice work, Dr. Hart. This is a very big deal." He glanced down at his beeping phone. "I've got to get this." He paused, pinning Sadie with a hard look before saying, "You're building quite the reputation here. You've been part of a team who's provided closure to Brian Russell's, Ray Grayson's, and Shauna White's families, as well as uncovering a tremendous archeological find. I look forward to seeing what else you can bring to the lab. Excuse me."

After both men left the room, Kimi jumped up, closed the door and began squealing. Sadie exhaled and shook her head, feeling the weight of the last few weeks release from her shoulders.

"You're not getting fired, Sadie!" Kimi bear-hugged her, then began jumping around like a kid on Christmas morning. "And I get to break the curse!"

Just then, the door opened and Sadie and Kimi froze like statues.

"I must've missed my invite to the party."

Leaning on a cane, Griffin grinned from the doorway. Kimi squeaked—*again*—and ran over and kissed his cheek.

"Sadie just had a Crypt update meeting with Ronnie, and you'll never believe who showed up."

"The ghost of Aaron Knapp."

"*Not* funny. No, worse, Allan Tedrick. And not only is Sadie not losing her job, they're going to release Atohi's bones."

"Nice," he squeezed Kimi's hand, then winked at Sadie as he propped a hip onto the edge of the conference table. "I told you he wouldn't can you."

She wished she would have believed it. Her face squeezed with concern. "How're you doing?"

Kimi frowned at the question, moved closer to Griffin,

and rubbed his back. Griffin and Kimi had gone from zero to sixty since the horrific day at Crypts Cavern, and Sadie wondered exactly how much had gone on before the little adventure.

"Really good." He tapped his cane on the floor. "Just came from therapy. My leg's getting better every day. Thanks to my beautiful Pocahontas here."

Kimi smiled, a tear glistening in her eye.

"Seriously, you helped save my life, Kimi, you know that. Owen couldn't plug both my wounds at the same time. I'd say the curse was lifted the moment you set foot in the cave."

Sadie stiffened hearing Owen's name.

Kimi kissed Griffin's cheek. "God, what a crazy few weeks it's been." She turned to Sadie and her face fell. "Have you spoken to Owen at all?"

Sadie looked down and began gathering her papers, ignoring the sinking in her stomach. "Nope." The single word was like a punch in the gut. She looked at the clock, "Hey, I gotta run guys," and forced a smile. "Griffin, I'm so glad you're doing so well... and that you've found your little Pocahontas."

Kimi smiled.

"I'll catch you guys later."

"Happy hour at Frank's in thirty," Griffin called out as she left the room. In an effort to avoid questions from the interns, Sadie clicked on her phone and pretended to be checking email as she weaved through the lab.

Victory.

She pushed out the lab door and heaved out a breath.

She should feel relieved that she was going to keep her job, and that Griffin was not only on the road to recovery, but that he and Kimi had found true love.

And she *was* glad, but the truth was, she'd spent the last two weeks trying to disperse a depressing gray, bleak cloud that had settled around her, growing darker with every hour that Owen didn't call. She'd spent the last two weeks doing everything she could to forget Owen Grayson.

It had been exactly fifteen days since they'd both almost died in the depths of Crypts Cavern.

Fifteen days since she'd had the best kisses of her life.

Fifteen days since she'd been whisked away in the back of an ambulance, watching Owen get strapped down on his own gurney with his dad by his side.

During the chaos, she'd learned that Owen's dad had heard about the bones and the rumor that they were his brother's while he was in rehab. He packed up and drove home, driving all night, straight to the cave where he'd arrived not a second too soon, and saved his son's life.

She hadn't heard from Owen since.

When she and Kimi had gone back to excavate Atohi's remains, Lieutenant Colson had told her Owen had recovered, and had gone back to Louisiana to rejoin the military, leaving Berry Springs for good.

Leaving her, for good.

Owen Grayson had sucked her in, rocked her world, and then disappeared into thin air like one of the Crypts ghosts.

Not a single call.

Not a single text.

Nothing.

With her stomach still twisting from the mere mention of his name, Sadie glanced at the clock on the wall—5:04 p.m.—and decided to screw working late, like she always did. She needed a warm bath, a massive glass of wine, and whatever mindless reality television was on that evening.

After grabbing her purse and computer from her office, Sadie pushed out the front doors of KT Crime Labs.

And her heart dropped to her feet.

Wearing a snug-fitting black T-shirt, worn jeans, and a sling over his left arm, Owen Grayson leaned against her SUV, his face shaded by dark sunglasses.

The late afternoon sun twinkled against the yellow leaves flittering down from the oak tree above him as their eyes met from across the parking lot.

A smile slowly curved his mouth. He pushed off her vehicle and met her at the top of the steps. "Here, let me..." and took the computer bag and purse from her hands.

She stared back at him, her mind racing to process the man standing in front of her. The man she thought she'd never see again.

His gaze drifted down to the dress she'd ordered online three days earlier. "You look good."

Warmth spread over her. She nodded to her walking boot. "Just missing my skis. Or, ski, I should say."

He frowned. "How's it doing?"

"Getting better. Doc says it should be off in two more weeks."

"That's good."

She looked at his sling. "How's your arm?"

"Will be good as new in about the same amount of time."

"Did you need surgery?"

"Nope. Just a box of staples."

"Well, I could have done that for free." If he'd been around, she meant in a thinly veiled joke.

A moment of silence slid between them.

"Headed to your car, I assume?"

She nodded.

He slung her purse over his shoulder and lightly grabbed her arm.

Butterflies.

He guided her down the steps. "Congratulations on the historic find. It's all over the news."

"Congratulations on morphing back into human form," she said, not bothering to hide the sarcasm.

They stopped at her SUV and he blew out a breath. "Vanished like a ghost, I get it." He tore off his sunglasses and ran his fingers through his hair. "I'm sorry."

Although her heart was racing, she crossed her arms over her chest and pretended to remain aloof.

He continued, "I tried to find you at the hospital after, but you'd already left."

The truth was, she'd tried to find him, too, in between taking turns with Kimi sitting next to Griffin in his room until his parents arrived. But somewhere after four in the morning, Griffin's mother arrived, and the doctors advised that she and Kimi go home to get some rest.

"I came back the next day... Kimi and I did to check on Griff."

"Why didn't you call or text?"

"Why didn't you?"

Sadie had written five—or was it five hundred—different texts to him, but could never hit the send button. By then, everything had hit the news, and it was a circus. Truthfully, she assumed he'd text or call her.

"Because..." he began pacing. "I had a lot going on with my Dad. We had a lot of catching up to do, and... well, I wasn't sure what I was going to do..."

"What do you mean, what you were going to do?"

"Go back to the Coast Guard or not."

"You did."

He nodded. "Once I was sure my dad was good, I went back to Louisiana."

She forced herself to hold his gaze, although every inch of her wanted to get in her car and drive away, exactly like he'd done to her. "Well, I'm glad things are better with your dad, and I know how much you loved the Guard, so I'm glad you were able to get back. Sounds like everything worked out." She started to push past him.

He stepped forward and reached for her hand. A cool breeze blew around them, spinning leaves around their legs.

"Sadie." He gripped both her hands. "I didn't go back."

She narrowed her eyes.

"I mean, technically I did, but I went back to officially leave the military."

Her heart froze. *"What?"*

A soft smile crossed his lips, and he stepped closer, inches from her. "My dad and I had a long talk. I'm going to take over the outfitters, buy him out, so I'll officially own it. I'm house hunting now; there's a cabin on the lake I'm going to check out later today. And dad's going to go back into the Navy, in a training capacity. It's what he loves. He's not himself without it, and I'm excited about running the business. I've got so many ideas." He squeezed her hand, then reached up and ran a finger down her cheek, sending a wave of goosebumps flying over her skin. "And I'm excited to see you again."

"Yeah?" She couldn't fight the smile.

"Yeah." He cupped her cheeks in his hand. "And, I'd like to take you on that date."

Her smile widened as she fought the sting of tears in her eyes. "Somewhere that doesn't involve creepy legends, ghosts, vampire bats, or see-through monster fish?"

"Well," A devilish grin flashed across his face. "I thought it could involve *something* see-through..."

She laughed. "Sorry to disappoint, but this cast has eliminated every shred of femininity left in me."

"Except for that dress." He reached down and swooped her off her feet.

"Owen." She tipped her head back and laughed, desperately trying to close her skirt. "Owen, put me *down."*

He kissed her forehead as he carried her to his truck.

"Where are we going?"

"On our date."

"Now?"

"Now."

"People are watching us. Put me down," she laughed.

"I like carrying you around." He opened his passenger door.

"You've done it enough already to last a lifetime, Owen."

He sat her inside and gave her a long, slow kiss. "Not nearly enough, Sadie, I can promise you that." With that, he kissed her nose, shut the door and took her out for a romantic dinner for two... that may or may not have ended with a peek at something see-through.

ABOUT THE AUTHOR

Amanda McKinney is the bestselling and multi-award-winning author of more than twenty romantic suspense and mystery novels. Her book, Rattlesnake Road, was named one of *POPSUGAR's 12 Best Romance Books,* and was featured on the *Today Show.* The fifth book in her Steele Shadows series was recently nominated for the prestigious *Daphne du Maurier Award for Excellence in Mystery/Suspense.* Amanda's books have received over fifteen literary awards and nominations.

Text **AMANDABOOKS to 66866** to sign up for Amanda's

Newsletter and get the latest on new releases, promos, and freebies!

www.amandamckinneyauthor.com

If you enjoyed The Cave, please write a review!

Made in the USA
Monee, IL
05 April 2025

15230442R00173